Books by Matthew Allen Dickerson

Prisoner of Silence
Twin Flame

Age of Shadows

Eclipse of the Sun
Silhouette of the Moon

Fables

Mystical Alliance
Knowing Gnowing

Human Born

Blood Oath
Arcane Inheritance
Emerald Intrigue
Garden of Gaia

Noble Souls

Trilogy:

Heart of Ice
Queen's Court
Dearly Beloved

Connected Novels:

Eye of the Beholder
In a Heartbeat

Primordial Quaternity

Seed of Earth
Crystal of Air

Revelations

Tapestry of the Second Born
Genesis of the First born

The Sunfire Chronicles

Lexia's Legacy
Tinker's Treasure
Parallax's Paradox
Dryad's Dream
Rua'So'Nid's Return
Liam's Legend

Dearly Beloved

Matthew Allen Dickerson

Dearly Beloved

© Matthew Allen Dickerson

All characters in this book are fictitious. Any resemblance to actual person, living or dead, is purely coincidental.

The book is protected under the copyright laws of the United States of America. Any reproduction or unauthorized use of the material or artwork contained herein is prohibited without the express written permission of Matthew Allen Dickerson.

The sale of this book without its cover has not been authorized by the publisher. If you purchased this book without a cover, you should be aware that neither the author nor the publisher has received payment for this "stripped book".

Cover art by Germancreative
First Publishing: October 2019

ISBN: 9781702373098

Chapter 1

"Mina, would you do the honor of marrying me?" Oliver was kneeling, the ring in his hand was held firmly within a hinged container. With tears sliding down his face, he tried to look through the blurred vision that his uncontrollable emotions had led to. He waited in silence for the answer, but none came.

"My dearest Mina, it would be an honor if you would be my wife." He mimicked the original gesture and once more, waited for a response that did not come.

"My dearest beloved, I cherish..." Oliver paused, trying to find the right wording, "I desire nothing more than to have your hand in marriage." He hung his head in frustration. Finally he looked up with a smile as he tried to again, "Would ya'll be wantin' ta' be hitched, darlin'?" He fell back into a sitting position in the middle of his living room laughing to himself, "No, that's just dreadful."

"My darling, my love, my dearest, my..." He sighed in frustration. This should be easy, it should just flow out of him, the ideal thing to say, the perfect words. Often Mina had said he spoke in poetry and yet he felt like he was stumbling for the right words. He had one chance to get it perfect and she deserved perfection. She was perfection.

Sitting on the floor of his living room, Oliver stared at the small box holding a ring that he had purchased as a gift for his girlfriend of three years. It was a beautiful design that had caught his eye and for the moment served as a temporary replacement for an engagement ring for when he practiced. It would do for now.

What weighed heavily on his mind was that he was not a rich man. He stared at the ring realizing just how humble it truly was when he thought of the woman it was meant for. Compared to him, she was so much more successful financially. Mina was a highly valued associate within her job, paid far more than Oliver was in his job at the front desk of a hotel. He was proud that he had worked his way up from a janitor, from where he had begun.

He felt embarrassed about his position, so told others that he was a manager. Which was true, in a way. Being around much more successful individuals such as Mina and her closest friend, Mitch, Oliver often struggled to feel worthy of her.

He regretted that he was unable to purchase something greater, more fitting for the finger it was destined for. He closed his eyes, leaning forward, a pain striking his chest. Touching the box to his forehead he considered his future. He wanted to propose, to make everything perfect, to have the ideal ring, poetry to be spoken in a setting that they would remember for countless decades to come.

Mina didn't care about his financial status. She knew of his past, concerning his family. She loved him for who he was, not what he could provide her in the form of material gifts. Oliver sighed deeply. She deserved better than what he could offer her. She deserved perfection, which he often felt he would never become.

A knock at the door drew him to quickly hide the ring box in his pocket and he began wiping way the tears from his face. Pulling himself to his feet, he moved quickly over to a box of facial tissues. Using them to regain some semblance of his composure, he tried to remember to breathe, to calm his nerves.

With a firm nod of his head, Oliver headed towards the door after the third attempt to gain his attention resounded. Opening it, relief washed over him at the sight of a pair of jade green eyes, the same color as he possessed. His younger sister Alice stood on the threshold of his home looking up at him from her five-foot, two-inch height. Compared to his six feet, she often commented that he towered over her.

"Greetings, Oliver." The smile on Alice's face quickly faded when she detected the details of his face, "You've been crying." She touched his upper arm delicately in concern, "Are you comfortable telling me what is distressing you?"

Oliver smiled warmly at the fact that he was grateful it was her and not someone else. He had much weighing heavily on his mind and she was the ideal person to speak to. Stepping back from the doorway, he motioned inside, "If you wouldn't mind coming inside before I tell you."

Concern shifted to curiosity as Alice's eyes narrowed, "Of course, I wouldn't want a private matter to be overheard by others."

Entering the house, Alice approached Oliver's couch. Standing before it she asked, "May I?"

It had been three years since Alice had departed their family home and yet she still behaved in a similar fashion to that of her twenty-five years of life under their mother's tutelage had engrained in her mind. Oliver gave a small nod of his head, "Of course." Once she sat, he joined her, "The reason for my emotional moment was that I was…" He nervously began digging into his pocket, withdrawing the ring box, "I was…"

Alice's eyes widened in surprise, her slender fingers covering her mouth as she practically trembled with excitement. Once she found her breath, she asked in a near whisper, "Engagement? I know you have spoken to me of wanting to do so…" Her hands lowered as she studied the box in his hand, "Is that the ring you wish to propose to her with?"

"No, this is a gift for her, unrelated to…" Oliver cradled it in both of his hands as it rested in his lap, "I was practicing with it." He scowled in concern, "I don't believe I'm ready."

The siblings were visibly related, both had inherited the strong high cheekbones and thin features of their mother. Each possessed pale skin coloration, hints of their Irish heritage on their father's side. Their hair color had been a near white blonde when they were born. Where Alice still possessed a similar color with only faint traces of yellow, her brother's hair had darkened to match their father's brown. The faint traces of blonde that remained were quickly fading into darker shades with each passing year. It was one of dozens of tiny details he was concerned with that made him less unique in Mina's eyes. When they had met, his hair was more colorful, the transition from dark blonde to brown hadn't taken over as predominantly and he thought maybe that was an attractive quality that she would miss.

Both siblings were naturally slender. Each possessing a restrained appetite, mostly due to the strict upbringing they both had endured. In Oliver's mind, a slender, petite woman was attractive. For a man, he often worried that Mina deserved someone more robust. Self-doubt was his worst enemy.

"I have often thought of what it would be like to be proposed to." Alice had known about Oliver's intentions concerning his desires to propose to Mina and had kept his secret ever since he first mentioned the desire to do so. "I am aware that women have been the one involved in a couple that proposed to the man in their life, but the concept seems foreign to me. I cannot grasp the idea of me proposing to…" She covered her mouth with her hand as she smiled, giggling at a thought, "Poor Hoven, I believe he would faint if I asked him."

Oliver sat up, his thoughts no longer on his own concerns but that of what was developing between his sister and the man in her life. "I hope you don't mind me asking, but what is the status of your relationship?" He suddenly stopped himself, feeling embarrassed for asking, an overly protective sense of wanting to make sure she was safe and happy led to his questions, "Is there a relationship?"

"I have confessed the love I feel for him." A light blush in the form of a faint red coloration touching upon her pale features led Alice to stare at her hands that rested in her lap, "His reaction was as I expected. He did not speak the words in return at the time, but I do believe he cares dearly for me. His past has made it difficult for him to feel such affection for me as generously as I do for him. He wants to but struggles to do so." Suddenly a thought crossed her mind as Alice looked up into her brother's green eyes, "Was it that way with Mina when you first told her that you loved her?"

It was only then she realized what had happened when Oliver had done so. He had confessed that he was in love with Mina and yet, she wasn't ready. He had taken the response with heartbreak.

Feeling terrible for bringing up such memories, Alice avoided eye contact, "I apologize, I remember how you told me of those events shortly after they took place. I'm happy that you confided in me, that you have someone to talk to about this when it feels that there is no one else to do so." She bit her lower lip, feeling deep concern, "It must feel strange to speak of such things with your sister. Possibly Hoven would be a more ideal person to do so with, he is another man that may…"

Alice felt a touch upon her hands which drew her to look up into her brother's eyes. Oliver gave her a reassuring smile, "I confide in you for many reasons. The first, you have always been my most trusted companion in life ever since we were children. You never gave up on me when I departed our family home despite the pressure of our mother to do so. You understand what I am enduring greater than anyone else, being the other child to choose the life of freedom rather than the destiny which our matriarch wanted for us. Lastly, your heart is pure, your vision of this world is idealized, and you help shield me from the potential for me to lose myself to what this world could have done to me. I trust you with my life as I know you do with me."

Pulling his hand away, Oliver sat back, continuing to watch his sister, "We each now have someone we care dearly for in our lives, someone we love and have expressed those feelings towards. I have had years to experience what it feels like to be in a long-term relationship, one that I hope will continue to blossom with time." He fell silent as he considered his concerns, "However, I don't know if that should involve marriage."

Alice reacted as if he had told her of the loss of a loved one, that someone close to her had died, "No..." She leaned forward, pain marring her features, "Why do you say that?"

"Early on in our relationship we spoke of marriage as if it were something that would naturally occur. We had grand plans in changing our last name to shed the past to build a brighter future. We each come from negative family experiences, but I thought we were both ready to build a family together in due time." An embarrassed smile crossed Oliver's face as he stared at his fidgeting fingers, "We certainly are not rushing into thoughts of children."

Alice fought back a giggle, enjoying her brother's reaction to his girlfriend's affections. He was a true gentleman in her mind, an ideal role model for her to mold her own life decisions after. "Go on, please?"

"Such discussions occurred often, like it was a fantasy that we enjoyed playing around with from time to time. We would even talk about what our children would be like. It was wonderful." Oliver scowled as he tried to think back to the past few months, "However, as Mina's job has taken over much of her time lately, which I'm incredibly proud of her accomplishments, it is as if the future between us is rarely brought up. I love her dearly and I believe that she still feels that same way towards me, it's just..."

Oliver took a deep breath, letting it out slowly to steady the growing anxiety concerning what was bothering him, "I feel like I'm reaching a point that I want to take that next step in our relationship and yet it feels like to me that she's comfortable with where we are now. She finds stability in our relationship."

"That's understandable. She may think of your relationship as the foundation to her life, which she can always rely on to give her strength. With so many changes happening in her career, it may make her uncomfortable to think about any alterations to the status of what she feels to be the one aspect of her life that isn't changing." Alice adored Mina and Oliver, as a couple she thought they were the ideal match. However, she was concerned about what the two individuals involved wanted to do with their future.

"I don't wish to harm you in any way, you know that. I will ask before I proceed if it is acceptable for me to speak frankly of what I have observed." The pain in Oliver's eyes broke Alice's heart for even hinting at trouble concerning his future with Mina. Yet, she had already set things in motion, therefore felt compelled to conclude, "I am certain these are observations that you yourself have already made, but it may help to have a secondary insight to such concerns?"

Oliver nodded slowly, acting as if he were about to receive grave news from a doctor, "Go on."

"You and I were born into privilege, wealth beyond our wildest imagination. If mother wished it, she had access to enough money and influence upon our society to gain whatever she wished. In turn, if we had decided to follow in her footsteps, we would have had a similar life. We would have wanted for nothing if we accepted the requirements of mother to be so blessed." Alice didn't wish to bring up their matriarch but felt compelled to begin with that aspect of their past, "When we both rejected such a life, monetary gain was never a concern for either of us."

Oliver nodded slowly, "I believe I know where you're going with this, but Mina doesn't do what she does for money. She may enjoy the perks of the wages she's paid for her efforts, but I would certainly never think of herself as a materialistic person."

"I agree, which is why I attempt to model my own life after her accomplishments and the motivations behind such deeds." Alice paused in silence to gather her thoughts, to make certain she wouldn't insult Mina or insinuate anything concerning the woman, "However, I do believe she feels that achieving a higher elevation of status in her career gives her a sense of accomplishment. She gains pride in these specific goals, where if you were in her position, you would not concern yourself with such things. You don't aspire to climb the proverbial ladder or to reach some higher level of authority in your career."

Oliver cracked a smile much to Alice's relief, "I don't have a career. I have a job that helps pay the bills, but that's it. Sometimes I'm worried that Mina thinks I'm unmotivated, that I don't want to do more with my life. It's not that, it's just..." His brow furrowed in consideration, "I find fulfillment in simple pleasures, a nice meal made for the woman I love, creating flowers out of paper to surprise her with..." He wiped away a tear at the thought of losing Mina, "She is my world. I want nothing else but to support her in her endeavors and to make her happy. I enjoy every moment I'm with her and yet, I know that's not enough for her. I respect that and I do what I can to give her the freedom she desires."

Alice smiled warmly, "You have found completion in your life through Mina, being in love with her, your relationship."

Oliver interjected, "A part of me thinks, why isn't that enough for her? Alternatively, I think to myself, why is it enough for me? Why am I not more driven to do more with my life?"

Alice had been considering related questions concerning her own life, "When I was still under our matriarch's tutelage, I felt as if my only value were as a bride and a mother to the children of a man who could provide for me. At the time, I felt such a life was restrictive, restrained. I was imprisoned by that potential future to the point that it terrified me. It was one of many motivations for me to break free from such a fate."

She held up her hand in defense even though she knew Oliver would not react aggressively, she still felt maybe she was potentially insulting his viewpoint, "I have spoken to multiple women and in rare cases, men who fulfill the role of a parent and nothing else. They find contentment as a caretaker and nurturer to their offspring. There is nothing wrong with finding happiness in such a role to play."

"We are meant to be equals. If we do have children, I want them to be as much a part of their mother's life as they are mine." Oliver hung his head in defeat, "I don't know. The more I think about the situation, the more I feel like it's self-doubt causing me to think such things." He was lost in a memory of Mina's dark, forest green eyes, "I love her dearly and I'm so scared that I'm going to lose her." Tears formed in his eyes as he stared at his hands resting in his lap.

"Oliver..." Alice gently touched his hands with hers, "You are perfect in Mina's eyes, I'm certain of it."

A smile tugged at Oliver's lips, "I know, and she tells me often but…" He closed his eyes, the weight of the world feeling as if it was resting upon his shoulders, "What if love isn't enough to keep a relationship from falling apart?"

~

"Why are you here with me and not that scrumptious man you like to keep all to yourself?" Mitch touched his chest with his fingertips with one hand while holding a glass of a colorful liquid in the other, "Don't get me wrong, lately it feels like I have to steal you away just to get five minutes alone time with my best friend, but don't you have to make time for Angel?"

Mina smiled as she watched Mitch in amusement. She needed this. Time spent with a man who could unravel the tension that had been building all week. She loved Oliver, adored spending time with him, but there was something about Mitch that made her laugh even when she was determined to be a foul mood. "I like to make time for everyone who is special in my life."

Mitch set down his drink as he leaned forward with a playful smile, "Awe, Kitten, I love that." His dark eyes had a perpetual twinkle of excitement in them that most found charming. His well-cared for face, flawless model level appearance and toned muscular body often led many to an instant attraction towards the man. Add in an admiration and flowing compliments towards those he met, he was always a welcome addition to any social gathering. "I could be at home curled up in the arms of my snuggle bunny or out here with your beautiful face." He acted as if he had been asked to make the hardest choice of his life, "To be honest, it was a hard decision."

Mina laughed, "Speaking of your snuggle bunny, how are you two doing?"

"Michael and I are…" Mitch made small gestures of his hands to accent what he was speaking of, "You know those warm chocolate fountains, constantly flowing with this warm, delicious, yummy delight that melts in your mouth, slides gently down your throat, and leaves an oh so warm and tantalizing feeling as it goes down?" He laughed, "That would be us. Yummy, good for my tummy, oh so warm and fuzzy…"

Mina laughed at his description, her dark, forest green eyes watching him in amusement, "You've come a long way from the man who said that he would live and die a bachelor."

"I'm like a born-again boyfriend. I changed my ways when it comes to affairs of the heart." Mitch motioned towards his friend, "It's all your fault. I had a taste, just a sliver of what you told me about your time with Oliver and how he swept you off your feet." He sipped at his drink before adding, "I admit, I was horrendously jealous, so I wanted a little bit of that myself."

Mina absently brushed her fingertips through her shoulder length light brown hair. She had recently cut it due to feeling as if she was spending too much time dealing with maintenance that she didn't wish to cope with. She remembered Oliver's reaction of disappointment before he tried to hide such feelings from her under a sweet, supportive smile. She knew he loved long hair, but she was trying to minimize the number of distractions to her job.

With her thoughts wondering, Mina asked, "Have you ever thought about getting married?"

"Okay then, straight to the point." Mitch set down his glass as he focused his full attention on Mina, "I knew something was bothering you, thought it would take me some time to work my way around other subjects before we delved into the heavier stuff but leap right in, why don't you?"

Mina scowled at her friend, "I'm being serious. You talk about how your relationship is going well and so I thought, have you considered getting married?"

"To begin with, for most of my life, it wasn't even an option for me. It was actually impossible for me to get legally married to the person I love." Mitch gave Mina a serious expression, any hints of amusement had vanished, "Did you know that a white man couldn't be legally married to a black woman in a lot of states until June of nineteen sixty-seven? Until then, police officers could arrest the woman, throw her in jail for being with her husband."

"Let's leap forward in time to about forty-eight years later when two people of the same gender were finally given the same legal rights of marriage as a man and a woman. Until then, the idea was denied to me." Mitch scowled, "Do you realize what that feels like? To essentially be told that while everyone else gets to enjoy the idea of planning their wedding, putting on those wonderful rings, getting the legal rights as a married couple that a man and woman get to enjoy, I was basically told I can't think about that because it's just not going to happen. Did that stop me from being who I am? Did that prevent me from loving someone that in my heart I wanted to get married to some day? No."

Mina started to reply, "I'm sorry, I shouldn't have…"

Mitch held up his hand to silence her, "My point is, I haven't thought about marriage because it's been denied to me for so long that it just never felt like an option. Now that it is, I don't know, I hadn't thought about it." He leaned forward, driving his intense gaze into Mina's eyes, "However, if I was thinking about marriage, I would talk to my significant other about the topic just like you should if it's on your mind."

"We've talked about marriage a lot early on in our relationship. It was something fun to bring up and play around with in our minds but lately…" Mina stared at the drink in her hand. Unlike Mitch, hers was non-alcoholic. "It feels like we're avoiding talking about it. I had a feeling that he was going to propose, I kept thinking he was working up the courage to do so but then suddenly, it's like he gave up."

Mitch sat back, watching Mina in concern, "Oh sweetie, you do give off that vibe I used to have when I was single." He quickly added, "Don't get me wrong, you love that man, you adore him, you speak of him with nothing but honey coated sweetness and for good reason, he is…" Mitch smiled for the first time before assuming his earlier serious tone, "He renewed my faith in the idea of being in love because he is so passionate, so heartfelt and…" He sighed, "See? Jealous, completely, and totally jealous of you. I admit to it."

"I'm not ready for marriage. My career is moving upward so quickly that I think trying to work around my busy schedule to make time for all the arrangements for something like that…" Mina noticed Mitch's disappointed expression, "What?"

He cringed, "You just referred to it as, something like that."

Mina fell back against her chair with a soft groan, "I know, I hate myself sometimes but it's how I feel."

"Then don't get married. Simple as that." Mitch pointed at her with a serious expression verging on threatening tone, "However, don't you dare hurt that poor man or let him slip through your fingers. If you lose him, you'll regret it for the rest of your life, and I will be heartbroken for both of you." He pouted for a moment before adding, "I can't take that kind of emotional damage, so even if you can handle it, know I can't." He touched his hand to his chest, "Do it for my sake, alright?"

Mina scowled at her friend, "Really? Do it for you? Oliver and I have nothing to do with the whole situation, just so you stay happy, is that it?"

"Now you're getting it." Mitch acted as if he was offended, "How long have we known one another, years and years, and you're only now understanding this about how the world works? Priority above all others, me of course. Then Oliver comes in second…"

Mina clasped her hands together as she stared at them intently, thinking about what it would be like to have a wedding band around her finger signifying that she was no longer Oliver's girlfriend, but his wife. The thought of the word led to her whispering it softly as if she were introducing the concept to the world by breathing life into it.

"I've lost you, Kitten, what was that?" Mitch watched Mina in curiosity, uncertain of what was happening, "What's going on inside that head of yours?"

"Wife…" Mina looked up at him, "Wife…"

"I may consider myself more so as one of you ladies than among those fine gentlemen here, there, and everywhere, but I am never going to be someone's wife. Husband, yes. Wife, no." Seeing that his joke was getting no reaction, he quickly dropped his attempt at humor, "I could try to figure you out by guessing, but I need something more than the word wife."

"Wife." Mina's eyes came into focus as she stared at Mitch, "I am comfortable with the idea of being Oliver's girlfriend. He's my boyfriend. We're in a relationship. We love each other. We tell one another how much we care all the time. I'm not worried about the future because we're happy where we are now. It's stable. It's reliable. No matter how chaotic my life gets, I know he'll always be there. I'm happy where I'm at in my life and I don't want anything to change."

Worry crept into her features as she looked around passively, "Wife? I feel like I must become something different, someone new to fulfill a role like that. I think about how my dad was married and had a wife. Then, because he got my mom pregnant with me, suddenly he had to divorce his first wife and marry my mom just to make it look like they were married when I was conceived. Marriage is just this piece of paper that tells the government that you're in some arrangement that affects you financially. Other times it's just for social status. If a man is married to a woman, he has control over her or if a woman is married to a man, she gets his money if they get divorced or if they die…"

Mitch clicked his fingers in front of her face, "Mina? Mina… Mina! Snap out of it, you're getting louder the longer you go on."

Burying her face in her hands, Mina groaned softly, "I'm not ready to be a wife, I may never be prepared for that. I thought I was, when it was just some sort of fun thing to think about, but now that it feels like it might actually happen, I don't…"

She looked up as if pleading with Mitch, "I love Oliver. Before I met him, I was so cut off from that part of myself. I hated the idea of love, I thought it was a waste of time. I didn't have any faith in it whatsoever. I didn't think it existed. If it did, it certainly wouldn't ever exist for me."

Mina stared at the table between the two of them, "Little by little, being this beautiful soul… He showed me what it was like to be loved, to be cared for, to feel safe… He allowed me to let down my guard, to think about what it would be like to be happy on that level that…" Tears formed in her eyes as she thought about Oliver's heartbreaking pain in his eyes when he first told her he loved her and she didn't say anything in return, "I can't hurt him, I can't… I refuse to do that to him again."

She looked up into Mitch's eyes, "I love him so much I would say yes not because I'm ready to get married or because I want to be his wife, all of that scares me. I would say yes because I know he would be so heartbroken if I said no or hesitated to respond to his proposal."

Mina wiped the tears from her eyes as she continued, "What's worse is that he would know. He would realize the truth and I would still hurt him despite me doing everything I could to prevent that from happening." She buried her face in the palms of her hands as she leaned forward with her elbows on the table with a soft groan.

"Sweetie?" Mitch tried to get through to her, "If he knows you as well as I do, which I'm guessing despite my best efforts, he does, then he's aware of your feelings on the subject. I'm sure he wouldn't pop the question unless he was hundred percent sure you were ready to say yes and not just because you felt obligated to."

Mina sighed, "We're so different when it comes to our life goals. He's happy with our relationship, being with me, spending time with me, and that's it. He has no goals concerning a career or doing something more with his life. Any time I mention him at work, often people will ask what he does for a living. What are his aspirations for the future when it comes to his career? I try to explain and it's like they pity me for not having someone more driven to do something more in his life. Some have even said that he's going to hold me back from accomplishing my goals."

"First of all, if I find out anyone, be those people you work with, your parents, your brother, even the mall Santa who I think is adorable in that bright red suit of his, convinces you that your career is more important than the love of that beautiful man..." Mitch pressed his lips tightly together in debate over what the repercussions would be, "Let's just say that I would not be a happy camper and I will make it well known to the one responsible for harming him and you by poisoning your thoughts that way."

Mina smiled at his reaction, "I'm trying to find a way to balance everything I want in my life. Oliver, you, Alice, my career, and..." She fell silent mid-sentence as a thought struck her, "I was going to say family, but I haven't talked to my parents in years or my brother for that matter."

"Hypothetically speaking, just for the fun of it, let's say that you and Oliver do get married." Mitch held up his hand to stop Mina from replying immediately, "You're sending out invitations. Who would you invite? I'm guessing your mom and dad are out, but what about your brother?"

Mina shook her head slowly, "I haven't heard from him in years, so no. You know my feelings about my parents, so..." Deflecting her concerns for the time being to think about other aspects of marriage, her brow furrowed in consideration, "You of course. Michael. I would say someone from work but I'm not exactly close to anyone and most of them don't approve of Oliver." She looked up from her thoughts with a smile, "It's definitely going to be a small wedding. You, Michael, Alice, Hoven, and I think that's it."

"To fill out the wedding party just a little bit, would it be alright if I invited my sister, her roommate, and their significant others? Not sure if Sparkle..." Seeing the confusion in Mina's eyes, Mitch explained, "I've been calling my sister Sparkle since we were kids. She was the first to ever earn herself one of my lovely nick names." He quickly shifted topics, "I'm not sure if Sparkle is with anyone at the moment, but..."

Mina nodded slowly, "Fine, but Oliver and I did discuss the idea of the size of our wedding, and we just want something small, just those closest to us."

Mitch grinned, "Excellent, I will call my sister tonight and give her the heads up of what the future will bring."

Chapter 2

Mina closed her eyes as she felt the soft, steady rhythm of Oliver's heartbeat underneath her fingertips. What had begun as dinner that he had prepared for her knowing that she would be getting off work late, had worked its way into an attempt at watching a movie which continued to play in the background of her mind. She had long since lost interest in television and was focused on the man she was curled up next to.

Home. That's what Oliver was to her. Home is where she felt safe, protected, content, relaxed, happy, and felt as if she not only belonged there but was welcomed with joy. Despite having her own apartment, she spent most of her time at his house. Often, she would find herself waking up in his bed, having fallen asleep on his couch. He would delicately lift her in his arms and take her to a more comfortable place to rest.

Much to her frustration, she would find him asleep on the couch each time. At this memory, her eyes opened. The side of her head touched his shoulder, her forehead gently pressed against the curve of his neck, her hand placed against his chest felt the warmth of his body through the fabric of his shirt. She scowled as if wanting to scold him, "Why don't you sleep next to me when you take me to your bed?"

Oliver gently brushed his fingers through her hair which lulled her into a half-awake state of blissful relaxation. She couldn't see his reaction but the tension in his body revealed that the question startled him, "I thought we discussed this already."

"We've been together for three years. There are couples who have done far more than we have after knowing each other for only three hours." Mina smiled as her fingertips gently played along the edge of the bottom of his shirt as she tried her best at a seductive smile, "Do you not trust me?"

"I trust you with my life." Oliver gently took her hand in his. He didn't remove her attempt at feeling his bare skin, but it was a gesture to stop her progress, "I find you to be incredibly attractive. My desire to be with you intimately can be so intoxicating at times that I don't trust myself."

Pulling away, Mina sat up, focusing her dark green eyes on her boyfriend, "Is it because of kids? Is that what you're worried about?" At first, she found the slow pace of their relationship as welcomed, wanted, and if she was honest with herself, needed. Her previous boyfriend had physically assaulted her when she had said no. She had barely escaped the situation and had disconnected herself from such interest in getting that close to a man again until she had met Oliver. "We can take steps to prevent that from happening."

After years of being with him, though, the lack of progress in their relationship began to grow from something she found comforting to a concern. Oliver calmly responded, having similar conversations in the past, he was prepared for what he wanted to say in response to related questions, "You know that's not why." He looked away, as if searching his memories, "I think about it often, what it would be like to be a father. At this point it's scary and exciting all at the same time."

Mina had been avoiding bringing up the topic, but she felt it was time to just get out of her system. Ever since her conversation with Mitch about marriage, being Oliver's wife, the idea had been sitting in her conscious thoughts for so long it was beginning to give her a headache. She was bottling up her emotions concerning the topic and they had promised one another not to hide anything from each other. "It's because we're not married, is that it?"

Oliver avoided eye contact when he felt uncomfortable, which was what he was doing now, "I know you don't think less of me for feeling that way, but I thought I had explained why I felt that…"

"Oliver?" His jade green eyes quickly shifted to focus on her as Mina continued, "I'm sorry." She leaned forward, kissing him softly before smiling at the exquisite pleasure it was to feel the warmth, passion, and intensity that he was able to express to her in such a small gesture. Often, after a single touch of his lips, she would feel like crying. He made every moment, especially when expressing his intimate care for her, incredibly beautiful.

Sitting back, she stared at him in silence before sighing in a mixture of frustration over the topic and the simple answer that Oliver had given to her. If it was only that easy for her. "Sex has always been such a weird topic for me. I had the usual mixed signals as a teenager. Sex is okay, just a natural expression of intimacy. Sex is just sex, whatever, just enjoy it and don't think too much about it. Sex should be only between a husband and wife for religious reasons. Sex was dirty, something to be ashamed of just thinking about it."

Oliver expressed so much without ever knowing he was doing so. During her speech, Mina noticed his arms were brought up close to his chest as if he were defending himself from something she had said, "Society has all these different viewpoints of sex. Some good, some bad, others think it's evil or it takes away from who we are spiritually, if we give into the physical world or something like that." Mina was rambling, she wasn't certain where she was going but once she started, it was hard to stop.

"Then of course there were my parents. My father cheated on his first wife with my mother. My mother wasn't much better, she was fully aware he was a married man, but she didn't care. I doubt that they loved each other, not once have I ever seen them together with a hint of warmth between them." Mina scowled at the memories of her childhood, "As an adult, I realized it was just about sex for them. That's all, two consenting adults who were attracted to one another so much that they were willing to ignore his marriage to another woman."

"Of course, all of that led to me. I exist because a husband ignored his pledge to his wife and wanted to have sex with another woman because..." Mina told her own story concerning her mental state with her actions. She pulled away from Oliver, turning to let her legs droop over the edge to allow her bare feet to touch the floor, "I'm the child created from lust, not love. My parents didn't love me. They blamed me for their mistake, their choice, that of a cheating husband and his mistress screwing up their lives. Somehow, because my mother got pregnant, it was the baby's fault, not her or the man she chose to be with."

"So, of course, as a teenager on her way to becoming an adult, I had a pretty screwed up viewpoint of sex. The idea of getting pregnant scared me so much that it was the main reason I avoided sex. I didn't want to get pregnant and ruin my life the way my parents blamed me for doing it to them." Mina felt Oliver moving to sit next to her, his arm sliding across her waist as he held her gently. She leaned against him, her head touching his shoulder, "By the time things went wrong with him..." She didn't want to name her ex-boyfriend, she mentioned him only as a painful memory, one she was trying to forget, "It was like a final reason to give up on the idea of sex, my sexuality, and intimacy."

Oliver spoke, barely above a whisper but loud enough for her to hear him, "Interesting..."

Pulling away from him, preparing herself to get mad over his peculiar behavior, if anything to have a path to channel her anger and frustration with her parents, Mina asked, "What was that for?"

Oliver removed his arm from Mina's back, leaving his hands resting in his lap. It was a defensive move he would make, like saying that he surrendered and didn't want a confrontation. He stared at his fingers as he thought about what she had said, "Sex, sexuality, and intimacy." He looked up into her eyes, "You separated the three. I thought that was interesting."

Mina reached over, sliding her hand over his as she inched closer to him. She hated the feeling of being separate from him. Whenever she was upset over something, which was never anything to do with him, she often took those bottled-up emotions and lashed out. Often, he was a victim of this, and his response broke her heart.

"Sex is the act of doing so. Sexuality is in my mind at least, how others see us and how we see ourselves. That involves self-confidence, how we view our bodies, our bodies themselves of course, and our ability to interact with others when it comes to the topic of sex." Mina squeezed Oliver's hand, "Intimacy is an emotional connection between two people. It doesn't have to involve sex but the best kind of sex, I would think at least, is when it's an expression of intimacy. It's because of that, and of course you, that I think about sex differently now than I did before."

Oliver stared at their joined hands, a lost look in his eyes, "I love you."

There was a lingering silence that worried Mina. After giving him what she felt was a long enough time to say something further, she replied, "I love you, Oliver. I don't want you ever to ever doubt that." She hesitated to continue but felt compelled to do so, "With that said, I don't know why you just told me that in response to what we were just talking about."

He looked up into her eyes with a faint smile. She knew that smile. It was unique, one that formed when he was lost in memories concerning the two of them. Mina loved how she could read him so easily, understand what little reactions to her meant. "I remember the first time you said those words. I never thought I would have a happier memory than that moment but each day I feel as if new experiences I have with you replace the previous ones with my favorite." He laughed nervously, "There is much of our future together that I think about. I consider what it would be like and will it live up to my expectations."

Concern worked its way into Mina's eyes and facial expressions, "Is that what you're worried about? You don't think it will be like, how you imagine it will be?"

A shy smile, a bashful expression washed across his face as he looked away, staring at their hands. It was moments like this which made Mina fell in love with Oliver, as if for the first time. She felt the yearning to cry, staring at such an incredibly beautiful man. He made her feel safe, protected, as if the world around them would never disrupt the happiness he brought into her life. Yet, he was vulnerable, delicate, like a flower that needed to be gently cared for. It was this side of him that she felt like the protector, his guardian angel, providing him the strength to endure the hardships that he encountered. It was this ideal balance that he offered her that made him perfect in her eyes.

"It's not that." Oliver laughed nervously, "Well, maybe a little." He fell silent, starting to speak only to stop himself as he struggled to find the right words to properly express himself. Mina watched him in concern but didn't want to rush him. She knew that he would tell her what was bothering him when he was ready. Finally he spoke in a near whisper, "I'm afraid..."

Mina's breathe caught in her chest when she saw the first signs of tears in his eyes. A pain struck her, the feeling of loss, sorrow, as if he were about to tell her that someone close to them had died. It was that form of heartbreak she felt whenever he cried. She wanted to sooth his troubled mind, to heal the pain he was experiencing, he deserved that and so much more for not only who he was, but all he had done for her.

"I'm afraid I won't be…" Oliver struggled to breath, his mind churning with trying to find the right words and yet when he spoke, it was blurting out the first thing that leaped to mind, "I won't be good enough for you."

Mina scowled in confusion, "What?"

"Not just when it comes to intimacy, but everything concerning our future. I want to be an ideal for you, perfect in every way, you deserve that. I've endeavored to be an ideal boyfriend, doing everything I can to make your life easier, to support you and give you strength when you needed it." Oliver felt it increasingly difficult to keep his breathing steady, "I'm afraid I won't ever be good enough for you as a husband." The first droplet fell from his eyes, "There are moments when I'm scared of the future, not certain if I'm ready for where life is taking me. Even if I'm able to be everything you want, need, and deserve as a lifelong partner, will I ever be a good enough father to our children? After what my mother did to me, and your parents hurt you…"

"Oliver…" Mina slid her arm around him, pulling him closely. He leaned over, touching his head to her shoulder as he released the pent-up emotions that had been building inside of him. No further words were needed to be spoken. What needed to be expressed was done so without sound, a loving embrace providing the comfort so dearly needed.

~

"I feel so embarrassed." Sitting on the front steps of his house, Oliver rested his elbows against his upper thighs as he buried his face in the palms of his hands.

"One should never feel embarrassed with the one they love. No matter what is said, or action taken, even by accident, your dearest will never judge you for such things. You should not feel concerned about their reaction." Alice touched her hand to Oliver's upper arm, "I am certain that Mina cherished your expression of emotion and is grateful that you were honest with her when telling her of your concerns."

Oliver looked up, dropping his hands into his lap as he avoided eye contact with his sister, "Telling Mina, I am happy I did so." He looked over at Alice with a playful smile, "Telling my sister about my experience with my girlfriend, that's what I find to be embarrassing."

Alice was confused by the statement, "All you said to me was that you and Mina were discussing your future and your concerns led to tears. You cried in the presence of the woman you love." She practically glowed at the thought of Hoven doing so with her, "I find that to be absolutely beautiful." Her smile faded as concern worked its way into her pristine features, "Men are often taught at an early age by our culture to not express themselves emotionally. It is comforting to know that you are able to do so."

Oliver had been doing lawn work when Alice had arrived. When she asked about how he was doing, he hesitated which she pursued the question in more depth. That led him to explain briefly and without any details as to what exactly they spoke of concerning the discussion he had with Mina the night before. Eventually the pair was sitting on the steps leading up to the front door of his house. In retrospect, he thought maybe he shouldn't have said so much.

Still, Alice was practically the only person he could talk to other than Mina. He was friends with Mitch but found it difficult to speak to the man about anything, especially personal topics. At the thought of others in his life, he remembered that it was Hoven, Alice's boyfriend, who had dropped her off. To change subjects, Oliver asked, "How are things with you and your own special someone?"

Alice blushed at the thought of such things being spoken of Hoven, "It is peculiar to me to think of him as my love. Some part of me knew he was the one the moment I first laid eyes upon his handsome face. Of course, it was not an easy journey for either of us, but I believe we have found a comfortable place for us to grow together." She giggled at memories of him, "He is so incredibly shy, I find it absolutely charming."

Oliver chuckled, "Mina says the same thing about me."

"I cannot speak for her, but for me, it allows me to feel as if I can be more assertive. More dominant personalities make me feel as if I have no voice, that I must remain silent or follow their lead." Alice considered a mutual friend of theirs, "As much as I care for Mitch and his role in my life, his personality can be challenging for me at times. We have had multiple instances in which he pushed me too far and I was forced to confront him due to his behavior."

"I think he's afraid to be that way with me." Oliver burst out laughing, "Mina may be a foot shorter than him and probably half his body weight, but he acts like he's scared of her sometimes. If he hurts me, even a little, he knows she will come after him with a vengeance."

Alice scowled at the idea, "That's peculiar. Yes, you are Mina's love and should be the most important in her life, but it was my understanding that I was under her protective guidance also. Why would she allow Mitch to run wild around me and yet he hesitates with you?" Oliver covered his mouth with his hand as he laughed leaving her to ask, "What is it that you find so humorous?"

Lowering his hand, Oliver stared into his sister's eyes, "I believe that the difference between the two of us is that Mitch's viewpoint of you may be different. He sees you as a potential sibling as opposed to me being something else in his mind?"

Staring at her brother with a narrow-eyed gaze, Alice studied his face as if trying to decipher what he was alluding to. "I don't understand your meaning."

"It's my understanding that before I formally met the man, he had seen me from afar and was aware of my appearance. Since then, he has not been subtle in his approval of me?" Oliver quickly concluded when he realized Alice didn't understand, "He isn't attracted to you."

Suddenly Alice's jade green eyes lit up with surprise as her mouth opened in shock, "Oh!" Her hands quickly covered her mouth as she burst into giggling at the realization of what her brother was speaking. When she lowered her hands, her face showing signs of her embarrassment with a red coloration across areas of her face, "Oh goodness, that is quite interesting to consider. Obviously, it is difficult for me to think of such things when you are concerned. Even when it comes to Mina's attraction to you, I only think of her love for you, not other aspects of such…"

Oliver laughed, looking away, he stared at his lawn, feeling awkward about the topic of the conversation, "Yeah, it has been an interesting journey when it comes to my interactions with Mitch, that's for certain."

"I can only imagine." Suddenly another thought struck Alice leading to a second shocked expression washing across her face, "What of Hoven? Do you believe he has been exposed to such a positive response to his appearance?"

Oliver barely interacted with Hoven. Since Alice had first met the man, they had crossed paths on rare occasions and often he did not speak much during such encounters. What he knew of him was from what his sister had spoken of. "I'm not certain, but it might be something you can bring up next time you see him."

"Oh no, I dare not. He may find that to be embarrassing. Not so much that a man shows interest in the beautiful person that he is, but he is uncomfortable being given compliments from anyone." Alice's brow furrowed in concern, "He continues to struggle with responding appropriately when I say something nice about him, especially when it pertains to his appearance."

Oliver smiled at what she was speaking of, "I used to be that way with Mina. Before we started dating, we had this lengthy discussion when she first visited my house. At one point she accused me of not having any self-confidence, even though I said I did."

"Oh yes, it is one her favorite compliments you have bestowed upon her." Alice paused as she searched her memories, "What was it you said? Even if I was a perfect ten before I met you, you've made me realize that a twenty exists, far beyond my reach."

"She told you?" Oliver's feelings of embarrassment grew, "Of course she told you." It was then he felt compelled to ask, "Just how much has she told you about me or us as a couple?"

"It is my understanding that I am the only female in her life she confides in. There are other women she interacts with concerning her job, but she does not share a personal connection with them and certainly wouldn't bring up her heartfelt moments. It saddens me to know that she feels isolated emotionally where she is employed." Alice shook her head in concern, "She says she is thriving in the environment, but to not have any devoted friends, to be emotionally detached from those around you I would feel would be rather unsatisfactory."

"Mina has two sides to her. The woman I met, fierce, determined, motivated, what I playfully call her work mode. She is emotionally cut off. She doesn't allow personal feelings to distract her and she's a force of nature when it comes to getting things done. It is why she was promoted so quickly in the last few years. She claims it's because of me." Oliver sighed, almost feeling guilty of doing something wrong, "She says until she met me, she was avoiding any attention from others as she hid away in her cubicle. After we got together, she was confident, comfortable, and able to speak her mind more often at work. That caught the attention of upper management, and the rest was her determination to accomplish her goals, to prove that she could overcome each new obstacle."

Alice could see the growing concern in his eyes, so she gently asked, "What of the other side of her? You said that she has two sides, her work being one. What of the other?"

Concern quickly faded to joy as Oliver answered, "The woman she is with me and I'm certain you. She's warm, affectionate, kind, generous, protective in an angel warrior sort of way, but…" His smile faded as memories flooded him, "She's vulnerable, fragile at times. She lets her guard down and opens herself up to being loved, to being in love, to connecting with others on a personal level. That's the Mina I fell in love with, the woman I love dearly, and the woman I want to…" He stared off into the distance, what his eyes were gazing upon the last thing on his mind.

"You wish to marry?" Alice touched her hand to his as she smiled sweetly, "Was that what the conversation you had with her last night was pertaining to?"

Oliver nodded, "Yes."

Concern grew as Alice asked, "It didn't go well?"

"Yes and no. I mean, I was able to talk about a lot of what was on my mind and release built up emotions concerning the topic, but I feel like we didn't resolve anything. We both want a future together, the destination is mutually agreed upon, but the path we take to reach that point feels like we are at odds with one another concerning how to do so. She's obviously not ready to move forward and when I think I am, I fall apart." Oliver sighed deeply, finally returning to the world around him as he turned to his sister, "I'm sorry, I don't mean to unload my concerns upon you like this."

"I am happy that I can bring you comfort in providing you someone to speak to about all of this." Alice smiled to reassure him before she asked, "May I ask, if it isn't too personal of an inquisitive curiosity on my part to do so, what did you mean by falling apart?"

"Oh…" Oliver turned away, his mind drifting once more, "I think I'm ready at times, but then I realize maybe I'm not. Maybe I never will be."

Alice gently squeezed his hand, "Please don't say that. It breaks my heart to even think of such a thing."

Before he had met Mina, Oliver had been in love with another woman. He had proposed to her, they began making plans for the wedding, everything felt like his world was perfect. That was when his mother intervened, speaking harshly of his fiancé, and saying that she was not good enough for their family. It was then that he was forced to choose between the woman he loved and his family. Of course, the choice was easy, he chose his future wife.

Turning his back upon his family also meant leaving behind the life of luxury. He was forcefully exiled from the mansion that he had grown up in, his possessions practically stripped from him. He had moved in with his fiancé, thinking that their love would endure, and they would create a new life together.

The truth quickly surfaced when their relationship became toxic in nature within the first month. As it was soon revealed, the only reason the woman he loved wanted to be with him was due to the wealth and luxury that his family would provide her. She only wanted to marry him for the materialistic offerings that would come with being a part of his family.

Shattered from the experience, the engagement was ended, and Oliver became a broken man. It was years until he finally withdrew from depression and began putting his life back together. He had given up on love until he met Mina.

"I trust her, I know she won't hurt me, but…" Oliver struggled with the idea that lurked in the back of his mind, "I put my faith in love once before and was betrayed. I can't help but fear that happening to me again." He quickly held up his hand to stop Alice from responding immediately, "I know, I shouldn't, but it's still there, like a weight upon my soul."

Alice was at a loss for words. When Oliver departed from her life to pursue a relationship with his former fiancé, she had felt betrayed by him at the time. It didn't help that their mother certainly painted him in such a terrible light, as if he were a scoundrel that had broken the trust and faith his family had in him. It wasn't until years later that she realized the truth and she made a similar decision. She desired the freedom to create her own life, to not be shackled by the expectations of her domineering matriarch.

"I'm sorry." Oliver's words broke Alice from her revere, "I shouldn't be speaking of all this to you. It's inappropriate and rude." He tried to clear his thoughts, "When you arrived, you mentioned that you wanted to talk to me about something and I interrupted you with my personal concerns."

"To begin with, speaking your concerns to someone that you trust and feel comforted by is never inappropriate. It certainly is not rude." Alice smiled in the hopes of cheering him up, "As for why I arrived, it is something we can speak of on another day. For now, you have more than enough weighing heavily upon you and I wish to alleviate that burden." She pulled herself to her feet, taking a moment to gently brush her hands across the light blue dress that rode just below her knees, "I wish to cheer you up."

Oliver hesitated, "What is it that you wanted to talk to me about? Does it involve you and Hoven?"

Alice smiled innocently, refusing to give in, "No, it does not. Enough of your questions for the time being concerning such matters. I am determined to find your smile even if it must take all day for me to do so." She held out her hand, "Now then, it may be a bit of a walk to reach our destination, so I wish to request for you to drive us to a location of my choosing."

Oliver looked down at his sister after he stood, "What do you have in mind?"

"Well, for starters, I know when I'm upset, I find that ice cream often turns my frown into a smile." Alice gently poked Oliver in the chest, "You need something extra special. I'm thinking your favorite with a light chocolate drizzle…" She giggled, "I so adore that word, drizzle." She laughed again, "Drizzle…" She made a series of strange faces as she sounded out the world in multiple unusual ways, "Drizzle… Drizzle…" The last time she said it with as a deep voice as she could muster with a deep frown, "Drizzle…"

Laughing at his sister's playful behavior, Oliver gave in, "Fine, you win. Cookie dough for me and…"

Alice clasped her hands behind her back as she smiled, "I like to be surprised with what they have to offer. I still have many new flavors to try out for the first time, so I will decide when we get there. Would that be alright with you?"

"It's your tummy." Oliver gently poked her in the stomach, "Alright, you accomplished your mission, you found my smile." He turned towards the house, "I need to wash my hands before we go."

Realizing that he had just touched her dress with dirty hands, Alice brushed away the spot where his finger had made contact. Thankfully, it wasn't covered in dirt at the time so there was no smudge to be found, "Would you have done that if you had soil upon your hands?"

"Of course not, that's one of the dresses that mother had tailor made for you. I wouldn't want to harm it." As the pair moved towards his house, Oliver concluded, "It was one of the few positive things that she did for you in allowing you to keep them."

~

"How did it go?" The moment Hoven asked the question, the answer revealed itself in Alice's eyes. It was one of the reasons he felt so comfortable around her, her honesty, it was as if it was impossible for her to hide anything from him. "That's bad, right?"

Alice carefully brushed her hands across her dress as she sat in the passenger seat of Hoven's car. Before they had met, the area was reserved for some of his belongings, but he had emptied the space just for her since he didn't allow anyone else in his vehicle. For most, a car was transportation from one location to another or possibly a symbol of one's social status. For him, it was his home, for he had been living there for years.

The gesture she had made was her attempt to avoid answering if only for a moment as she gathered her thoughts, "It went well in one aspect." She smiled, "I was able to cheer him up, for he was struggling with personal concerns involving his relationship." She quickly looked up in concern, "I didn't mean that negatively, they love one another and are happy together."

Hoven's dark blue eyes watched Alice in confusion for a moment before shaking his head, "Sometimes it takes more than love and being happy with one another for a relationship to work." He grinned, "Not that I would know, you're the closest thing to a whatever I've ever had in my life." He stared at his steering wheel, "I didn't exactly do well with women before I met you."

"Sometimes when I am shopping for a new dress, it takes hours to find something that fits me ideally. I browse, I consider style and design, color scheme, and of course size is important. Then, the way each garment is created, how it presses against my body here or is too loose there can lead to discomfort. If I'm lucky, I eventually find one that fits me." Alice looked over at Hoven, "Sometimes a person spends a lifetime searching, trying out what it would be like in a relationship with multiple people and never find something ideal."

Hoven stared into her jade green eyes with growing confusion, "Did you just compare me to clothes?"

Alice suddenly covered her face in embarrassment, "Oh goodness, no!" Lowering her hands, she gave him a pleading look, "I'm so sorry, I never meant to offend you with my attempt at a metaphor. What I meant was that there is the rare occasion when I pick out a dress and it fits me perfectly the first time, without need to search further." She gently placed her hands into her lap as she smiled sweetly, "You are blessed in that you did not have to search the world over, spending multiple years and enduring heartbreak from relationships that did not work out well, before you found your one true love."

Hoven sat back in his chair, staring out the front window of his car, "It sounds weird when you say it like that."

Alice stuck out her lower lip as if pouting in disappointment, "You do not believe I am your one true love?"

"Yeah... Of course... But..." Suddenly he sat up and turned towards her, "I meant, it's weird when you talk like that. At least it is to me." He sighed, "I'm sorry, I don't know how to talk about this."

Alice grinned playfully, "It's quite alright, I will be your guide into this beautiful realm of majestic tranquility that is true love."

Growing frustrated with her straightforward optimism, Hoven felt like he needed to make a few things clear first, "I enjoy the fact that you like me..."

Alice smiled warmly, "Not like, I love you." She kissed her fingertips before touching them to Hoven's mouth. Seeing his stunned reaction, she giggled at his reaction. A few seconds later, her smile faded when she realized something was wrong, "Are you breathing?" She tapped his chest, "Breathe!"

Snapping out of a trance, Hoven took in a sudden deep breath, "Okay... Right..." He swallowed before nodding, "Warn a guy next time before you do that."

"It wouldn't be as romantic or playfully flirtatious if I did." Alice smiled before giggling at his reaction to the words romantic and flirtatious. Hoven suffered from a form of social anxiety. When overwhelmed he was known to faint, a complete shutdown of his mental processes which led to what he referred to as blacking out. Other symptoms were forgetting to breathe or dizziness.

Alice theorized that his mental state was due to years of physical and emotional abuse from an early age. He never knew his parents, his mother put him up for adoption shortly after he was born. Years of being moved from one foster home to another led to an endless stream of abuse by the other children he lived with. His smaller size led to ridicule and an erosion of his self-esteem as an adult. Standing at five foot four, he was shorter than most men he encountered and often felt discouraged because of it.

For Alice, who was only five foot two, she found his height being closer to her own was comforting. Often, she found taller men intimidating. She was grateful women like Mina, who was Hoven's height, enjoyed the company of taller men for her brother was six-foot-tall, she was grateful that the man she adored was exactly the way he was, perfect in every way in her eyes.

"What?" Hoven noticed Alice was staring at a part of him that wasn't his eyes. He tried to figure out what it was, "What are you looking at?"

Realizing she had been caught, she felt embarrassed, "My deepest apologies, I didn't mean to stare." She hesitated but felt like she had been found guilty, "I am not accustomed to your shorter hair."

When they had met, his brown hair reached nearly the middle of his back. One day he had surprised Alice by cutting it shorter, barely brushing past his shoulders. He had asked Mitch for help and their mutual friend was more than happy to find him the ideal hair stylist to help give him a fresh look. Alice gently touched her fingertips to Hoven's chin, "Your skin is so soft."

Instinctively he turned away from her touch, he was trying to get comfortable with her small gestures of physical contact but each time it felt like his heart was about to exploded in his chest, "Yeah, Mitch taught me how to shave better than I have been."

Wanting to change the subject, Hoven quickly shifted topics, "Anyway, back to what I asked earlier. Did you tell your brother about what's going on between you and your mom?"

Alice sat back in her chair, deep concern washing over her, "No, I haven't, which troubles me. I'm not certain if Oliver would understand, the damage done may have been too severe to seek salvation." She looked over at Hoven, "I know that mother requested to speak to him, but I am afraid that it will be too much for him." Alice took in a deep breath to steady herself as she added, "The last time they spoke was when she dismissed him from her home, saying that she no longer considered him a son and one unworthy of the world she provided."

Chapter 3

"You're going to have to tell him eventually." Mitch stood in the middle of his living room staring at his closest and dearest friend, "This is kind of a big deal that will affect your relationship."

Mina shifted between sitting on the edge of his couch to standing, pacing a short while before sitting again, "Nothing is final at this point, I can't say for certain how things will certainly play out. I don't want to drop all of this on Oliver only to come back a few days later with news that it fell through, and it wouldn't be affecting me."

It was then that Mitch realized some element to the whole situation, "Hold on a second, I just realized that you came to me with this news before your sweetie baby, what's going on there?" He quickly moved forward to sit next to Mina, "Are you two doing alright? Is there something wrong that you're not telling me?" His eyes flared wide, "Are you pregnant!"

Anger suddenly flared across Mina's face, "What!" She hit him in the shoulder hard enough to make her point, "Don't you think that would be the first thing out of my mouth when I got here?"

"Well, yeah..." Mitch laughed, "I had to snap you out of this downward spiral you were heading down. It was the first thing that leaped to mind that would get you to focus on something else."

Mina's dark green eyes narrowed as she studied Mitch's face, "Sometimes I hate you. You know that?"

"You find me frustrating at worst." Mitch grinned, "You love me, and you know it. You wouldn't put up with me if you didn't."

"I came to you because you're a lot like me, your mind focused on your career. Your relationship with Michael is amazing but you don't let it distract you from your life goals." Mina felt a twinge of guilt, "I love Oliver, I would never risk losing him, especially for a job. At the same time, this is incredibly important to me."

"I'm certain that he's fully aware of that fact and he's three gazillion percent in your corner supporting you." Mitch shook his head, studying Mina closely, "I just don't get why you brought this up with me before him. That's so unlike you. Yeah, before you two were a couple, I get that, but now? I always got the feeling I was getting secondhand information when it came to all the stuff going in your life." With a dramatic pose, he tilted his head back, resting the back of one hand on his forehead as if he were dying on stage during a play, "My fairest Mina, how I have lost you to such a beautiful man. Woe is me! Woe... Is... Me..." He lowered his hand as he grinned, "And... Scene." He gave a small bow of his head, "Thank you, thank you."

Mina shook her head in frustration, "You're incorrigible."

"Don't talk like I don't know what that means. I may have gone to a public school and barely scratched out a passing grade when I was there, but I have spent more than enough time around my precious Alice and that lady's vocabulary is so far out there. I've had to look up so many words just to know just what she's talking about half the time. Which is a good thing, of course, I'm learning but still." He suddenly stopped himself, "I'm sorry, where what we were talking about?"

"My situation at work?" Mina stared at him in disbelief, "This is why I talk about these things with Oliver. He listens to me, intently, he doesn't get distracted with random thoughts like you do. He makes me feel like everything I say, even the boring stuff that I think is stupid for me to even mention, is the most important thing he's ever heard in his life." She looked away, staring at the floor before her, "Why am I not over at his house telling him about all of this? Why am I here with you?"

"Ouch." Mitch touched his chest, biting his lip as if he was about to cry before continuing, "Right here, deep within my feels, that hurt. Shame on you Ice Queen."

As if ignoring him, Mina continued talking to herself, "I should be over there talking to him, I shouldn't be running over to your apartment to tell you about something so important." Suddenly she stood up, a moment of determination driving her, "I'm going over there right now and just…" She began to lose her strength, "Tell him everything."

Mitch leaned back in his couch, watching her with raised eyebrows, "You're not all that convincing to me, so I highly doubt you're doing a decent job doing that for yourself."

Mina didn't look over at him as she held up a hand, "Shut up, you're not helping."

Mitch touched his hands to his opposite upper arms as he lightly rubbed them, "Did a chill just run through here? I think I have the air conditioner on too high because it's getting frosty."

Mina turned slowly, tears forming in her eyes, "I shouldn't be with him. That's it, isn't it?"

Mitch bolted to his feet, grasping her firmly on the shoulders, "Don't you dare say that!"

Mina's eyes flared wide in shock, startled by his sudden reaction, "It's true, though. If we were meant to be together as a couple, I would turn to him first about everything. I would tell him everything, no matter how painful it may be for him to hear. I shouldn't be sheltering him from the things in our lives that may be difficult to cope with. We should find strength within each other, but instead, I'm hiding here with you rather than just telling him."

"That's it, you've given me no choice." Mitch walked over to where he had left his phone. Picking it up, he began looking for Oliver's number.

Mina grabbed the phone out of his hand, "What are you doing?"

"I'm doing what you should have done. I'm calling him, telling him about this whole situation, and telling him his girlfriend needs him." Mitch looked down at his phone, "Now, are you going to give me my phone back or are you going to do the right thing and march your sexy little butt over there?"

Mina shoved the phone back into his hands, nearly jabbing him in the stomach with it, "It's weird when you say things like that."

Mitch laughed, "Just because I don't want a piece of that sexy little bit of yumminess doesn't mean I can't admire it for the perfectly sculped delight that I'm sure a certain ravishingly beautiful man in your life knows it to be."

Mina shook her head, "That's just not right, you know that?"

Mitch grinned playfully, "At least I'm willing to say it." A strange thought flickered across his mind, "Does he say that to you? Does Oliver tell you about just how delicious your sensual curves are in his eyes?"

Mina folded her arms across her chest as she stared up at Mitch's dark eyes with a deep scowl, "If you must know, he focuses on other things like my eyes and smile."

"Awe, sugary sweet loveliness, I'm sure, but a woman needs to feel attractive in the eyes of her man. I'm just making sure he's doing his job properly in elevating you to the status of goddess that each pure of heart, delightfully lovable woman in this world deserves to feel like." He suddenly frowned, "Not all the foul, nasty, pieces of trash that are more street walkers than deserving the status of a lady. Those don't deserve it only because they're not only toxic to themselves but everyone around them. I cannot stand people that. Men or women, they're just disgusting people."

Suddenly he smiled, making a motion as if he were zipping his lips closed, "That's enough out of me about that, I won't let their negativity take away my sparkle." Placing his hands on his hips, he gave Mina a long hard stare before speaking, "Now then, about Oliver proving to you beyond a shadow of a doubt that you are a scrumptious delight that he cannot wait to taste all the flavors that you have to offer him."

Mina held up her hands, "No! That's disgusting!" She cringed at the thought of being something someone could taste like she was some sort of meal or desert. Lowering her arms she shook her head, "Oliver isn't like that, so stopping implying that he is."

Mitch's eyes narrowed as he looked into her eyes, "In all seriousness, is there something I need to know about?" His eyes lit up with excitement, "As heartbreaking as it would be for you, I absolutely would be there holding your hand throughout the experience, but I do have to admit, I would be delighted if he…"

Mina threatened to punch him in the chest but slowed her fist until she barely tapped his body, "No. That's not it at all." She turned, pressing her arms against her chest as she muttered softly, "That isn't it. Oliver makes me feel attractive every moment he's around me, from the way he looks at me to the way he touches me, even little moments when he places his hand against the middle of my back or gently pushes a strand of hair away from my face."

"He doesn't just make me feel attractive. He makes me feel beautiful. Not just in a model sort of way or a piece of artwork kind of beauty, but…" Mina struggled to find the right words, "He loves every detail about me, mind, body, and soul. He's attracted to me, that much is obvious, but the way he expresses it, the way he tells me so much without words is so beautiful. It's like the rest of the world melts away the moment he notices me. He acknowledges things going on around him and interacts with others, but the whole time he's focused on me, what I'm saying, what I'm doing, anything I may want or need before I even say something about it."

She turned slowly, looking up at Mitch, "I know he will make me feel this beautiful, this attractive to him when we're eighty. It's so much more than what he sees with his eyes. He said that what makes me uniquely beautiful is not the body he sees, which he enjoys gazing at, but it's the soul he sees within."

Mina turned away once more, "Physical attraction is not a problem, I can assure you. The way his fingertips glide across my body, the way he holds me, tiny details he does when we're together that…" For a moment she felt the strength giving out in her legs. Only by clearing her thoughts was she able to stay standing.

Twin tears, one from each eye broke free form the lower rims or her eyes, sliding down the sides of her face, "You say that he should make me feel like a goddess, but he does so much more than that. He makes me feel like his one true love… He gives meaning to words that I had no faith in, that I thought were silly sounding and things ignorant people said to one another to make themselves feel better. When Oliver is with me, I don't want to be a goddess. Any woman can feel like a goddess, but only one can be his true love and that is more precious to me than anything I could ever hope to be." Mina struggled to breathe as she was lost in thought, memories of her time spent with her boyfriend flooding her mind.

The touch of Mitch's hand brought her out of her revere as she turned to face him, "I'm sorry I said what I did. Obviously, Oliver takes whatever I could ever hope to inspire in you to a whole new level." He was tempted to brush away her tears but knew in his heart only one man in her life deserved such an honor, "You know what you need to do. Now go do it."

Mina wiped away her tears as she tried to regain her composure, "He'll know I've been crying."

Mitch smiled, "Good, then he'll know how hard it was for you to struggle with all of this. It also shows that you are deeply upset for not coming to him first."

"I'll tell him everything." Mina nodded slowly, "Not only what I told you but the fact that I came here first and my regret for not telling him before you." She looked up, trying to muster a smile, "However, I'm leaving out the part about my delicious body and you talking about my butt."

Mitch leaned forward, whispering softly, "Things are going alright in that area of your relationship, though, right? Are you getting the scrumptious yummy goodness that you deserve from that sensually delightful perfection that you get to call your own?"

Mina refused to give in as she gave him a cold, hard glare, "Mitch Frederick Bulsara, we discussed this. The intimate details of my personal life are private. That is between me and Oliver. Even if I wanted to talk to you about that, which let me make it abundantly clear that I don't, I won't ever reveal anything about that part of my life with you or anyone else because of the man I love. He feels uncomfortable talking about this subject let alone discussing such details with someone other than the woman he has devoted his heart to. So, out of respect to him, you'll never hear anything of the sort from me. Out of respect for me, stop asking because I don't want to talk about it."

Mina grabbed a fistful of Mitch's shirt, bringing him lower until her nose touched the tip of his, "There are few things in this world I'm willing to do anything for. Protecting Oliver is one of those things and right now you're threatening to cross a line in intruding upon our privacy, do I make myself clear?" He started to speak but she quickly slapped her hand across his mouth, "Don't you dare mention Ice Queen to me."

Mitch slowly nodded before she removed her hand. He spoke softly, "I'm sorry, I was just joking. I didn't know it was that important to you or I wouldn't have ever even mentioned that. You know I respect and adore you. I certainly would never do anything to hurt you."

Releasing her hold on his shirt, Mina stepped back, "Sorry, but it felt like you were threatening to hurt Oliver by asking about that sort of thing." She gently wiped her hand slowly across her face, "I don't know why I was ready to punch you just now."

Mitch felt he shouldn't in that moment, but he was practically glowing with pride, "My precious Kitten transforming into a tiger to protect her man, I love it!" He laughed, "You know what's weird? You're what, five four, a hundred and ten pounds. Me, I'm six four, well built, practically every inch of me slender muscle, and yet..." He held up his hands in defense, "You nearly scared the pee out of me just now."

Mina held up her hand, pointing at Mitch with a serious expression, "Don't you forget it, either." She turned quickly on her heel before she departed.

~

"You've been crying." Before Mina had a chance to response, Oliver's hand gently caressed her cheek as he stared into her eyes, searching for answers as to what was bothering her, "What's wrong?" He withdrew his hand as he stepped back, "I'm so sorry, please come in." He waited for her to pass by as he continued nervously, mostly worried about her mental and emotional state but knowing never to intrude, "I was washing dishes when you arrived."

"I didn't mind waiting." The response to her knocking at the door wasn't immediate, but he had explained the delay. Once inside, Mina turned to face him. "I love you."

Seeing the pain in her eyes left an emptiness building within him. Moving closer, he brushed his hand across her cheeks, "I love you..." He kissed her softly, to reassure her that his words were not spoken simply because she said them to him. It was meant as an expression of comfort, to show that she should feel safe with whatever it was that was concerning her.

Pulling away from his heartfelt expression of emotion, Mina tried to regain her breath as she touched her hands to his chest, gently pushing him away, "Please stop..."

Her reaction to him caused heartbreak in his eyes which nearly brought her to tears. Mina tried to quickly explain, "I'm sorry, it's just... I'm trying to stay focused on what I wanted to tell you and that is making it so incredibly hard for me to..." She lightly tapped him on the chest, "Concentrate. Not thinking about..." She smiled sweetly, "You are wonderful, and I adore you but there is something I need to tell you."

Oliver felt embarrassed for responding to her distress incorrectly, "I'm sorry, I thought..." He looked away as he motioned towards the couch, "Would you like a seat?"

"Thank you." Mina held onto his hand as she guided them over to a sitting position. Once there, she tried again with what she wanted to tell him, "I have a feeling that you'll think I'm silly about overreacting concerning all of this, but I feel like I made this horrible mistake and I wanted to ask for your forgiveness."

"You have it." Oliver didn't need to ask what it was that she was apologizing for, he knew she would never do anything to harm him or break his unwavering faith in her.

At times, Mina felt frustrated with herself which she admitted she often projected onto Oliver concerning his incredible purity concerning her. She could do no wrong. If she made a mistake, he forgave her without hesitation. He never once thought there was a problem they could not resolve and more than likely had their entire future planned out from engagement to their golden years in retirement. She wished she could feel that way towards him and most of the time she did. However, as she said when she had visited her closest friend, she felt that maybe they shouldn't be together because she wasn't good enough for him.

"I went over to Mitch's apartment earlier with news of something that I learned about today instead of coming over here first. I regret doing so and I feel horrible for not telling you before him, but I was worried about your reaction." Mina held his hands in hers as her eyes focused on them rather than watching the range of emotions washing across Oliver's face. "We talked and he essentially told me what I should have done in the first place and that was coming over here and telling you what I needed to say."

"Mina..." Hearing Oliver say her name was one of the most beautiful moments she ever experienced in her life. Somehow, he was able to say a single word and make it embody the essence of love. Not just the emotion, but the purity of what it represented. She looked up into his eyes as he continued, "There is nothing to forgive because you didn't do anything wrong."

"I did. From the moment I first told you that I loved you, I have always come to you first with everything going on in my life." Mina scowled, thinking about the few exceptions, "Well, there were the times I wanted to surprise you which forced me to hold back something from you but that was because it was the only way to make it an unexpected event."

"I understand." Oliver gently squeezed her hands, "I'm sure there are other occasions in which you told Mitch something before me, but you just can't think about them because at the time, it wasn't a big deal. It might have been something minor you mentioned in passing not realizing I didn't know about it yet." He smiled warmly, his jade green eyes making her feel as if he were searching the depths of her soul for areas of her mind that were troubled so that he could soothe and heal what worried her. "When you're ready to tell me, I'm here for you."

Mina slid closer, slipping her arm around him, pressing the side of her face against his chest as he returned the embrace, "I love you, Oliver. I don't want to ever lose you. I'm so afraid I'm going to do something wrong at one point and screw up what we have."

Oliver gently brushed his fingers through her hair which he knew had a calming effect on her, "My love for you, my dearest Mina, is unconditional. It will not change, it will not fade with time, and it certainly will never vanish from this world. Not even death will eliminate its existence, for it is eternal."

Mina tapped her fist gently against the available space on his chest as she spoke softly, "Don't say that. Don't ever talk about death, especially your death, okay?"

"I'm sorry, it was rude of me to even say such a thing. I just…" Oliver felt ashamed, "I wished to make a point, but you're right." He paused before shifting focus of what he was saying, "What is it you wished to tell me?"

Pulling away, Mina looked up into his eyes, "My job…" Why was it so difficult to tell him? She felt like it was so silly to feel this way. "You're aware of how I am viewed positively at work, right? I've been involved with several projects that have proven successful lately and that has caught the attention of one of the team leaders of this branch of the company. They have been working towards expanding beyond their current operations here in the United States. I don't know all the details at this point, but it may involve an acquisition of the operations of a small business in Europe. They are wanting to sell to a larger company and expand their potential."

Oliver wasn't certain what she was alluding to. Often, she would be, in a term she hated him using, dumbing things down for him to understand. Mina would avoid using technical terms and explaining too much in depth concerning topics that he had little understanding of. He would often rely on a process he had been taught as a child when given information. He was to recite back a version of what he had been told in his words to express that he understood. "Alright, according to what you told me so far, a small business in Europe wishes to sell their operations. I'm guessing it involves the brick-and-mortar aspect of their business along with their employees, manufacturing abilities, and so forth? It's not a liquidation of assets, but a merging of them and your company?"

Mina smiled at his attempt to understand, "Yes, something like that, but it's a lot more complicated to go into detail. The biggest obstacle is the financial aspect of it and negotiating just how much the business being sold will stay as is without too many alterations with how they run things. A lot of the local workers are against the sale and..." She quickly waved her hands in front of her, "Those are details that don't matter at the moment, that's not the point of what I wanted to tell you."

"Just to summarize, everything you described concerning what is happening related to this merger is the cause for what is troubling you?" It felt as if the answer was tugging at him in the back of his mind, but Oliver was so focused on trying to soothe Mina's concerns that he didn't think too seriously about where her train of thought was leading.

She brushed her hand across his cheek, savoring the soft texture underneath her fingertips. He put forth such effort to connect with her, to understand and sympathize with what she talked to him about. "Yes." Her hand dropped back to his where they were joined together, "Before I tell you, though, I want to make sure that you know that this isn't final, just rumors at this point. For all I know they won't even consider me and I'm going through all of this for nothing. I feel kind of silly even getting this upset..."

"Mina?" Oliver noticed Mina was avoiding eye contact which told him that she was struggling to get to the point of what she wanted to say, "What would Mitch say in this situation? Spill it?"

Mina smiled as she looked up at him, "Yeah, he says that a lot, doesn't he?"

Oliver was eagerly wanting to learn what she wished to tell him but knew that to pressure her in any way would be inconsiderate of her feelings. Instead, he watched her in silence, enjoying the beautiful woman before him. He couldn't help but feel as if somehow, by some miracle, he was more in love with her with each passing moment he spent with her.

Mina knew that look. He wasn't going to say anything until she did. It wasn't that he was trying to play emotional games with her in forcing her to speak. He was enjoying being there with her in silence, which made her a little uncomfortable as she felt like she was being put on the spot, a giant light shining down upon her. It was her fault, not just speaking what was on her mind instead of avoiding it as much as she had been. Fine. Just do it already!

"I may be asked to go to Europe." Mina blurted it out, like removing a band aid, just rip it off in one quick motion.

Oliver's eyes lit up with excitement, "That's incredible!"

Of all the reactions she expected, joy was not on the list. She had expected him to get upset, sorrow that she would be gone. Confusion took dominance in her mind, "You're happy for me?"

"Why wouldn't I be? I traveled to Europe myself when I was younger. Mother loved Great Britain and wanted us to immerse ourselves in its culture. I spent every summer throughout my childhood in our home there. France, Italy, so many wonders to explore." Oliver felt so excited for her, "It is an opportunity you cannot turn down if it is to be offered to you. You will love every moment of it." He brought up her hands, kissing her fingers before speaking, "You are so incredibly blessed."

"I am…" It had nothing to do with a trip to Europe. It was because of him that she felt that way, "Thank you."

Despite what should have been positive news, Mina's reaction to the situation confused Oliver forcing him to ask, "I'm sorry, I'm feeling a little at a loss. You were crying before you arrived. You've been struggling to convey this news to me. Yet, in my mind, this is a positive experience that is being offered to you. What is it about you visiting Europe that is causing you to feel so upset?" He curled his fingers around her hand as he watched her intently for some understanding of what was happening.

Mina wanted to kiss him, to lose herself in the passionate delight that was being with the man she loved dearly. He was intoxicating to be around, a single touch of his hand made her forget about anything but what such a sensation felt like to her. Her body tingled with anticipation of what else he could do with a gentle caress across her skin. She desired nothing more than to lose herself in the moment, to forget about the world around her and enjoy the pleasures Oliver had to offer.

Closing her eyes, forcing herself to think about what was troubling her, Mina spoke softly, "I won't be visiting. I will be taking up a permanent residence there."

At first the news didn't sink in, it was like being told something that would forever change your life, as if she had just told him that they were going to have a baby. The initial shock faded as he realized why she was so troubled by the fact, "Oh… I see why this concerns you." He nodded slowly, "I'll begin preparations immediately, starting tomorrow I'll take the necessary steps…"

"Wait, what?" Mina looked up at him, confused as to what he was talking about, "What preparations?"

"I'll contact a realtor tomorrow and begin taking the necessary steps to sell my home." Oliver's mind was racing ahead for all that would be required of him, "I'll have to renew my passport, I haven't been out of the country since I left mother's home which was years ago, I'm certain it isn't any good at the moment." He smiled as his eyes met Mina's gaze, "I have experience with the region. What area of Europe will you be moving? I may know it well and can provide some guidance."

"Oliver..." Mina squeezed his hand in attempt to regain his focus. "I don't know if this is final yet. It was mentioned in passing. I haven't been given the promotion or assigned to the project. At this point it's more of a rumor circulating around the office, there is no certainty to it. We shouldn't make any major decisions." She stared at his hands, a pain welling up in her chest, "I'm not moving my life permanently there. It will only be for a few months." She looked up at his beautiful jade green eyes, "I want a home to come back to when this is over."

"Oh..." Oliver studied Mina's face as his mind put together the last remaining pieces to the puzzle. She was upset before she arrived. She had avoided speaking to him about what had happened and was feeling guilt in speaking to Mitch about the news. She didn't find joy in spending time in Europe, and she was assuring him not to make any drastic changes in his own life even though he had no desire to... It was then that everything clicked into place as his eyes flared wide in surprise, "I see."

Mina realized that until that moment, Oliver didn't grasp what was bothering her. Seeing that he now understood, she felt like she had betrayed him in some way. "We won't be able to spend much time together when I'm there. We can still stay in touch, of course, I'll find every way possible to keep our connection, but…"

Oliver smiled, trying to be optimistic, "I can visit. I may not have the money to do so every week or month, but…" He would never ask her for money, even though he was certain she made much more than he ever dreamed of making in his current job, "It will make our time together all that more precious in the meantime."

Mina felt the first of her tears sliding down her face as she stared into his eyes. "I don't want you to spend your money to visit me. I'll find a way for you to see me as often as we can." She held onto his hands tightly, she felt that she didn't deserve him, that he was too good to her and that she didn't deserve such generosity concerning all that was happening, "Thank you."

She felt his arms slide around her as he moved closer. Holding Oliver tightly, she pressed the side of her face against his shoulder, allowing her emotions to flow out of her without restraint. He was a haven in world that felt to be on the edge of chaos. She found excitement in her job, but there was never a moment's rest, always pushing forward. The man she now held in her arms provided her a moment to stop, close her eyes, and rest knowing she was home, safe, and cared for.

Chapter 4

"I don't get it." Hoven yawned as he sat on the bench in the park, staring across the open field as people enjoyed the early morning hours of the summer day. He had only been awake for about an hour before he was joined by his girlfriend. They considered themselves as being in a relationship and yet, it was hard for him to think of it as being true. It was like a dream he was afraid to wake up from.

In a half-awake state of mind, he attempted to react to what Alice had told him, "What's the big deal? She goes on a trip to Europe for a few months. She does whatever it is she's doing there, then comes back. They keep in touch by phone, right? There are dozens of ways to talk to each other online, photos, video chat, all sorts of ways. It's not like it's the nineteen forties and they have to write letters to each other that may take weeks to reach each other."

He scratched at his hair as he yawned again, "Are you afraid their relationship is going to fall apart because they're separated like that for a little while?" Hoven shook his head slowly, "If being apart for a few months breaks them up, then obviously they shouldn't get married."

Alice's jade green eyes flared wide in concern, "Hoven, please do not speak so casually of such an important detail. I spoke to you about Oliver's intentions in confidence." She stared at her hands that were resting in her lap, "If my brother wishes to speak about such intimate details concerning the future of their relationship, I wish for Mina to learn such things from him."

"Okay, fine, I'm sorry." Hoven yawned again before growling at himself in frustration, "I wish this would stop."

Noticing his distress, Alice gently touched her hand to his, "I'm sorry for waking you so early, I know today is your day off and that you had an opportunity to sleep longer than is typically allowed for you to do so."

Hoven smiled. He loved the way her skin felt against his. It was the softest texture he had ever experienced in his life. It sent waves of pleasure coursing through his body, relaxing any tension, "I would have woken up around this time anyway, the summer heat makes it unbearable in my car by the early hours anyway. I just didn't sleep well at all last night. I tried to get comfortable, but I kept tossing and turning. I rammed my knee into the side at one point."

"I'm concerned about your living situation. I know that you wished to remain in your vehicle, that it allows you a sense of freedom. I have attempted to respect your wishes." Alice shifted her body from sitting next to him to angling her legs towards him as she turned her body to face the man next to her, "I must encourage you once more to consider finding a permanent home in the form of an apartment, even a small…" She tried to remember the term used, "Studio apartment?" She nodded once she concluded, she had used the proper terminology, "It would greatly reduce my concern for your wellbeing if you did so."

Hoven didn't like the idea of forcing himself to be locked into paying someone to live somewhere for any extended period. He felt trapped by long term obligations such as loans to pay off large expenditures. He had bought his car in full when he got it.

"I'll think about it." Hoven quickly shifted subjects, "Say Mina does get this job, goes off to Europe for a few months to a year, so what? They don't get to see each other for a while. From what you've told me, there isn't anything that would break them apart, so…" He noticed concern in Alice's eyes, "Okay, so I'm missing something here, right? What don't I know about?"

Alice pressed her lips firmly together in consideration of revealing much more than she was prepared to do so. She wished to respect the privacy of both what Oliver and Mina had separately confided in her, but at the same time, she felt compelled that she should trust the man she loved unconditionally. No secrets should be withheld and maybe due to his unique insight concerning life, he may find a solution that she had not considered before.

Finally, after a deep breath and a firm nod as if agreeing with her decision to do so, Alice looked up into Hoven's dark blue eyes, "Know that what I am about to tell you must never speak of to anyone, not Mina, not Oliver, and certainly not Mitch. What I have been told and information I have ascertained on my own through observation and study of their behavior, is to be considered private."

Hoven felt like laughing but instead chose to smile instead, "If it's private, why are you telling me?"

"I wish to confide in you as a lover would for the man she cares dearly for." Alice paused, confused by the flaring of Hoven's eyes showing signs of sudden shock, "What's wrong? What did I say to alarm you?"

Hoven avoided eye contact, which translated as signs of his anxiety, "You said the word…" He cleared his throat, "Lover."

"Oh." Alice did not consider the multitude of interpretations of the word. She blushed as she looked down at her hands, "My apologies for speaking of such a word so lightly. In my mind, when I speak of the word lover, it expresses the bond two people share with one another through the emotion of eternal care for one another. I did not mean it as a reference of two individuals that were intimately close together by sharing…"

"Stop." Hoven quickly added, "Please stop." Seeing concern in her eyes, he revealed a nervous smile, "I get it, you don't need to go into detail."

"Oh goodness." Alice's embarrassment grew in intensity, "You're correct, of course, I did not realize I had spoken so plainly of the act in which two people express their love for one another in such a personal manner. It was dreadfully rude of me to do so, especially in such a public setting."

Hoven curled his fingers around her hands as he gently squeezed them as he spoke in a soft tone, "You know what I like about you…" He laughed nervously, "I mean, on top of everything else I like about you, but…" He wilted in frustration, "Sorry, it's just… Okay, let me try again. What I like about you is that you are shyer about this topic than I am, which makes me feel better about how awkward I get about that topic." He muttered in conclusion, "I hope that makes sense. I'm not so good at talking to you sometimes."

"Hoven?" He looked up to find Alice watching him with a heartfelt warmth in her eyes, "I love you." She leaned forward, kissing him gently upon the cheek, "Thank you for your kindness."

Feeling as if all the air around him had vanished, Hoven struggled to breath. Closing his eyes tightly, he nodded in response since he was incapable of forming words. His heart was beating heavily in his chest as his foot began tapping rapidly. He didn't realize he was squeezing Alice's hands tightly until she pulled them free. Looking up, he tried to speak in between short gasps of air, "Sorry..."

Alice felt such sorrow watching his intense reaction to such signs of affection. His social anxiety, as he had described it to her, often caused intense physical reactions to certain situations. Brushing her hand gently across his cheek where she had kissed him, she quickly withdrew it when she realized she was only making things worse, "It is I who should apologize to you. I become so overwhelmed with emotion that I wished to express it, to show you the affection and kindness that you show me. I forgot for a fleeting moment that it may cause you harm."

Pressing his arms tightly against his chest, Hoven smiled, "Not harm..." Thankfully his breathing was returning to normal, "I hate the fact that my body does this to me." He had his eyes closed as he tried to calm himself, "I'm sorry if I make you uncomfortable because this happens."

"Hoven?" He peeked his eyes open to see Alice, "You are precious to me. Even if you are uncomfortable with such signs of affection, I will still love you for who you are, not what you may become in the future. I will always be here for you."

He smiled as he closed his eyes, "Could we talk about something else? It would help get my mind off this."

"Of course, there is the subject matter I mentioned earlier." Alice tried again, first asking a question, "Would it be acceptable if I touched my hands to yours?"

Feeling embarrassed about his body overreacting the way it did, Hoven smiled, "Yeah, here…" He held out his hands.

It broke her heart to see them shaking, as if fear were clutching at his thoughts. Gently taking them in her own, Alice carefully brought them down to touch upon his lap, "Thank you." She nodded firmly as if assuring herself that she was making the right decision once more, "What you do not know concerning both Mina and Oliver is that on the surface, they do appear to be an ideal couple. They are each confident in their own way and strong individuals when it comes to confronting obstacles and resolving adversity that they encounter throughout their lives."

Alice took in a deep breath, letting it out slowly. Speaking it out loud made it more real in her mind as if she couldn't deny the truth any longer, "Despite this appearance, each possess deeply rooted hesitations, doubts, and insecurities. To begin with, my brother experienced the same mental and psychological conditioning that my mother forced upon all four of her children. Oliver considered it torture, breaking down his self-confidence to a point where he felt mother remolded him to fulfill some ideal in her mind."

Alice considered the fact that recent events concerning her mother but did not wish to delve into that subject matter for the time being, "I do believe he has recovered from those experiences, but it still left him feeling vulnerable because of it."

"Then there is what he had with his fiancé." This wasn't the first time she had mentioned such details of Oliver's past to Hoven, so she felt it was more so a review of information rather than a revelation to him, "She wished to marry into our family, to become a part of the wealth and social status that would come with being Oliver's wife. When mother did not approve of the engagement and forced him to choose between love and family, he chose the woman he cared dearly for. Without the rewards she was seeking in becoming his wife, the engagement ended in tragedy. It forever left a deep wound within him that he has struggled with for years ever since. I feel such incredible pride to know that he has overcome his fears and suffering from that experience and is wishing to pursue marriage with Mina."

"Meanwhile, the woman he loves is one of the strongest, most confident women I have ever met. She is fierce in response to threats, and I believe possesses an iron will when it comes to achieving her goal and overcoming obstacles set before her. However, her parents stripped her of her self-confidence throughout her life, blaming her for all their personal concerns and troubles. It was as if somehow it was her existence to be blamed, her birth setting into motion such hardship." Alice gently squeezed Hoven's hands. It was because of speaking of such troubling memories that she needed his emotional support."

Alice felt tears form in her eyes, "Mina has confided in me that she feels that she is unworthy of Oliver. She described it to me as not feeling brave enough to open herself completely to him. She said that she struggles to allow herself to be that vulnerable."

Alice watched Hoven in silence, his eyes closed, he was listening, but he was lost in thought. She wasn't certain if he was focused on what was troubling him or what she was telling him. Still, she felt compelled to continue, "Both Mina and Oliver are ideal for one another, they love each other unconditionally, yet both have had a terrible journey fraught with emotionally destructive family members, painful experiences of trust broken, and love denied to them. It is as if all this pain, suffering, and scars of the past are threatening to tear them apart. Each afraid to allow themselves the happily ever after they deserve."

"Life isn't that way, though." Hoven opened his eyes and he looked up at her. He wanted to use the word never but knew to do so would be pessimistic. Ever since meeting Alice, he had been trying to let go of negative and toxic viewpoints that nearly destroyed his life. He took a more neutral approach, "Happily ever after may happen, I don't know. I..." A nervous smile spread across his face, "Before I met you, I would have said that it never happens and thinking that way was being ignorant of the way the world works."

Hoven's foot began tapping as his anxiety began creeping back into his mind, "Having you in my life, I began to think otherwise. I hope that I can have that one day, without..." It felt like his body was betraying him, making his attempts to open himself up to her as much as he wanted to was difficult. Tears formed in his eyes before he realized it happened as he pushed himself to finish, "I want to believe that I will have happily ever after with you. You give me hope that it exists and the only thing holding me back right now is me. I struggle to let go of my insecurities, too, so I get it."

It wor Swallowing hard, Hoven fought with himself to not fall apart before he could conclude, "It's a fight that each of them will have to deal with on their own. From what you've told me, they have given each other a way out of the worlds they built around themselves, the doubt, and fears. It's up to them to follow the light, to escape whatever it is that is holding them back. They have to choose to do that on their own like am trying to do with you."

Suddenly Hoven pulled away, moving quickly to his feet as he took a few steps away, his arms pressed tightly against his body. "I'm sorry…"

Alice wanted to follow him, to provide comfort but knew keeping her distance was the only way to help. "Thank you. I realize how hard it was for you to express this to me and how dearly you understand their struggle." She wiped away tears from her eyes, "It is beautiful that you think of me as a guiding light in your life."

"I once read something that inspired me and gave me hope at a time I had nearly given up. It was written by a storyteller, a man I greatly admire for what his words meant to me." Alice smiled sweetly as she did her best to remember what she had read, "True love will not fix the damage done in the past. It won't erase the scars upon the soul or heal the tortured existence created within the mind. However, it will provide a guiding light to escape the mental prison that many are trapped within. It will give strength to shed the darkness that cloaks many as a second skin. In the end, it is up to us to follow that path, to seek that guiding light, and to take the first steps towards something beautiful that each of us can in turn, share with another, equally wonderous soul."

As she concluded, Alice looked up to see Hoven extending his hand for her to take. She smiled warmly as she stood, taking his hand in her own, "It is my greatest desire that Mina and Oliver follow the beacon of hope that each of them represents in one another's life and find the happily ever after that they truly deserve."

~

"Alice isn't here." Mina stood at the door to her apartment. She had just finished lacing up her shoes when she heard someone knocking at the door. Considering that Mitch and Oliver were both at their respective jobs, none of her coworkers knew where she lived or shouldn't know at least, she wasn't certain who would be on the other side. To her surprise, she found Hoven waiting her arrival.

"Yeah, I know." Hoven held up his phone, "We talk all the time. She knows I don't like talking on the phone, so we text each other whenever we can." Lowering it, he continued, "She went to work about an hour ago." He grinned, "She loves her job, which is weird. I never knew someone who enjoyed dealing with customers as much as she does, but whatever makes her happy."

Mina was still at a loss as to what he was doing there, "I was about to go out for a run…" It was the first time Hoven had ever made any attempt to contact her without Alice being an intermediary connecting the two. She didn't mind that he was aware of where she lived, she had told Alice it would be okay to convey that information to him in case there was an emergency, but she never dreamed that he would show up at her front door.

"Why?" Hoven stared at her in confusion, "You're going to run to get something?" He motioned behind him, "I could drive…"

"For exercise?" Mina had come across several people who didn't understand her routines. Because of this, she knew how to respond politely, "It helps reduce stress, improve my heart health, and keep me in shape."

Hoven nodded slowly, "Oh, that's cool." Mina watched him closely, curious as to his reaction concerning her outfit and yet she didn't catch him looking down beyond eye contact, "I wonder how Alice stays so slender." He motioned towards himself, "Me, I admit, I don't eat well." He grinned, "She's trying to encourage me to eat better, a more balanced diet which is helping me with my energy, and I don't feel sick as often as I used to."

Mina smiled, realizing that she hadn't taken notice of the changes in his appearance since she had first met the man, "Take this as a compliment that I mean it to be, but you do look better then when I first saw you."

"Yeah, Alice is doing a lot of things to help change my life around. I admit, at the time, I was kind of giving up on my life when I met her. I wasn't trying to stay healthy or anything, I wouldn't have minded to just…" Hoven made a waving motion of his hand, "Sorry, I shouldn't talk about that." He smiled, once again nodding slowly, "So, you're going to go running." He sighed as if giving into a situation he wanted nothing to do with but was willing to participate if it provided him what he was seeking, "Maybe I could go with you? I needed to talk to you about something and if you're going to be running, then, I guess…"

Mina was confused, "How about we start off for a walk and you can talk to me along the way, how about that?"

Hoven's face lit up with a smile along with an expression of relief, "Yeah, a walk, that's much better. That I think I can do." His eyes lit up, "Alice walks! She walks all the time, no wonder she's…" His mind began wondering, "I want to look as good as she does." A strange flicker of sadness flickered across his face, "She's so beautiful… I don't…" His breathing increased, soon becoming short gasps of air, "I shouldn't…"

Mina touched her hand to his shoulder, having been warned of how his body often reacted to anxiety. "Hoven?" Getting him to make eye contact with her rather than the gaze of someone lost in thought, she continued, "Why don't we go for that walk, okay?" She stepped forward, hinting that he should step back to allow her through. He followed her request giving her the chance to close her apartment door and lock it behind her. Slipping the key into a bracelet she wore just for that purpose to keep it safe, Mina turned back to the man that appeared to be lost in a trance, "Ready to go?"

"Hold on…" Hoven pulled up his phone before him as he typed out a quick message. After reading to make sure it sounded right, he clicked send before lowering his arms, "Wanted to ask her what she did for exercise since you run."

Mina smiled as she motioned towards the hallway leading to the stairwell, "Talk on the way?"

"Yeah, sure…" Mina couldn't help but think that Hoven appeared lost in thought. As to what, she couldn't figure out. Either that or he was staring directly into her eyes as if trying to learn something about her, "Should I go? Am I bothering you?"

Mina shook her head, "No, why?"

"I don't know, you seem busy." Hoven commented, "I heard that about you, that you're always doing something."

Mina wasn't certain how much about her he knew. However, she was curious about his assessment of her, "Can't help but feel like that you think that's a terrible thing?"

Hoven kept his gaze on where they were headed as they moved down the stairs towards the first floor, "Defensive, I get that. You like being in control too, not in a dominating sort of way, just you don't like being thrown off balance. I was that way early on with Alice, I didn't want to let her get too close to me that I kind of pushed her away."

"May I ask you something?" Hoven looked over at Mina as the pair exited her apartment building. She glanced over to see a man walking by giving her the reaction she was accustomed to. A smile, a quick look at her appearance, obvious interest in what he was seeing. If it wasn't for Hoven, he may have even approached her to say something. Without waiting for a response, she looked over at him, "Did you ever notice what I was wearing?"

Looking down for the first time she he had arrived, his face scrunched up in confusion, "I never understood why women dress like that. How is that comfortable?"

Mina was wearing a form fitting pair of pants that fit snuggly around her hips. A small gap in her clothing revealed her exposed stomach and waistline while her sports bra comfortably fit around her chest allowing freedom of movement for her arms. She was confident in her appearance, wearing clothing that both felt comfortable and minimized chances of becoming overheated.

Hoven had given her appearance a passive glance before looking back up into Mina's eyes, "Doesn't that feel like you're wearing just underwear? I think it would." He shrugged, looking away, "Where are we going?"

Mina pressed her lips firmly together to keep from laughing. The more she was around the man, the greater her understanding as to the fact that he was perfect for Alice who was modest in her appearance, often wearing dresses that accented her feminine body but at the same time, would never be considered too revealing. She pointed towards her right, waiting for them to begin moving before she asked, "Are you in love with Alice?"

Hoven buried his hands into his pants pockets as he stared at the sidewalk, "If I said yes, would you tell her?" He glanced over at Mina, "I'm still struggling with that part of me, so I want to say yes, but I'm so broken inside, I don't think I can say that yet. I want to, but at the same time, I'm always honest with her about everything. So, I wish it were that simple. I just feel like I'm not capable of being in love because I don't love myself."

Mina nodded slowly, thinking about her own personal struggles with opening her heart to Oliver. It had been a hard journey to finally let her proverbial walls fall away to accept how she felt about him. However, it felt like Hoven was fighting with a much worse condition, one of self-abuse that was preventing him from experiencing what Alice had to offer him. She struggled with how best to respond, "Feels like members of their family have that effect on others. They draw out the best us in us."

Hoven smiled, "Yeah, she's really good at that."

The sound of a car horn blasting for nearly thirty seconds drew their attention. The driver of the car that had come to an abrupt halt, leaned out of his window, and shouted obscenities at a woman who was struggling to parallel park. Mina was tempted to get involved but the guy moved around the woman before roaring down the road, "I hate people like that."

Hoven shook his head as they resumed their walk, "Alice taught me never to use the word hate. It takes a lot to hate something or someone, to experience something like that let alone hold onto those feelings creates poison in the world."

Mina found Hoven's unique perspective and his response to Alice both fascinating and charming. Beneath the rough exterior and reserved personality, once he revealed more of himself, she was beginning to understand the allure that his girlfriend had seen in him. "You're right, I don't hate people like that." She smiled, laughing at something that flickered through her mind, "Oliver said that you should never be angry at the person. You should be upset with what they do. Something about how the human soul is creation, love, and life. What we do with our lives is what leads to all the harmful stuff, so I should love the person, but dislike what they do." She shook her head at what she had thought was a naïve viewpoint the first time she heard it, "Where do you think they learn all of this?"

"Don't know." Hoven glanced over at Mina, "I find it beautiful. It's what I…" He wanted to say the word love, but a tightness in his chest made it difficult to speak of such things even casually. He wanted the focus of such emotions to be the first to hear him say it, so was forced to correct himself, "…like about Alice."

Mina noticed his hesitation, smiling at his reaction to Alice. Clearly the pair affected one another the way Oliver brought out the best in her, often teaching her things she didn't realize she was learning about until it was already a part of her. "I know it's not genetics, their mother was a horrible person, and their older brothers weren't much better."

"Yeah, about that…" Hoven was tossing around a problem he was struggling with, "I want to protect her and yet, at the same time, I know I shouldn't because she's stronger than me."

Mina stopped, grabbing onto Hoven's upper sleeve to get his attention, "What's wrong? Who is trying to hurt her?"

Hoven avoided eye contact, feeling uncomfortable revealing anything, "It's why I needed to talk to you. From what Alice says about you, you're the strongest person she knows, fierce in a kind of warrior woman sort of way. I thought, if anyone would know how to deal with a threat to Alice, you would be the one to talk to."

Worry quickly grew in her mind as Mina pushed for answers, "Just tell me what's going on." She realized she was being too forceful with him, "Please?"

"I'm worried that I'm going to lose her." Hoven looked up into Mina's eyes, "She's been in contact with her mother recently and I am worried that she might be drawn back into that old life. It took everything, every little drop of strength and courage to finally free herself of that world and here she is going right back." He pressed his folded arms against his chest, "I'm scared about what's going to happen. She acts like everything is going well, that nothing is wrong, and I shouldn't be concerned, but…"

Why didn't Oliver mention any of this? Unless of course… A strange sensation flowed across her body leaving her to shiver despite the warmth of the summer day, "She hasn't told anyone, has she? She hasn't even told her brother yet, am I right?"

Hoven shook his head slowly, "She said she didn't want to upset him, that what's happening should be kept private and that she confided in me only because she loved me and that she felt that I should know everything, even things she withheld from others."

Mina's immediate response was accusing in tone, "Why are you telling me if it is supposed to be a secret? If someone loves you and confides something that personal to you, you shouldn't…" She bit her lip realizing that if Oliver were involved in a comparable situation, she would have more than likely asked Mitch for advice on how to handle the situation. "That's why you're telling me, because I'm the only other person in the world who might understand what you're going through. If his mother had contacted him and I was worried that…" She slowly nodded as if saying yes to everything she was saying, "Fine, you're right, I'm sorry, I might have done something similar."

Hoven shrugged his shoulders, staring at Mina, "What do you think I should do? I'm worried about her. I…" Again, the pain in his chest prevented him from saying it, "…care about Alice. I'm scared I'm going to lose her, that who she is will be changed. She told me about how she used to be like when she was a part of her mother's family. She was becoming this cold, uncaring, emotionless, kind of person. She said she was pretty rude at times to Oliver which came as a shock to me."

Mina remembered how her boyfriend had described his sister's behavior before she left her mother's home. "It's strange but Oliver has a part of his personality that still comes and goes from his time with his mother training him to be a certain way. When he feels threatened, he becomes someone else. It's almost like this…"

Hoven nodded in agreement, "Yeah, I've seen Alice do it a few times." He sighed deeply, "That's the part of her that scares me. It's not her, it's not the woman that I…" He cringed, the pain in his chest getting worse each time he nearly said it, "I just want her to be safe, to not be sucked back into that world again."

"I'm worried about how Oliver would react to all of this. Not only would he be worried about his sister, but the stress of knowing his mother was trying to invade what was such a wonderful part of his life would be devastating to him." Mina pressed her hands against her face as she paced back and forth a few steps each direction before turning back across the original path, "I get why you came to me with all of this, but I don't…" Lowering her hands, she stared at the man, "Is there anything else you can tell me? Is there something I should know about what's happening with her mother?"

Hoven shook his head in response, "I don't know, the time spent with her mother or what they talk about is private according to Alice. Which is weird as she never hides anything from me." He stopped for a moment before adding, "Well, before this happened."

~

"What do you see in him?" Alice's mother sat in an ornately crafted chair upon a stone platform that had taken nearly a week to make certain as to its perfection in appearance.

She wore an elegant, hand-crafted dress as light blue eyes observed her youngest child and only daughter with an intense, dissecting gaze. She had attempted to soften her response to Alice, but old habits were hard to quickly let go of. Long dark blonde hair was carefully combed back behind her back, not a trace of gray or white hairs could be found. Despite her eldest son being in his late thirties, she appeared not much older than in her early forties.

Alice delicately sipped at the cup in her hand, enjoying the flavor of a tea that was her favorite from when she was younger. She had been unable to obtain it once she had left her mother's home due to its rarity and expense involved. "Please be respectful of the man I love, or I will be forced to depart prematurely. I don't wish to be rude to you, for you have been a gracious host, but I will not ignore any harm done to him."

"No disrespect meant, my dear." Setting the cup into the saucer she held with her other hand, Alice's mother placed it upon the small table in front of her. The surface had been covered by silk cloth, a shade of red that matched the roses surrounding the pair. "I am attempting to better understand the woman you have become. I thought it best to inquire about those within your life."

Setting down the cup and saucer, Alice carefully interlaced her fingers and placed them in her lap. "He is beautiful to me. He does not fulfill the conventional sense of masculinity due to his shorter than average stature and lack of physical strength, but in my eyes, he is a wonderous human being worthy of the admiration and love I am able to provide to him." She realized that may not be what her mother was seeking as to an answer, "Why do you ask?"

"As you well know, I had him investigated at length. I provided you the information concerning his troubled past and yet you ignored such warnings." Alice's mother watched her daughter in curiosity. "He was abandoned by his parents. Moved about from one foster home to another. In his youth, he was involved with several criminal activities that led to his arrest on multiple occasions. Despite this potential to cause you harm, you still welcome him into your life with open arms." A faint smile tugged at the corners of her thin lips, "I am concerned for your wellbeing."

"To be clear, I may have forgiven you for taking such an action in invading his privacy due to your interest in protecting me from what you considered a threat, I am not pleased with your actions. You have been interfering with my life all too often and as requested, it is my hope that you have remained at a distance." Alice met her mother's gaze with equal strength, refusing to be intimidated. "As to your inquiry, you must know that he has not been involved in such activities since he was able to withdraw himself from the foster homes in which he lived in his youth. As an adult, freed from the influence of others that forced him into such scenarios, he has been virtuous in his interactions with others."

"I will not make any potentially slanderous remarks concerning his lifestyle. However, have you considered encouraging him to alter his current situation? If you love this man, then I am certain you desire for him to lead more suitable life than what he now chooses." Alice's mother held up her hand as if to interrupt an objection, "It can't be safe for him living in a vehicle, exposed to the dangers of this world. His health must be a concern as well."

Alice wasn't certain if her mother was attempting to criticize Hoven or if she was genuinely concerned for his wellbeing, "I have spoken to him concerning his lifestyle. I wish to be supportive of his decisions in life but at the same time, express my concerns. He finds the idea of creating a permanent home as restrictive. He speaks of being trapped in such a scenario. However, he has taken steps in providing his body proper nourishment and I believe it has altered his physical condition positively." She smiled, "I did not think it possible, but I believe that he becomes more handsome with each passing day."

Alice's mother did not wish to accept Hoven as a potential mate for her daughter. In her mind, she deserved a tall, muscular man with broad shoulders, barrel chest, and one of high breeding coming from a family with wealth and power. It was those kinds of individuals she had been encouraging before the pair had separated from one another's lives for nearly two years. By comparison to this vision, Hoven was small, skinny, nothing about him fit what she considered ideal. The fact that he was homeless, living out of his car, working with animals of all things, it was disgusting.

However, since her reconciliation with her daughter, Alice's mother had been doing her best to set aside her presumptions and attempts to see the world from a new perspective, "If I invited you to a social gathering in the future, would you be interested in attending with your gentleman caller?"

"Mother, he is not merely a man who is seeking a romantic connection to me." Alice felt frustrated that her mother would not accept the truth, "He is my boyfriend. I love him dearly."

"Has he spoken such things to you in return?" The concept of love was foreign to Alice's mother. She had never experienced such emotions in any form from her parents and certainly not from her husband. Their connection to one another was purely for social status, creating a stronger bond between two families, and in her mind, elevating herself to a higher position of authority. The moment he died, she quickly took control of the vacancy he left, eliminating anyone who attempted to treat her as anything less than a force to be reckoned with throughout the company she had authority over.

Alice wasn't certain if her mother had spies to learn of such things or it was merely an accidental guess as to what had or in this case, not occurred, "No, he has not." She quickly looked up from staring at her hands, "However, I believe he feels such a connection with me even if he struggles to speak the words. He was emotionally damaged throughout his youth. The idea of opening himself to the concept of being loved and loving someone in return is difficult for him." Alice leaned forward to take tea kettle to pour herself another cup, "I had thought you would understand."

Was that a biting remark concerning her own past? Alice's mother was impressed. She held up her hand, "Don't exert yourself in such a way, dearest daughter." A woman dressed in formal attire who was standing nearby silently waited for the slightest movement from her benefactor. Seeing the gesture, she moved forward to refill the empty cups.

Alice looked up, speaking firmly, "I have no need for your assistance, thank you." The woman who had approached the table stopped, pausing to look over at the elder of the pair.

Alice's mother smiled, enjoying the expression of power and control that her daughter was exhibiting. Ignoring the individuals that she considered as nothing more than a servant in the presence of a queen, she made a small brushing motion of her fingertips. Immediately the woman stepped back, resuming her position a few feet away. All the while the elder woman watched Alice, "I am happy to see that not all that I have taught you has been lost with the passage of time."

Alice poured the tea into her cup and began to stand to offer to do the same for her mother who held up her hand in a signal to stop. With a small nod, she set down the kettle and took the cup and saucer in hand, "This is delicious, thank you dearly for providing me such a luxury. I appreciate that you remembered I enjoyed this particular tea when I was younger."

"Despite what you may think of me, I was keenly interested in your childhood as much as I am now focused on your life as the mature woman that you have proven yourself to be." Alice's mother shifted topics, "Have you considered my request?"

Alice set down her cup, concern etching itself into her features, "Yes, I have at great length. I am worried about his reaction. I don't wish to cause him undue stress in his life, but at the same time, I do not wish to remove the potential of resolving what has been a troubling aspect in his past."

"Is your brother aware of our interactions?" Alice's mother watched her intently, despite her training to do so, her daughter was not as reserved in expressing her feelings as she once was. Such response to her questions often provided her the answers she sought.

Alice shook her head slowly, "He knew of our first meeting but not any other since then. I have kept such information from him until I feel that it is the ideal time. As of this moment, he has more pressing concerns weighing heavily upon him."

Alice's mother studied her daughter's face to see how she would react to her statement, "Yes, I'm aware of the opportunities that are opening up in Europe."

Surprise struck Alice as she stared at her mother with an accusing tone to her voice, "Are you responsible for what is happening?"

A smile spread across her mother's lips as she found amusement in her daughter's response, "Whether you wish to believe me or not, I do not influence all things throughout the world. I like to keep track of what is happening to all my family members to prepare myself for a public inquiry concerning their lifestyles should I need to either defend or distance myself from their activities. The fact that the company that the woman in his life works for is expanding their operations intrigued me." She paused, considering a peculiar notion, "She intrigues me."

"Is that why you are seeking an audience with Oliver, because of Mina?" Alice wasn't certain what her mother's motivations were.

"I had no interest in him until recent events. Because of you, I wish to alter my stance concerning my viewpoint of his life choices. Upon investigating him in greater detail than I had before, I learned more of the woman he wishes to spend his life with." Alice's mother smiled, "As I said, she intrigues me."

Alice gave her mother a stern look in her eyes, "Please do not contact Oliver until I have had the opportunity to speak to him concerning our interactions as well as your wish to create a connection with him. I will attempt to find an ideal moment to convey this information to him when the time is right."

"So be it." Alice's mother turned her head, gazing across the vast garden behind her mansion, "Shall we go for a walk? The flowers to the north recently bloomed and are rather beautiful."

"Thank you, mother, but you have left me much to think about and I do not believe I am in the mood to gaze upon your flowers." Alice carefully moved to her feet, "It has been a pleasant experiencing having this opportunity to spend time with you and I hope to do so in the future. Please do not take my abrupt departure as an insult. With what all that weighs upon my mind, I do not believe I would be acceptable company in my current emotional state."

"If that is how you feel, then so be it." Alice's mother rose to her feet out of respect for the woman before her, "Do you wish an escort to the entrance, or would you prefer to do so on your own?"

Alice was startled that she was given the option, typically she was provided someone to show her the way out. "I wish to depart alone, if you do not mind."

"So be it." Alice's mother turned away from the table, making a brushing motion towards the surface. The woman who had been waiting nearby quickly moved forward to clean up what remained as the mistress of the home began walking towards the north end of her garden, "Fare thee well, Alice, until next we meet."

Chapter 5

"You and I need to talk." Mitch stood near Oliver's car that was parked a few blocks away from where Mina worked. It was his day off and he visited her during her lunch, providing her with a hot meal he had picked up at a small shop along the way from where he left his car.

Oliver looked around confused, "How did you know I would be here?"

"Don't take this wrong way, but you're predictable. I could practically set my watch to the routines you follow. Every Wednesday you visit your lady where she works. You park here or over there…" Mitch motioned to a parking lot across the street, "Then walk to where she is, picking up something from that cute little place on the corner. One of the few remaining mom and pop café style places. I love the ambiance, the whole environment is warm and cozy, but the food isn't all that great. However, I know you get it from there so that it will be nice and warm for when you show up a few minutes later in the lobby patiently waiting for Mina to arrive since security prevents you from going up and meeting her at her office."

Oliver scowled, feeling uncomfortable with the fact that Mitch knew his routine so well. Folding his arms across his chest, he stared slightly up at the taller of the two men. "How do you know all of this about me?"

Mitch laughed, "Partly from what Mina has told me, little bit of boredom, and a healthy dose of curiosity to see if it was all true."

"How did you know where I parked?" Oliver motioned towards the city around them, "It could have been anywhere nearby, even if you knew where I got food from."

"Oh, that's easy. You like to avoid paying the costs of parking fees, which I totally get, they can be dreadful at times for someone on a budget." A firm expression formed across Oliver's face as his eyes became like solid steel doors. Mina had talked often that if her boyfriend felt threatened or insulted, another side of him surfaced that hinted at the man his mother had taught him to become. Although he had turned his back on such a strict upbringing, often it returned when he needed to show strength. "Oh, I have to admit, I get a little tingly when I see that fierce look in your eyes." He lightly patted his chest just about his heart, "I can see why you drive Mina wild with such intense passion…"

"Stop." Oliver held up his hand, "Your point has been made concerning me finding somewhere within range of where Mina works that is free to park here. It may take a bit of walking to reach her location, but it's worth it to me. However, know that your statement edged closely towards an insulting tone in derision concerning my financial status. That I do not appreciate and secondly, don't speak of any aspect of intimacy with Mina. Please respect her privacy, even if you don't show such respect for me."

Mitch bit his lower lip, feeling a warmth rising across his body. The intensity, the passion, the fire in those eyes in defending the lady of his life. "If I were a teapot, I would be whistling loudly right about now. Oh my…"

Oliver firmly asked, "What is it you want?"

"Obviously, we got off on the wrong foot here, so let's start again…" Mitch smiled before waving his hand, "Hi. We need to talk about your situation."

Oliver wasn't certain what the other man was alluding to, "What situation?"

Mitch looked around, "Can we do this in private? My car is right over there next to yours which will be safe for now. I need to steal you away for a while and I thought this was going to be a wonderful time to go into depth about what's going on."

Already feeling exhausted dealing with the man for the brief period they had been interacting, Oliver nodded slowly, "Alright, after you."

Mitch mimicked how Alice would, in his opinion was the cutest thing ever, curtsey. Since he wasn't wearing a dress, it looked a little odd, especially for a six foot, four-inch-tall man doing so. "You are as ever, a gentleman, dear sir."

Knowing what Mitch was doing, Oliver reserved judgement as he asked, "Why did you do that? I hope you weren't insulting my sister's behavior by doing so."

"No! Of course not." Clearly Oliver was already worked up about something, which was the exact reason Mitch felt they needed to talk. He was going on the defensive about everything. Man needed to unwind a little. Normally Mitch would recommend some personal time with his lady, but from what he knew of them, they hadn't explored that level of their relationship just yet. That, and he knew that the other man would practically rip his head off for even speaking of their sex life. "I adore Alice, she's my Precious."

Oliver turned away, "I see."

Feeling a bit of a chill in the air, which reminded him of Mina's frosty disposition when they had first met, Mitch kept silent as he reached the driver's side of his car. By then Oliver was standing on the other side. With a click of a button of his keys in his pocket, the doors unlocked. Once inside, he tried a different approach the conversation, "Mina loves you."

"I'm aware of this." Oliver buckled himself in before continuing, "You didn't have to stalk me to learn my routines to ambush me at my vehicle to tell me that."

"Do you not like me? I thought we got along before." Mitch pulled his car into reverse and began pulling out of his parking spot, "I'm sensing a lot of hostility over there, what's going on in that head of yours?"

"We have rarely interacted with one another in the past. I am not accustomed to your behavioral patterns. That, I must apologize for. I don't wish to be rude due to my lack of understanding of how you are around others." Oliver sighed deeply, feeling it necessary to clear the air on a topic that was bothering him, "In the past, you upset my sister. Two separate occasions specifically come to mind. The first, you implied that someone without experience when it came to relationships and to a further extent, physical intimacy, was to be thought less of." Mitch started to speak but he was interrupted by a raise of a hand, "Secondly, you picked her up without her permission which was a violation of her privacy."

"In my defense, she forgave me for both of these situations." Mitch cringed, "This is not going the way I was hoping for."

"There are only two people in this world that I care about. I would give my life to protect either one without hesitation. Mina tolerates your behavior, often speaking of it as something that amuses her. She speaks highly of you and trusts you with nearly as much as what she confides in me. I respect the relationship you share with her and her reaction to your potentially insulting commentary is what my understanding is…" Oliver struggled to properly explain himself, "There is a saying, she gives as good as she takes? Something like that."

"Oh yeah…" Mitch laughed, "That gal can fight me toe to toe and win. Just recently she nearly scared the pee out of me. She's a fierce lady that I have learned to be careful around." He laughed again, "Still, I never hold back around her until I trigger something, then I bring it back a notch. Until then, she's like all my friends, she can handle whatever I throw and her, no problem."

"As for my sister, I am not pleased with your disrespect of her." Oliver kept his gaze forward, "I am concerned about your influence upon her life, and it worries me that you are the cause of unnecessary grief." He sighed deeply, "However, she enjoys your company and speaks highly of you. She has discussed with me the incidents that we both agree went too far and crossed a line when it came to social interaction. She was upset with you at the time, but as you said, she forgave you. However, I am deeply worried that your behavior will eventually lead to a statement that will harm her on a personal level that she will not recover from and will not forgive you for." Finally, he turned his head to face Mitch, "What guarantee can I have from you that you will not reach such an extreme with her?"

"There are no guarantees in life, and you're certainly not going to get something like that from me." Mitch had enough defending himself or the way he was, "I respect you. From what Mina says about you, you're perfect in every way. I wish nothing but sunshine for you and Mina. I get why you're coming at me about all the stupidity on my part when it comes to your sister. Yeah, I totally take full blame for that, my bad. I get that." He held up one hand while holding the steering wheel firmly with the other, "I'm guilty of all crimes I have been accused of your honor."

Lowering his hand, Mitch continued, "However, don't you dare sit there and talk down to me like you're better than me. You may not think you are coming across that way, but in the few minutes I had in the presence of the illustrious wannabe queen that is your mother, I am getting a lot of that vibe from you just now. Don't let her sassy little vicious…"

"Please don't speak of her." Oliver closed his eyes and he leaned back in his chair. "You're right, I apologize for my behavior."

"Oh thank goodness…" Mitch felt a sudden relief, getting into a fight with Mina's boyfriend was the last thing he ever wanted to do. Yet, he felt he had to defend himself from what was beginning to feel more like round two with Oliver's mother more so than speaking to the man that was sitting next to him. "Don't take this the wrong way, but I did not believe the whole split personality thing that Mina mentioned."

Oliver turned, a scowl forming across his brow, "What are you talking about?"

Mitch grinned, "You know, good cop, bad cop?"

At first Oliver didn't understand but quickly realized what he was alluding to, "Oh that…"

"Yeah, that." Mitch tried to relax after the tension had built between the two men, "I suddenly felt like you were attacking me, things starting to turn ugly, and then I thought to myself, when was the last time I felt this way? That's when I realized, a certain someone who won't be named, made me feel that way. Must be your years of being trained to be a certain way was seeping through, not the sweet and kind man that Mina loves."

"I wish I had transitioned as smoothly to my new life the way Alice did. I feel like it takes over sometimes, like a subliminal message that is triggered by stress." Oliver glanced over at Mitch, "My point is still true, though. I'm not pleased that Alice has shed tears over your behavior."

Thankfully they had come to a light allowing Mitch to touch both hands to his chest as he reacted with a deep pain in his eyes, "She cried? I made Precious cry? She never told me that."

"She didn't wish to hurt your feelings further once the two of you had resolved your dispute." Seeing Mitch's reaction, Oliver felt that he had made his point, "Do you see why I'm upset?"

"I guess I'm so used to dealing with people with a tougher outer shell. They are soft on the inside, sure, but tough as nails on the outside. It takes a lot to get through to them. My comments just slide right off like rain off a frog's butt." Mitch laughed, "That last one is due to my papaw, something he used to say."

"I apologize for interrupting you earlier." Oliver tried to shift topics, "What is it you wished to talk to me about?"

"Oh yeah..." Mitch laughed, "Boy, did we get sidetracked. We went on a little trip to tension town, quick stop to the anger shop, smoothed things out at a relaxing spa of getting things out of our system, and now here we are back at serious topic city."

Oliver shook his head slowly, "I am not certain what you meant by any of that."

"You and your sister are so alike sometimes." Mitch grinned for a moment before assuming a more serious tone, "Mina loves you and you love her, so don't let what is happening ruin that, okay? If this opportunity for her does happen, not sure if it is a thing yet, but if it does, don't think she's getting cold feet."

"Cold feet?" Oliver felt like he had heard the term before, "What do you mean?"

Mitch tried to keep the conversation friendly, "She's not avoiding you proposing to her, so don't think that."

Oliver's eyes widened in shock, "What do you mean, me proposing to her? What do you know about that?" It was then that Mitch realized he had said too much, so chose to keep his eyes on the road in front of him as he kept his lips firmly pressed together. "What does she know?"

"I shouldn't have said anything." Mitch avoided eye contact, "I am so sorry for even saying a word. I never..."

Oliver felt anxiety building within him as he asked, "Does she know...? Alice, did she say something?"

Seeing a place for him to pull over, Mitch quickly moved into an empty parking spot before responding, "Alice didn't say a word about it. She would never break your trust."

"What does Mina know or thinks she knows about my intentions?" Until that moment, he was under the impression that she had no inkling that he was considering proposing to her. They had spoken of getting married someday, but never was there any hint that she knew that he was practicing or planning to do so soon rather than within the next few years.

"First of all, how well do you know your girlfriend?" Before Oliver could respond, Mitch held up his hand, "Don't answer that. Just think to yourself, what if she knew you as well as you know her. Based off that alone, if she was thinking about proposing to you, her behavior would change, details would add up, right? You would be able to figure it out on your own, no one else involved to piece it together. That's the downside of being with someone that can read you like a book and knows you probably better than you know yourself." He smiled wide, "Which I love that about you two. Michael and I, we still have awhile to go to reach that point, but you two? It's like you two are so in tune with one another."

Oliver sighed deeply as he scowled in consideration of what had been presented to him. Of course, Mina knew. Her keen intellect was one of many reasons he highly respected and admired her. He had to admit to himself his behavior had changed. He had not been as restrained in his affection towards her. Some part of him felt less reserved knowing that they may become husband and wife. Nodding slowly, he forced to conclude, "What are her feelings on the subject, if you don't mind me asking?"

"Honestly? Not what you want to hear, but..." Mitch hesitated, "She's scared."

"Scared?" Looking up, Oliver felt a deep pain in his chest, "Not excited or joyous over the possibility?" It was yet another element to the situation he wasn't willing to accept and yet knew was the truth. He was scared himself, worried about the future, fearful of history repeating itself in being rejected by the woman he loved after proposing to her. He nodded slowly, "She feels fear?"

"She loves you, you know that, but considering her past, you got to understand that she's got a lot of scars buried so deep that I don't think anyone has seen them before." Mitch was hoping his talk with Oliver would help the situation, but he was afraid he was only making things worse. "I love Kitten. I would do anything for her. You know that. Just give her some time. Don't pop the question prematurely. You know how the ladies respond to things when a man does something prematurely."

"The woman I love fears a future with me and you're making an inappropriate joke?" Oliver unbuckled his seat belt, "Thank you for telling me. I knew of her concerns, I sensed that was the truth, but you confirmed my suspicions. However, it's obvious to me that you're not the one to speak of about this further. I don't wish to be rude, but your continuing attempts at humor make it evident that you're not the ideal audience for what I wish to say in response." He opened the door.

Mitch called out, "I was trying to help."

Closing the door, Oliver spoke through the open window, "You did. Just not in the way you had hoped." He turned away, heading down the sidewalk, not caring how he would find his way back to his car, he just needed time alone.

Groaning softly, Mitch fell back in his chair, "Some fairy godmother I'm turning out to be. Evil queen disrupting the wedding, that's more like it. How do these fairy tale folks do it? They make it seem like it's just so easy." He took in a deep breath before letting it out slowly to calm his nerves, "Alright, need to go to the source when it comes to this happily ever after stuff. I need an expert on the subject matter because obviously, I don't know what I'm doing."

~

"You did what? Why!" Alice fought back a surge of an emotion she rarely felt, typically reserved only for her mother's behavior. It was a form of anger born from deep rooted frustration with a situation. She wanted to gently poke him in the chest but felt that such an action would only cause harm and perpetuate the need for physical violence in response a loss of temper. "Mitch Frederick Bulsara, how could you be so naïve!"

"Me! Naive?" Mitch wasn't sure if he wanted to burst out laughing considering who it was that was calling him such a thing, "Sweetie…"

Alice held up her hand to silence him, "Please do not interrupt me." Lowering her hand, she continued, "If you are the root cause of my brother and Mina ending their relationship, I will not forgive you. We will no longer be friends, for you will have hurt Oliver deeply, even if your intentions were benevolent in nature."

"That's why I came to you immediately afterwards, you know more about this once upon a time, happily ever after, fairy tale happiness a lot more than I do." Mitch held up his hands as if trying to stop Alice, "I live in the real world, not in your fantasy world."

Alice scowled at the remark, "What are you implying? I cannot help but feel that there is a potential insult to be found within your statement."

"What is up with your family today? First Oliver, now you? Where did I go wrong?" Mitch started to turn away, "That's it, I obviously got up on the wrong side of the bed this afternoon. My mojo is all but gone today."

"I too live in the real world as you do." Alice scowled, restraining her emotions for the time being, "I am not a little girl immersed in a fantasy world. I thought you respected me greater than that to say such a thing."

"What happened to me? It's like I just can't say the right thing today, what is up with this?" Mitch muttered before addressing Alice's statement, "I love the way you see the world. I really do. It's this beautiful fantasy that you created around yourself that you can trust strangers, that everyone deep down is good inside, the fact that when two people say they love one another, all of them are being honest about it. You have this rose-colored glass viewpoint of everything going on around you that I would give anything if it was true, but it isn't. Oliver is a lot like you. It's why Mina finally stopped being the Ice Queen and is now Kitten around her man."

"Just because I have an optimistic viewpoint that I refuse to allow the harshness of reality to tarnish, does not mean I am naïve of the truth." Alice shook her head slowly, "I am fully aware of what is going on around me, how so many believe this viewpoint of yours that because the world is a certain way, that we must merely accept it and work within the restrictions of such toxic behavior."

"What I meant with all of that is that you understand your brother better than me, his viewpoint, his idealized feelings towards true love and how the world should work." Mitch sighed in frustration, "Then there is Mina, who is more like me, realistic in how the world works and how happily ever after isn't easy."

"It should be." Alice was confused, "Did you not say something similar in the presence of Mina? She stated that real life isn't a fairy tale. Love isn't always a beautiful fantasy. You told her that it should be. The only reason it isn't is because we've convinced ourselves that it can't be and that outside influence of our society has convinced us that it isn't. Why have you suddenly changed your mind about this subject?"

"Because Mina's leaving." Mitch felt his heart breaking the moment he saw Alice's reaction. He wanted to hug her but knew not to do so without being invited to do so, "The company has a media outlet page where people like me can keep up to date with what her company is doing and any news to come from events concerning where she works. Since I needed to know what's going on just in case Mina feels like suddenly keeping me out of the loop, I signed up for any updates. I get a message that shows a picture of the team moving to Europe for the next six months to a year to establish their new branch there. Mina's name is right there in the list. She hasn't told me, of course, she's waiting to tell Oliver later tonight but news travels fast. So, I thought, well, let me intervene, try to get him ready for the news and I failed on an epic level I am not proud of."

A woman with shoulder length jet black hair and matching dark eyes entered the room, "Hey there toy boy."

"Hi there, Vixen, long time no see." Mitch gave Alice's roommate a playful smile and a wink.

Knowing that she had zero chance with a man that she admittedly found incredibly attractive, Cara tolerated him as eye candy. Beyond that, she didn't really like having him in her apartment since he tended to disrupt what was typically a quite space for her to enjoy reading. Alice was the perfect roommate, keeping the apartment spotless clean, well-organized, and always quiet. "I heard a lot of noise, should have known it was you."

"Oh boo on you. Just because you never go anywhere or do anything, doesn't mean Alice can't have a life." Mitch loved playing around with Cara, she was like an annoying little sister and a woman trying to flirt with him at a bar all rolled into one.

"You do realize the only reason I put up with you is that I'm mentally undressing you right now." Turning from the conversation, Cara went into the small kitchen area, "That and I don't have to worry about putting on clothes or you mentally undressing me when you're here." She paused, smiling at Mitch, "It's weird, but I like it."

Mitch kissed his fingers before blowing her a kiss, "Love you too, sweetie." Returning to the conversation with Alice, he continued, "I screwed up."

Cara paused with a bottle of water in hand as she laughed, "It must be the end of the world, the almighty Mitch made a mistake. We're all doomed…" She said the last part with a deadpan expression and a monotone voice.

Mitch held up his hand for silence, "You need to be quiet. The adults are talking."

Cara stared at him with an opened mouth shocked expression before replying, "I don't have to take this."

Mitch made a brushing motion of his hand, "No, you don't, so you should just go back to your room and let me finish."

"It's my apartment!" Cara glared, "If you weren't so hot and my body didn't seriously need something to compensate for the fact that I can't find…"

"Shocker." Mitch shook his head, "Men aren't flocking to a woman with a snarky attitude and biting remarks?"

Alice interrupted their interlude, "Mitch, apologize to her."

Seeing Alice's stern expression, he turned back to Cara as he recited what he had been told to say, "I apologize for my behavior, and I did not mean to offend you."

Cara laughed, knowing that was Alice's words coming out of his mouth, "Fine, whatever."

Alice spoke to her roommate, "Would you mind giving us a moment alone? I promise that it will not be for much longer and the gentleman will be leaving shortly."

"Gentleman? Him?" Again, Cara laughed, "Right, sure…" She touched two fingertips to her forehead and motioned towards Mitch in a solute, "See you around, sir."

"You take that back. The term sir is reserved for my father, not me. I am way too young for that." As Cara headed back to her room, Mitch asked, "So, what should we do?"

"Wait patiently and let Oliver and Mina resolve their situation without any further interference." Alice smiled confidently, "I do believe that love will prevail."

Chapter 6

"I'll miss you." Tears formed in Oliver's eyes as he stared at the ground, "I'm sorry. I don't mean to ruin this moment for you."

Mina brushed her hand gently across his cheek facing away from where she was sitting next to him as she kissed him softly on the other, "Don't feel guilty for feeling the way you do. The only thing keeping me from reacting the same way is because I'm nervous, scared, worried about the flight, what it's going to be like when I get there, all of this is new to me." Mina had flown before, but it was the first time she had traveled outside the country. She had gotten a passport when she graduated college, updating it as necessary with grand plans in traveling the world but she had never done so.

The pair was waiting for the announcement that boarding of her plane would begin. The seating area was filled with other members of the group that had been selected by her company to aid in setting up the new location in England. A few had families, others were either seated alone by choice or grouped together discussing the future they were about to embark on.

For Oliver, the world around him had melted away. In that moment it was just the two of them sitting together for what would be the last time in weeks, possibly months. He spoke of plans of visiting her often but knew it may never come to be. Mina would be extremely busy, either involved with some project or traveling from one location to another that would require her attention. What little free time she had would be to catch up on much needed rest.

That is how it was described to him at least, how it would play out. Mina wasn't certain. She was comforting in that she offered to purchase him plane tickets to fit in a visit whenever possible. It wasn't the first time their roles were reversed but it was certainly a rare occasion when Oliver was the pessimist, considering what he felt to be realistic expectations and Mina was optimistic in what would turn out to be a positive experience.

Oliver gently squeezed her hand, his mind wondering as to how the future of his life would play out without her by his side. He couldn't help but compare this experience to her passing away, becoming a… He scowled, he wouldn't be a widower, they weren't married but he certainly would feel that level of loss.

No, he shouldn't think that way. She was alive, with that there was hope that he would see her again. They could call each other every day and keep in touch in dozens of separate ways. The modern world offered multiple options that generations before had been denied. He was tempted to create handwritten letters as his grandfather may have done for his grandmother but thought such a gesture was silly. When would she have time to read it? Would she even receive it properly what with her moving about so often?

"Oliver?" All other thoughts quickly vanished as he turned to Mina, his mind fixated on memorizing every detail of her face, to preserve each memory as if it would be his last of her. "Thank you for being so supportive throughout all of this."

A part of him wanted to shed tears, but he withheld his yearning to do so as he smiled, "You're welcome, my love."

Mina looked away, "Stop it. You're going to make me cry."

Oliver started to apologize, "I didn't mean to…"

"I'm sorry for saying that. All of this…" He saw the tears in her eyes, guilt weighing heavily on him for being the cause. Mina smiled, "I've been trying to hold back, to be strong for both of us but then I realized that is unfair to you. You deserve..." The first of many broke free, sliding down the side of her face, "We deserve…" She struggled to find the right words, "I want you to know how much I'll miss you and not letting all of this out now, I'll regret it."

Oliver slid one hand behind her back. The other caressed her cheek before he kissed her softly. After what felt like eternity for both, he pulled away just enough to touch his forehead to hers, "I love you Mina. I will miss you and cherish every moment you can provide me when you're gone. I'll do everything I can to keep in contact with you." He drew in a shuddered breath, "With each beat of my heart, I will feel your presence."

Mina wanted to speak, say something beautiful, but nothing felt it would be enough to express what she wanted to tell him. "I love you…" The first announcement that her airplane would begin boarding sounded, drawing her to pull away, turning her head she watched as others began to stand and prepare to make their departure. Looking up into Oliver's eyes, she whispered, "I should stay, I can't do this to you…"

"I want what is best for you above all else. You should and need to do this. You'll regret every moment if you don't." Oliver slid his hands down to meet hers. He clasped them firmly, "This isn't goodbye. Think of it more as until next we meet. Where there is true love, there is hope. I will be with you again someday."

Oliver slid out of his chair into a standing position. Mina joined him, hugging him tightly, pressing the side of her face against his chest as she cried uncontrollably as she released the pent-up sorrow she felt in leaving him for so long. "This won't be forever, I promise." She pulled away, looking up into his tear-streaked face, "You are my forever. You always will be."

Touching his chest with his fingertips, Oliver smiled, "You will always be with me." He touched his hand above her heart, "If you ever need me, you know where to find me."

Mina knew her time was running out, she had to leave soon, "I love you, my sweet Oliver."

He leaned forward, kissing her with a heartfelt passion that nearly made it impossible for her to remain standing by the time their embrace concluded. He held her one last time, speaking softly in her ear, "I love you, my precious Mina."

~

"Thank you for providing us a moment alone." Oliver had time to regain his composure before returning to the main area of the airport. Mitch, Alice, and Hoven had joined the couple, saying goodbye to her before the pair went on through the security check point to reach the boarding area for the plane.

Mitch grinned playfully, "No problem, security is a nightmare to get through sometimes."

Alice shoved her elbow into the man's stomach, "Humor is his defense mechanism. If you would be so kind to excuse his potential rude behavior."

Shocked, Mitch stared down at Alice, "You just hit me."

Alice smiled sweetly, "Mina said I could do so in her absence. I normally do not encourage such behavior, but she taught me what is acceptable concerning..." She tried to remember what she had been told, "To keep you in check?" Her brow furrowed, "I am not certain what that means exactly."

Mitch slipped his arm across Alice's shoulders as tears formed in his eyes, "You did it just like Mina would, I'm so proud of you." He tried to avoid eye contact, "I thought I had cried myself out last night but here I go again."

Alice gently patted Mitch on the back as she smiled, "I knew that there was a pure soul and a gentle heart found within that tough exterior." She shifted her gaze to Oliver, her expression of happiness fading as she assumed a more serious tone. "Is there something I can do to help you?"

Hoven cleared his throat, feeling like he didn't belong to the group, not knowing Mina as well as the others, "What can we...?" He motioned towards the three-standing opposite of Oliver, "...do to help you out? I know how I would feel if it was Alice that was on that plane, so..." He shrugged as he buried his hands in his pockets, nodding slowly since he wasn't sure what he was doing, "Want something to drink?"

Alice looked over at Hoven in shock, "Are you suggesting he an consumption of alcohol?" She quickly shifted her focus to Oliver, "Do you wish to partake in the consumption of distilled beverages?"

Oliver smiled, enjoying the reactions of his friends, "No, I do not wish to do so."

Alice turned back to Hoven, "Why would you say that?"

Hoven reacted defensively, "I don't know, I just... I don't have a lot of experience with someone who is a positive part of my life going away. Everyone I've ever known before you was horrible to me, so when they were gone, I was happy." He motioned towards Oliver, "This? I have never gone through anything like this. I mean, I just have to think to myself, what I would feel like if you were going away for a few months." He felt his mouth going dry as dizziness began affecting him, "I saw it in movies and television, when something like this happens, people get drunk."

Mitch interrupted, trying to pull away some attention from Hoven, "I plan on getting drunk, that's my coping mechanism in dealing with stuff like this. However, that's just me." He pointed to Oliver and Alice, "These two don't drink. Ever."

"I knew that about Alice, I just..." Hoven shrugged, "I'm just going to shut up now."

Alice took a step towards Hoven, "I'm sorry for my accusation. You were just trying to provide comfort in a scenario you have no experience with. I should have realized that before..." She touched her hand to his cheek, "Please, forgive me?"

"Sure." Hoven felt a warmth coursing across his cheek, "It's no big deal, I'm used to it."

"You shouldn't be." Alice hugged him, even with his arms still at his side and his hands in his pocket, she pinned them into place as she held him firmly for a moment as she spoke softly, "You deserve nothing but kindness, love, and generosity." She pulled away, enough to kiss him softly on the cheek before returning her focus to her brother, "What would you like to do next?"

"I need to go home for a while, deal with what just happened." Oliver nodded slowly, "I haven't slept much at all in the past few days knowing this was coming. I think I just need rest, recover the best I can and start again." He steadied his breathing, doing what he could to keep from crying again, "She's going to keep in touch the best she can, update me on what's happening. She may not have much of a chance to call me once she lands, there is a lot happening once she arrives." He struggled to smile, to try to remain stoic in the face of all that was happening, "I guess I just need some time alone, to be available for Mina should she wish to reach out to me in the meantime."

Mitch touched his hand to Oliver's shoulder, "Know that if you ever need someone to talk to, you have my number, so…" He wiped tears from his eyes, "I miss her so much right now. She would know what to say right now. Me of all people at a loss for words, you know?"

Oliver nodded in response, "Thank you."

Alice held out her hand, "You are not alone." Oliver took her hand, smiling at the comfort she provided him, "If you need anything, we'll all do what we can to help you through this time in your life."

Hoven spoke without thinking, "Except for me, I don't know what I'm doing. Probably best if I don't get too involved."

"Shush." Alice took Hoven's hand, soon holding onto her brother on her right and her boyfriend on her left, escorting them both, "You never know what you have to offer until you try. A true hero knows their limitations but is not hindered by such restraints."

"A true hero?" Mitch was walking beside Oliver, a smirk crossing his lips, "Sounds like something my sister would say. That reminds me, I need to call her. She's been so busy with her career lately." He looked over at the man next to him, "You're lucky to have Alice close by so you can see her every day."

Oliver scowled at the thought that he wouldn't be able to see Mina as often he was accustomed to, "Yeah…"

"Oh no, I did it again, didn't I?" Mitch held up his hands, "Hoven, my man, you think you have trouble saying the right thing at the right time, try being the mess I have been lately." He shifted his focus to Oliver, "I'm sorry, I didn't mean bring up Mina. It's just… I give up, I should just keep my luscious lips sealed."

Oliver laughed at Mitch's reaction to what he had said, "It's alright. Mina left explicit instructions on how to respond to you whenever it felt inappropriate."

Mitch fell silent, his mind racing as to what that may mean, "What did she tell you?"

Smiling at the memory, Oliver stated, "It was something along the lines of the patience parents show towards their toddlers."

Shock washed across Mitch's face a moment before he burst out laughing, "That's exactly something Mina would say!"

~

"Thank you for accepting my invitation." Alice smiled warmly as she motioned inside, "Please come in."

Oliver stepped inside his sister's apartment, his gaze slowly sweeping across the room. Little had changed since he had last visited. His sister was not known for her chaotic nature.

"Your home is as lovely as ever. I wish I was as organized with my own house." Oliver had been procrastinating concerning the upkeep of where he lived ever since Mina had departed. His energy levels had dropped dramatically. He was vigilant in getting to work on time, putting forth his full focus and attention at excelling at his tasks when it came to his job so that no one was aware of any changes in his behavior. However, once he was clocked out for the day and had returned home, who he was quickly changed.

Where he would typically prepare meals, buying the ingredients at a grocery store, making sure his pantry and refrigerator were well stocked, he now often bought things he could heat in a microwave for a quick meal. Time spent reading, cleaning his house, maintaining the exterior appearance, things that kept him busy had soon faded as the weeks passed. Often, he would find himself waking from falling asleep on his couch, a movie or television show he had been watching having concluded without his knowledge before pushing himself to go to bed.

What had begun as getting a phone call from Mina once a day soon became a few days in between. In the first few weeks, attempts to get through to her was successful every time he made the attempt to do so, working around her schedule that she kept him informed of. Now it was next to impossible to get through to her. Either he was linked to a personal voice mail, told by someone that she was currently detained, and it was increasingly difficult to plan for something he had no knowledge of. It wasn't that she didn't attempt to do so, she just had no clue how each day would play out as the week progressed.

With communication between them becoming difficult, Oliver had begun creating handwritten letters whenever he felt lonely, wishing to express what was on his mind. Mina had said she had begun to receive them, showing her gratitude in such beautiful words written to her, but didn't have the time to return the gesture. He wasn't upset with her, he knew her job was demanding, and it was something he had thought he had prepared for emotionally but after a month, he was forced to face the reality of what would more than likely be what would be standard in the future.

He was grateful that Alice found time for him. She was currently the only social outlet for him. Receiving an invitation from her to visit her apartment was welcomed. He stood in the middle of the living room uncertain of what to do next, "Is your roommate present? I wished to greet her, say hello so that she knows I'm acknowledging that this is also her home and would like to thank her for the opportunity to spend time here."

Alice smiled, "Cara is currently at our mutual place of work. She will be there for the next few hours. I did warn her that you may be remaining until her arrival and that she should be expecting company when she comes home."

"May I?" Oliver motioned towards one of three chairs set up in the room. He had asked her once why there was such a unique set up. Alice explained that two chairs were for the two residents who were renting the apartment while a third was open for visitor. They had both agreed that they would not have more than one visitor at a time. Cara rarely wanted anyone around, often spending her time in her room playing an online game.

"Of course." Alice enjoyed being around her brother, their mutual formal training when they were younger, softened by life beyond their childhood home, made for the most pleasant of interactions. "Would you be interested in something to eat or a beverage to drink?"

"No, thank you." Taking a seat, Oliver waited until his sister joined him before continuing, "I'm sorry if I have come across as rather distant lately, I don't mean to. I just..." He frowned, "I'm troubled by the lack of communication I have with Mina lately. It feels like the only time I get to speak of what is in my heart is in my letters that I write to her."

Alice rested her hands in her lap as she sat on the edge of her chair, her posture rigid as she watched her brother in concern, "It's quite understandable. I would feel that way if I lost touch with you or Hoven. Whom we love and cherish in this world can dramatically affect our mental state."

"After I was forcefully disconnected with our family and..." Oliver didn't want to speak her name, to do so felt like drawing about too painful of memories, "...after my fiancé ended our relationship, I was isolated worse than I am now. I should be grateful for what I have." He tried to smile, "I have you in my life, which I didn't have at the time. Mina is difficult to reach, our time spent communicating is brief, but she is out there, alive and well." His attempt to smile bloomed at the thought of her, "Most importantly, she is here..." He touched his chest, "We once said that we gave one another our hearts. We each needed someone to protect that part of us, to heal that broken part of us."

Alice loved hearing stories about her brother's relationship with Mina, "That is beautiful."

"I often say that wherever she is, a part of her is always with me. Every beat of the heart in my chest is a reminder that she is a part of my life." Oliver's smile faded, "That is metaphorical of course. We don't actually..." He laughed nervously, "I'm sorry, I shouldn't ruin the evening with my sulking."

Alice scowled, feeling terrible that he would think such a thing, "You need someone to speak to of such things and I am the only one you turn to. I know your friendship with Mitch is not a comfortable one and that you communicate with him because of Mina. Hoven is a part of your life, in a way, but only because of me." She paused, asking something she didn't wish to bring up but felt it was information that may aid in her, "Do you confide in anyone at work? Do you have someone that you would consider a friend if only at the place of business in which you have a job at?"

"No. I feel rather isolated at work, which I don't mind. I enjoy my brief interactions with customers who are checking in or out or who need help and is more than enough for me to enjoy my day-to-day experiences." Oliver fell silent for a moment before clearing his throat, "Enough about me, how are you doing?" He smiled as he looked around the apartment, "I envy you. This is a truly beautiful place you live in and from what you've told me, you get along well with your roommate."

Alice glanced around her personal space, not having put much thought into what others would think of where she lived. She simply did what she thought best, "Yes, we are, thank you."

Uncertain of what to talk about, Oliver asked, "How are your other relationships fairing? I take it Mitch keeps in touch often?"

"Oh yes, he visits at least once a week to check in on me." Alice giggled at a memory, "I believe he enjoys the company of Cara, my roommate, whether he admits to it or not. In Mina's absence, I believe she fulfills the role of being firm with him in ways I do not know how. I only do so when he has upset me, and it does not last long. Either I depart, or we resolve our differences quickly."

"How is your relationship with Hoven?" Oliver hesitated to speak of the man since they had such little interaction. The brief times he had been near him were when he was accompanying Alice at a social gathering and often, he would shadow her, rarely speaking.

"Mitch would describe it as complicated. However, when it comes to love, I do not believe any connection between two people can be that way. Hoven would respond with, it is going okay, not good, but not great. He would then proceed to blame himself for it not being better." Alice gently slid her hand across the skirt of her dress, smoothing out a wrinkle as she stared at the motion, her mind drifting to other things, "To me, he is beautiful. He is flawed, yes, but that makes our connection possible. A truly perfect individual has no need of others, no want or desire to connect with someone else. They are complete by themselves. As human beings, we are flawed, every one of us, and that is why we need to connect with others, to find those missing pieces to make us whole. Friends, family, those we love in a romantic way, and even pets." She looked up with a smile, "I have thought about getting a cat."

Oliver's eyes lit up at the concept, "Oh really?" He looked around the apartment before asking, "Are you allowed pets here?"

"No, we are not." Alice laughed at what she pictured Cara's reaction would be, "My roommate is not an animal person." She giggled at something and said, "She claims to not be a people person and since people are animals, she groups us all together."

"Yet, you get along well with her, right?" Oliver was enjoying the fact that the conversation no longer felt forced and that it was beginning to flow more easily.

Alice nodded quickly, "She claims we have an ideal living scenario, one that is apparently rare according to her. We both like to maintain a clean, organized living space. She spends most of her time in her room and when she is wishing for social interaction, she finds the fact that I don't watch television, movies, and prefer listening to music through my headphones, as ideal. She enjoys the peace and quiet, as she has stated."

Oliver noticed a comic book resting on the table, "I see you are keeping up with Mystery Alliance. Do you have a place in your room for your collection?"

Alice turned, motioning towards a bookshelf where a series of comic books carefully contained within a plastic sleeve and a cardboard backing was next to her collection of novels. "I'm proud to know the woman who is the writer of the series." She smiled brightly, "She is such a wonderful person and an inspiration to me to aspire to do remarkable things in my life. Mitch is lucky to have her as a sister." Oliver bowed his head, quickly wiping away tears which led her to ask, "What's wrong? Did I say something to upset you?"

Smiling, Oliver looked up, "You said Mitch is lucky to have this woman as his sister. I was thinking, I felt the same way to have you as my sibling."

A blush began to cross her cheeks a moment before Alice covered her face with her hands, "You are too kind, I have yet to accomplish such amazing things as she has."

"We each move forward at our own pace, accomplishing goals and finding success in our own unique way." Oliver nodded slowly before continuing, "You have done so much in such a brief time. I've been on my own for longer than you have and already it feels as if you have surpassed me in achieving all that you hoped to accomplish."

Lowering her hands, feeling that she had regained her composure, Alice quickly responded, "As you just told me, we move forward at our own pace. I did not have the hardship that you had to deal with. Your concerns which weighed you down were multiplied by many factors. You were alone, where I wasn't. Without you, I would have been like a ship lost on a stormy night out at sea with no knowledge of where to go next."

"I'm lost without her, and I shouldn't be." Oliver fell back against the chair he was sitting in, staring at the wall that just happened to be across from him, "My life shouldn't be defined by our relationship. Obviously, her life is incredibly full without me, she doesn't need me to find purpose." He turned his head, focusing on Alice, "You don't. You're driven to achieve goals you've set for yourself. Hoven is a part of your life but not the only aspect that gives your life meaning."

"Obviously, Mitch has friends, a career, and his relationship is one component of a multifaceted experience which I admit, a part of me is envious of." Oliver shook his head as if disagreeing with his own statement, "I say that and yet, I know I don't want that life. I would feel exhausted trying to keep up with so many friends, constantly going out every night for some social event, and trying to juggle that pressure to respond to others around my job. I would never have any time to myself which I enjoy."

He lightly rubbed his hands across his face in frustration, "I was happy when Mina was here. We would spend time together. She would encourage me to come out and socialize with her friends. She was much more active, but she understood my need for time alone." Oliver looked over at his sister, "I don't mean to make assumptions, but it feels as if you agree with this concerning your own life?"

Alice nodded in response, "Yes, I enjoy my time walking around the city alone during the day, making certain I am around crowded areas where I feel safe. It's my way to interact with new people, see familiar faces that have grown accustomed to seeing me on my journey. I yearn to socialize, but I don't wish to be pressured to maintain the volume of interpersonal relationships that others maintain. Mitch more so his personal life while Mina does so through her work life. I would find the task rather daunting."

"I have been reacting to Mina's absence as if it were purely a negative experience, that I should hold my breath for her…" Oliver noticed his sister's eyes widen as concern washed over her face, "It's an idiom, meaning to wait for a prolonged period of time."

Alice was still concerned, "You aren't going to do so?"

Oliver smiled at her response, "No, not in actuality." He quickly moved forward, "What I was leading to was that I have defined my life by Mina's presence in my life. I have done much to please her and devote every waking moment to try to help make her life more ideal. As I have done this, I've lost sight of who I am and what I'm going to do with my life. She deserves an equal, someone who doesn't exist merely as a part of her life." He concluded with a deep sigh, "The problem is, I don't know what to do with my life or how to define it."

"I brought up a similar topic concerning how one defines success. Often we do so through various means that typically coincide with how we focus our energy towards." Alice motioned towards her brother, "You did so with your love of Mina and your relationship." She touched her chest with her fingertips, "I do so through exploration, learning, and trying to figure out where my life is going next. For me, it is the journey that matters most."

She let her hand fallback into her lap, "For Mitch, it is his career and elevating himself above the humble beginnings in which he was born into. For his sister, it is her career as a writer. For Mina, she finds fulfillment in her own career as well." She fell silent, realizing she didn't have an answer for the next person on her mind.

Uncertain if it was alright to do so, Oliver asked innocently, "What of Hoven?"

"That's what troubles me." Alice looked up from her thoughts into her brother's eyes, "I don't know."

~

"What is your purpose in life?" Alice asked in curiosity.

"Do what now?" Hoven had been forced to swallow the portion of his drink that was in his mouth before answering, "What is my what?"

"Your purpose in life, what drives you, what keeps you focused, and what inspires you to move forward in your life?" Alice was careful to monitor Hoven's mood, knowing that he was sensitive to such a subject, and she didn't wish to cause him distress, "My brother and I were involved in a discussion concerning the topic and after listing the answers to others in my life, I didn't have the response for you since I did not know what to say."

"Okay…" The pair had been sitting on a bench in a park they visited often when Alice had brought up the topic. Uncertain of how to answer, Hoven considered the question seriously before answering, "Going back a few years, my goal was to survive until the next day. Sometimes that meant defending myself against what others were doing to me, other times it was trying to avoid getting into too much trouble when I was being forced to do something that I didn't want to do…" He shrugged, "Survive, I guess?"

"That was then, what about now?" Concern worked its way across her face, "Do you still feel that way?"

Hoven avoided eye contact, staring at the drink that Alice had bought him held firmly in between his hands, "I'm trying to answer, just working my way up, thinking about it one step at a time if that's okay?"

Alice felt ashamed for rushing him, "My apologies, take your time. Thank you for answering, I know how this is troubling you."

"It's okay." Hoven cleared his throat, "I don't know."

"Oh..." Alice was hoping for more of an answer but didn't want to make him feel pressured, "That's alright, you don't have..."

"Wait, I said I don't know because..." Hoven looked over at Alice, "I hadn't thought about it. Until I met you, I was sliding downhill fast. It scares me now to think that if you hadn't been there, I wouldn't be alive right now. I would have gone through with what I wanted to do at the time. You saved my life."

Tears formed in Alice's eyes, she wanted to embrace him, hold him tightly in her arms until she absorbed the pain that he was enduring but knew to do so would make him feel uncomfortable and possibly lead to an anxiety induced seizure. "I'm glad you chose to stay here in this world with me."

Hoven smiled, "To answer your question, I guess what motivates me, what gets me up every day, what is my goal and all of that, is to make my life worthy of what you did for me. I want my life to be good enough for you, for what you did, that I deserve to live. My purpose, I guess, is to prove I deserve to be alive, that there is a reason for me to be alive, and that..." He struggled to find the right words, "You saved my life. There must be a reason why I was saved, that you were there at the right moment to intervene, to stop me from going ahead with what I wanted to do, what I felt at the time was the only thing I could do, what was best for the world. If there is some sort of reason for that to happen, then my life must have a purpose. Now it's up to me to figure out what that purpose is or at least, be worthy of that, I guess? I don't know."

Alice touched her hand to his as he held his cup, "That was beautiful, thank you. I think we are all seeking something similar."

"I'm not a hero. Nothing about me is heroic. I'm not comedy relief. I guess if someone were writing a story about me, I would be the…" Hoven laughed, which was rare for him to do so which startled Alice. She was happy that he had a reason to, but she wasn't certain what he found funny.

Confused by his reaction, she asked, "What is it that you find so humorous?"

"I was just thinking that I…" He laughed again, "I'm the damsel in distress and you're the hero." He nodded slowly, "Maybe that's my purpose in life, be saved by my knight in shining armor and I don't know." He wilted as he concluded, "I'm just a victim that needs saving, maybe that's my purpose."

"Hoven." Alice touched him gently upon the cheek drawing him to instantly turn to face her. Normally she would pull away, not wishing to cause discomfort but she didn't wish for him to accept his words. She continued to caress his cheek as she stared into his dark blue eyes, "You're a victim of your past, that is true, but you are heroic in that you endured such hardships and emerged with a nobility that shines through your eyes with such brilliant light that drew me to you. You are my hero, for you have survived far worse than I can ever imagine and did not become stained by such atrocities. The scars of your memories are etched upon your soul, but they do not define who you are."

"In my head I want to say something as awesome sounding as that, but all I can think about is how you were a victim and now you're a hero to me. I was a victim, but somehow I'm a hero to you." Hoven looked away, "I wish I knew how to talk better."

Alice smiled sweetly, "It is not in one's eloquence that words find their meaning, it is in the passion of the speaker that they are given true strength."

Hoven grinned, all the while avoiding eye contact with her, "That's not fair, you know how to talk, I don't." He was careful to follow the three rules she had established for him early on in their friendship, before it developed into a romantic relationship. First, don't ever speak of suicide as an option. The second, don't be mean to others. Just because he had a hard life, didn't give him the excuse or right to lash out at others in anger or with poisonous words.

The hardest was to not be mean to himself. It was okay to think such things, it was hard to stop the way the mind works, but he shouldn't bully himself. He didn't have to speak positively of himself, but he had to stop being so hurtful in his own self derision. Therefore he was forced to carefully choose his words, "I wish I was better at speaking the way you are."

Alice touched her hand to his with an encouraging smile, "Speak from the heart, don't hold back, and let whatever is on your mind form the words. Often we over think what we want to say and end up stopping ourselves from saying what we hope to express."

Hoven nodded as he took in a shuddered breath. Tears formed in his eyes as he thought about the one thing he had been struggling to speak. Fear had held him back. A lifetime of suffering had suffocated his ability to communicate what was on his mind. They broke free from his eyes as he turned to Alice. He smiled nervously before opening his mouth, "I love you."

Chapter 7

"I made a mistake. I admit to this fact. Now that the circumstances of those choices have developed, I wish to resolve them before causing further harm." Alice was in the living room of Mitch's apartment, sitting across from a pair of men that she was seeking guidance from, "I need consultation as to how to proceed."

Michael looked over at Mitch, confusion revealed in his dark blue eyes. "I'm missing a piece to this puzzle, what did she say?"

Alice was comforted by his presence as he reminded her of a taller, more traditionally masculine version of Hoven. It was as if the two men could be siblings, complete with a matching shade of brown hair. She understood her friend's attraction to his boyfriend, but none would compare to her own true love in her eyes.

Mitch patted his boyfriend's hand as he smiled at Alice, "What's bothering you sweetie? Between the two of us, I'm sure we can figure out something. Just throw it all at us, we're a pair of big strong men." He glanced over at Michael and made a growling noise before playfully smiling. Returning to his original audience, he continued, "We can handle it."

"I have been withholding information from everyone." Alice stared at her hands as they rested in her lap, "The exception being is Hoven, of course, he knows everything about my personal life, even details I may feel uncomfortable telling others." She looked up, shifting her focus from Mitch's dark eyes to Michael's blue gaze, "I have been meeting with mother on a weekly basis since our first interaction shortly after my first attempt at karaoke."

Mitch felt the breath catch in his throat as his mouth lost all tension keeping it close. Noticing the reaction of his boyfriend, Michael asked, "I'm missing something here. I know a little bit about your situation, he has filled me in with some details but other than your mother being a…"

"Don't say it." Mitch quickly turned to his boyfriend, "Remember, we don't use that kind of language around my sweeties, that includes Alice and Oliver, both are pure as a baby's smile, and I don't want to ruin that. Besides, her relationship with her mother is complicated, so better keep opinions about the woman between us." Returning to the woman before him, he asked, "You've been doing this after the trip we took together?"

Alice nodded slowly, "The first time I went after you accompanied me was to seek final resolution to our conflict. I wished to tell her how I felt and to conclude our connection with one another. Something I said caused a change within her. Since then, she reached out to me, and I wished to seek a cordial relationship with the woman who raised me. Thus far, it has led to fruitful discussions that are often brief, only an hour or so, but I feel like we have made great progress. A part of me feels that she is still the woman that she was when I was younger, but she is making attempts to be a better person."

"My instant reaction is to not trust her, run away, she's like a vicious ex-boyfriend or ex-girlfriend trying to get back with you, claiming they've changed and all of that." Mitch raised his hand, "However, with that in mind, she is your momma. I was lucky enough to have a loving and supportive momma myself."

"I love your mother, she's adorable." Michael smiled, "My mom is still awkward about my life. She's accepting of it all, but I avoid family reunions for a reason, it just gets so weird."

"For the moment, I'll accept your mother's wish to fix what she's done to her family. I'm a firm believer of it never being too late to fix the bad choices we've made in life, so optimistically speaking, let's just say I blindly accept that her intentions are not some super villain's plan to finally destroy your lives once and for all." Seeing the startled look on Alice's face, he quickly added, "What? When I met the woman, she was sitting on an actual throne in some giant empty room with a group of security guards behind her that you said would kill me if I threatened her. I'm sorry, but that screams super villain. At least an evil queen like in those fairy tales."

"Yeah, I still can't believe she did that." Michael shook his head in disbelief, "What he told me about his visit with her was like out of some sort of movie, it was so bizarre."

"Please be respectful of the woman even if you do not agree with her life choices or behavior." Alice was growing uncomfortable with the direction the conversation was going in, "Even if you do not wish to show such a response to her, then do so on my behalf."

"You're right, I'm sorry." Mitch tried again, "Your momma is trying to patch things up between you and…" Suddenly his eyes widened, "Oliver doesn't know!"

Michael quickly joined in, "I thought you two were close."

"We are." Alice felt as if the world itself was pressing down upon her from the guilt and shame she was experiencing, "I feel like I have betrayed his trust in making this choice of not telling him."

Michael responded, "I have nine siblings, my family is practically modeled after that show where a man met a lady, and two families became one. If only things played out as charming and sweet as that seventy's sitcom. I have a spectrum of relationships with my brothers and sisters. Some great, I trust them with my life. Others I would worry were trying to steal my wallet out of my pocket for drug money." Alice's eyes flared wide in shock, "Short version, I get where you're coming from. You don't want to hurt your brother with this news, so you kept it a secret. Now that it's been going on longer than you expected, you think to yourself, now what? Eventually he's going to find out, better come from you."

Alice nodded slowly, "That is correct." She sighed as she focused on Mitch, "She wishes to speak to him, to try to correct past mistakes as she is attempting to do so with me."

Mitch fell back against the couch he was sitting on, "Where is Mina when I need her? I've only been told a smidgen of everything that went down between Oliver's momma and him. She was nice to you compared to the brutal stuff she did to him."

"Okay, again, I don't know about all of this drama which at this point I'm beginning to feel like I need a tub of popcorn and something to drink because this is developing into a better story than what some soap operas have to offer." Michael shifted his focus between the pair, "Which of you are going to fill me in?"

Sitting up, Mitch quickly intervened, "Sweetie, I'll tell him what I know so that you don't have to go through some of those painful memories yourself. Also, that way you don't give away anything new that maybe is best kept secret, how about that?"

Alice smiled, comforted by Mitch's gesture, "Thank you."

Turning to his boyfriend, Mitch began, "Here is how it went down according to what I know of the situation. Their family started out with two sons, then their father wanted a daughter. First attempt to do so didn't turn out as expected and so they ended up with Oliver. Alice came along afterwards but by then, his mother essentially had an extra son she didn't want."

"No…" Michael's jaw fell open for a moment in shock, "You are not being serious with me."

"Dead serious, he was the child that neither one of his parents wanted and they made it pretty clear that he was lucky to even exist." Seeing Michael's reaction, Mitch nodded in agreement, "First time Precious told me that, I cried. I can only imagine just how much pain that poor boy has gone through."

Michael looked over at Alice, "Why are you trying to be nice to this woman? I was warned to be polite about your mother, but I'm not feeling it."

Alice struggled with her response, "I have no desire to defend my mother's past actions, she has much to be held accountable for, but she is making attempts to alter her behavior and make up for her past mistakes. That is why I am in communication with her. I feel that if Oliver holds onto the suffering that he endured because of her, there will be this wound within him that will never heal. I am afraid it may affect his future. If he chooses to have children one day, I don't want memories of his childhood to affect the way he would behave as a father."

"Awe…" Mitch smiled wide, "Daddy Oliver. I love it!"

Michael laughed, "Oh, I see how it is, you are going around calling someone else daddy."

Mitch shoved his boyfriend, "Oh whatever, there is only one person in this world I call my daddy and it sure isn't you. He is married to my momma, and I am not into that kind stuff and you know it."

"You're so much fun to get a rise out of." Michael continued laughing at Mitch's reaction.

"Oh shush, there is a lady present, no need to be talking about that." Mitch gave Michael a knowing look.

"You know perfectly well I wasn't talking about that." Michael turned to Alice, "Are you sure you want him telling me all of this, because he may never finish at this rate."

Mitch scowled at his boyfriend, "I will so make you sleep on the couch."

"Oh whatever, I have my own apartment." Michael sighed, "A certain someone has commitment issues."

"You know perfectly well the leaps and bounds I've made since we first met." Mitch held up his hand as if putting a stop on the topic, "Anyway! Where was I? Oh yeah, so, Oliver had that hanging over his head going into it. Then his childhood was okay since his mother didn't interfere much until he hit puberty. Suddenly the whole training him to become the ideal son began. That's why Alice and Oliver are so formal." He turned to Alice, "Don't get me wrong, I love that about both of you."

Returning to Michael, Mitch continued, "Everything was going according to plan until Oliver got himself engaged."

Michael didn't know about that part, "Wait, what? I didn't know his girlfriend and him had gotten engaged?"

"No, not Mina, this was years before Oliver met her. He fell head over heels in love with a woman who seemed perfect, their relationship was going well until his mother comes along and says, no, she doesn't fit the bill as to what I want in this family." Mitch held up his hands, "Either she thought she wasn't good enough or she suspected her to be a gold digger."

"He was given the ultimatum, your fiancé, or your family, by that I mean all the wealth and the life that he grew up with. Of course, Oliver being the romantic that he is, he chose love. He decided to risk everything and walked away from his family. He even bought a house for his fiancé and himself to live in. He was preparing for a potential family once they were married. It should have been happily ever after." Sitting back in his chair, Mitch shook his head, "That's when the truth was revealed."

"I can probably fill in the blanks. His mother was right about her being a gold digger. The second she found out he was no longer a part of the wealth of his parents, she was out." Michael nodded slowly, "My youngest sister, as much as I hate to say this, she's that way. She married this one guy because he had money, twice her age, total slob but she didn't care. I think she's cheating on him on the side, nasty business. I want nothing to do with it."

"So, that happened." Mitch made a motion towards Michael to acknowledge what was said, "Oliver becomes a broken man. Meanwhile, his mother goes above and beyond to not only cut him off from his family fortune, but essentially ruin his life."

Michael scowled deeply, he hadn't even met the woman and he was beginning to hate her. He looked over at Alice who was acting like a puppy that had been found guilty of chewing up its owner's shoes, "What more could she do to him?"

"Don't worry, sweetie, I got this." Mitch intervened, "Since she claimed that she paid for his higher education, she found ways to have his records eliminated from the college he attended. Suddenly his degree vanished. They claimed he didn't get enough credits and that his whole graduation was a mistake. It got ugly."

"Then the company he was with for the longest time went under. Not sure how much his mother was involved in on that one." Mitch looked over Alice, "Did she do that?"

Alice looked up, shaking her head slowly, "No, by then she felt she did not deem him worthy of further effort. I was to keep in touch with him in a passing hope that he would return to the family, but..." She smiled at the memory, "Her attempt at manipulation did not conclude the way she had hoped."

"It totally backfired. Oliver was able to get through to Alice, past all that nonsense her mother put into her head, and she walked away a few years ago. She's been a free lady ever since then, not looking back." Mitch touched himself on the cheek, "So proud." Returning to his boyfriend, he continued, "With the company he had been a part of gone, his work experience records lost to the wind, no contact info, it was just a mess. So, he got a job at a temp agency that hooked him up with janitorial duties at a hotel. That was about the time he met Mina and he's been working his way up ever since. He's now a manager where he works."

"Riches to rags and then rags to what?" Michael's face scrunched up in confusion, "Probably not important, but anyway. So, abridged version of all of this is that Oliver has a list longer than Santa has concerning naughty and nice as to why he should hate his mother? Does that about sum it up?"

Mitch nodded enthusiastically, "The one and only time I met the woman, I almost blew up on her with the fiery passion of every angry little tidbit I had bubbling up inside of me." He looked over at Alice with a smile, "If it weren't for Precious, I would have done just that, but she did the right thing. She stood up against her mother just like a queen would another member of royalty, it was a thing of beauty." He shifted his attention to Michael, "She may look like a dainty little flower, but she's more like one of those giant trees that a car could smash into and it would be all destroyed on impact while the tree is just like, yeah, whatever, you got nothing on me."

Michael laughed, "That's the strangest metaphor I think you've ever said, and you've said some bizarre ones before."

"I'm colorful with my descriptions, I thought you liked that about me." Mitch grinned playfully at his boyfriend before turning back to Alice, "So, Precious, what do you need from us?"

After a momentary pause to consider exactly what she was hoping to gain in addressing her concerns with the pair of men, Alice finally spoke, "How should I proceed?"

Mitch was the first to respond, "Tell your brother. It's not what you want to hear. It's going to be the hardest thing you'll ever do, but you need to tell him about what's going on. Especially if your mother wants to talk to him."

Michael quickly agreed, "From what little I know of your mother, if she wants something to happen, she'll make it happen. She may try to play nice with you right now, but if she wants to get in contact with your brother, she'll do so with or without your permission. She'll find some way around whatever reason may hold her back from doing so because of something you said, but she will get her way eventually."

Alice nodded slowly, that had been her assessment of the situation as well, but she needed the emotional support of others to encourage her choice. Looking up she sighed softly before speaking, "I agree with you both, of course. I fear what will happen next, but it is my hope that Oliver will forgive me for my poor decisions concerning mother in the recent past and that together we shall find a solution to this situation."

~

"Is it Hoven?" Alice had sent a message requesting to visit Oliver at his home at his convenience. There was something peculiar about her wording in the message which hinted that she had something to speak of urgently. When she arrived, much of her expression and subtle mannerisms confirmed his suspicions. Once they were seated, he was quick to ask, "Is there something wrong with your roommate?" Studying her face, he quickly realized that look that only one person could be responsible for. Resuming a firm expression, he sighed, "What has she done now?"

Alice was surprised that despite her best efforts to mask what she was thinking, her brother had deciphered what she was wishing to speak of, "I need clarification as to whom you are referring to?"

"That's interesting." Sitting back in his chair, knowing that he shouldn't be confrontational when it came to their mother due to Alice's personal feelings on the subject matter, Oliver tried a different approach, "Something involving our mother is bothering you and yet you're upset over something she has done specifically which means..." Dozens of suspicions ranging from worst case scenarios to the most farfetched of concepts leaped through his mind before he asked, "I believe you need to tell me something?"

"I am in communication with mother." Alice had been instructed to say what it was that she needed to tell Oliver right away, to be one of the first things spoken. The longer she waited, the more difficult it would be to say the words. "I have visited her home on multiple occasions since my first interaction when I was accompanied by Mitch."

Oliver leaned forward, resting his elbows against his upper legs as he rested his face against his open hands. He tried his best to hide that his hands were shaking as fear was clutching at his chest. This could mean any number of things, the worst was confirming his greatest concern that Alice was returning to her old life that she had left behind years ago, becoming what their mother wished of her, and that he would essentially be losing her forever.

Alice expressed her anguish, "I beg of you, Oliver, please forgive me for not telling you sooner. Shortly after my first attempt at doing karaoke in front of an audience, I returned to confront her, to tell her what I felt one last time before closing that part of my life off completely. It was my way of finding resolution to what happened between the two of us and my childhood."

Oliver looked up, interlacing his fingers together as he touched his lips to his combined hands, "Are you going back to your old life?"

Alice felt like crying, seeing the pain in his eyes, "No, of course not. I am stronger than that. I don't wish to be ruled over by anyone, especially her. I showed her I am worthy of the respect of a queen in the eyes of another. I possess dominion over my own life and would resist her attempts to manipulate me with equal force of will power. When I spoke to her that second time, what I felt to be the last moment in her presence, she cried."

Oliver's eyes narrowed, "She has never cried, not even at father's funeral. I suspect crocodile tears."

"As did I, but when I looked into her eyes, I saw what she was feeling was genuine, something she has never expressed in all my life. Regret. I don't know how but I somehow was able to connect with a part of her that we did not think existed." Alice stood, taking a few steps forward before kneeling in front of her brother, looking into his eyes as she touched her hands to his, "Please forgive me for not telling you sooner. I would be lost in this world without you. I have been racked with guilt all these months…"

"Months? You've been…" Oliver suddenly pulled away as he slid to the right so he could stand without bumping into his sister. He paced the room as she got to her feet, "Why didn't you tell me sooner?"

"When it first began, it was out of curiosity. That led to exploration of what could be." Alice's brow furrowed in concern, "I expected it to conclude long before now."

Oliver folded his arms across his chest, creating a protective barrier between himself and what his sister was revealing to him, "I need an answer. Why did you not tell me sooner? Who else knows?"

Alice did not back down from his unyielding stare, she felt she deserved his wrath, "Hoven, he was the first since I trust him completely with all that is my life and who I am as my dearest love. I am certain you would agree that you would have done the same with Mina, am I correct?"

Oliver nodded in agreement before asking, "Yes, of course, but am I the last to know? What of Mina or Mitch?"

"Hoven confessed to me that he spoke to Mina without my knowledge. He was concerned as I am certain you are, that mother would be attempting to alter my perception of the world and my way of thinking. He was worried that she was going to change who I am, the woman he..." Alice struggled to conclude her statement, "The woman he loves."

At first Oliver didn't understand why such a fact was hard for her to say. It was obvious to anyone who saw them together that Hoven cared for her, but... Suddenly his eyes flared wide as his arms dropped to his side, "He spoke the words to you?"

Alice nodded slowly, "Yes, a few days ago. You are the first to know, not even Mitch has heard of this."

Despite the weight of concerns involving their mother, Oliver's face lit up with a wide smile, "Congratulations." He reached out with arms, "May I?"

"Yes, please." Tears had formed before Alice spoke as she rushed towards him, soon hugging her brother tightly. "Thank you."

After a lingering embrace, the brother and sister parted as they were both smiling at the joyous news, "I'm so happy for you. I know how it felt when Mina first told me she loved me so long after I told her how I felt."

"I will forever cherish the moment. It was beautiful and he was so adorable when he said it. He was incredibly bashful when he did so, it was with such charm that it won my heart once again." Alice felt a warmth crossing her face, "I'm so sorry for everything, I wish I had told you from the beginning."

"I feel that I may collapse if I don't sit." Oliver gestured to one of his chairs, "Would you join me?"

"Yes, of course." The pair sat on two adjoining cushions on his couch, turned slightly to face one another as Alice continued, "Do you forgive me?"

"Yes, of course, I'm sorry that I reacted the way I did." Oliver felt dizzy from all that had been revealed to him, "I'm glad that I am not the only one concerned about your wellbeing when it comes to mother. Hoven is a good man with a noble soul. He is an ideal choice for you."

"Thank you." Alice smiled sweetly, "As is Mina for you." She quickly asked, "How is she, by the way?"

"Exhausted. I haven't been able to keep in touch with her as much as I hoped, as you know. She calls me late at night, often falling asleep on the phone while we are speaking to one another shortly after we begin. I think she enjoys listening to my voice in the same way a child listens to bedtime stories from their parents. It puts her mind at ease, which I am flattered by."

"Awe..." Alice covered her mouth with her fingertips, "That is so romantic."

Oliver smiled, laughing to himself, "Thank you. I feel blessed by whatever aspect in her life I can be a part of." He cleared his throat before continuing, "Returning to the original topic, I must ask what it is that is going on between you and mother during your interactions with her. Why are you telling me now?"

"This has been of growing concern. The longer I've waited, the worst I have felt. I felt I needed to tell you soon before I break under the weight of guilt that was growing with each passing day." Alice didn't want him to think that the only reason she was telling him now was for a specific reason, as if without it she would have continued not speaking of it to him, but she needed to tell him everything, "Mother wishes to speak to you."

Since departing his mother's home, Oliver had not heard anything from her directly. What little knowledge he gained about the woman was through his sister, there was never any firsthand information until a letter arrived claiming she was facing a terminal illness. It was a ruse to get Alice to speak to their mother. The first time in years she speaks to him directly only to focus her desire on someone else. This was the first time she had shown any interest in him personally, "What game is she attempting to play with me? What new cruelty is she wishing to unleash upon me?"

Alice hated to feel like she had to choose between her mother and brother, "You may not believe her for good reason, I sympathize, but I do believe she has changed. She may not be coping with a terminal illness, but she realizes her time is limited."

Oliver watched Alice with a narrow eyed distrustful look aimed at his mother in his mind, "Is she in good health? Has she shown signs of deterioration that may warrant such concerns?"

"No. She appears and behaves with the same firm vibrancy she did when we were children. Little has changed." Alice didn't want to bring up such details but felt to do so may explain the change in behavior, "Our two eldest brothers are each married, both with children. Mother knows full well that they are loyal to her and the upbringing that she instilled within them. However, they are doing everything possible to distance themselves from her. They respond when called upon and fulfill whatever duties she requests, but all attempts to prevent her from interacting with her grandchildren does occur. She is aware that both families are withdrawing as far back as they can without breaking any rules she set forth or being obvious about their behavior. Mother is intelligent enough to know the truth."

If Mina was present, she would warn him to be careful, to put up his guard and to protect himself from this potential threat. Then again, she was protective of him, refusing to take no for an answer in accompanying him should he choose to meet with his mother. However, she was in another country practically cut off from him due to her demanding schedule. It had been so long that he hadn't considered his mother's influence in his life, that it was one among many painful experiences he endured.

Oliver stared into his sister's eyes, trying to find some answer as to why she would choose to communicate with their mother, "What would you have me do?"

"Accompany me to speak with her as Mitch did for me. The two of them were rather confrontational." Oliver smiled, soon laughing at what she had said which startled Alice, "Why are you reacting this way?"

"I can imagine just how volatile those two personalities would be towards one another. Each strong dominant alpha type personalities, mother greeting him on her terms of course would make her feel that he should be submissive to her. Mitch being himself would not allow for such behavior." Oliver felt good to laugh, for it eased the tension he had been feeling, "I apologize, I shouldn't have reacted the way I did. I know it must have been uncomfortable for you to be exposed to such animosity."

"I firmly intervened, telling Mitch to leave and continued to speak to Mother concerning her behavior. I left on my own terms, feeling a newfound strength in confronting her and speaking to her as an equal. I was no longer her devoted daughter, but a peer worthy of her respect. Whether she agreed with me about such matters, it did not concern me anymore. I deserved her respect and if she did not show it, then I would have nothing to do with her." Alice looked down at her hands resting in her lap, "After singing the song that Hoven chose for me, I realized that she was also my mother, not just an adversary to defeat. I wished to express my thoughts about what I had learned, what I felt about her, and that it was her last chance to have me as a part of her life. That is when something in her changed."

Alice looked up at Oliver, "I gave her another chance, one that you may choose to provide her or not, that is your choice."

"It is clear to me that you wish for me to make the attempt." Oliver struggled with the idea of confronting what was the source of much of his animosity in life. He did not wish to begin a new life with Mina with so much darkness buried deep within him that he was holding onto due to his lack of resolution of his past. Finally, he sighed deeply before addressing his sister, "Promise me that you'll go with me?"

Alice smiled, "Of course." She touched her hands to his, "You don't have to do this, I don't want you to feel like I'm pressuring for you to do so."

"If I am going to build a family with Mina, should she so choose to create such a future with me, I need to let go of my past completely when it comes to these lingering elements that I don't have resolution to. When I left, it was abrupt, without warning and I never truly recovered. To me, you are a much stronger person for doing what you did in speaking to her. You stood up to not only mother but Mitch at the same time, which is incredible." Oliver smiled, "I don't believe I would have the strength to do so."

Alice squeezed his hand in reassurance, "You're stronger than you think. You must remember that you confronted mother first, before I ever had the courage to do so. You in turn, gave me the ability to follow through with my own dreams in separating myself from the role she would have had me play in her life. You are an inspiration to me. Without you, I would not be the woman I am today for I would not have been given the freedom to grow and learn to become who I desire to be."

Oliver bowed his head, "Thank you."

"I will speak to her on my behalf if you wish." Alice wasn't certain if this were one of those scenarios where the sooner one did it, the easier it would be or if he needed to gather strength to go forward with his decision.

"No. She reached out to you through me by sending me a handwritten letter." Oliver assumed a serious expression, "We shall see how she'll react to receiving a similar gesture."

Chapter 8

"Could you stop staring at me?" Hoven would look away only to find that the woman across from him was still watching. It was beginning to make him uncomfortable. "Why did you ask me to come inside if you were just going to stare at me like that?"

"I didn't ask you, I told you to come inside. One is a request. One is a demand." Cara shrugged her shoulders, "I was curious if it would work, and it did." Her eyes narrowed as she searched for something, "You're submissive. You don't put up much of a fight. That's probably why Alice likes you."

"I took it as an invitation. I was trying to be nice." Hoven started to stand, "I think it would be better if I waited in my car for her to get here." Alice had sent him a message, requesting for him to visit her at her apartment for them to talk about what would occur the next day. He had arrived sooner than expected and she was delayed at work. By the time he received her reply, he had already knocked on her door. Moments later he had been greeted by Cara, her roommate.

"Sit down." Hoven ignored her, leading Cara to add, "Please?" He looked over at her as she formed a forced fake looking smile, "I said please."

Hoven hesitated, "You're weird."

Cara laughed, "I know." She motioned to the chair across from her, "Seriously, Alice is going to be mad if you leave because of me and I'd rather not deal with that." She settled back in her seat, "Besides, you seem cool from what I've heard."

"Thanks?" Hoven wasn't sure what to make of Cara. She hadn't even taken time out to get dressed. She was still wearing a shirt that appeared to be made for a man twice her size, it drooped down to nearly her knees with it hanging off one exposed shoulder. Knowing Cara was a part of Alice's life, and he was trying hard to be more connected to his girlfriend, he hesitantly took a seat.

"Does the fact that I'm naked underneath this make you uncomfortable?" Cara grabbed a bit of fabric between her fingers, holding it out to make it clear she was talking about the shirt before letting it go, "Wow, I'm impressed, not even a twitch in the eyes." She finally smiled, "Alice is lucky to have you. You are that into her, huh? Other women just don't do anything for you."

"Too many women in my past tried to use their sexuality, their bodies, whatever to manipulate me, control me, and essentially get whatever they wanted. They made me feel like they were interested in me only to break me, sometimes just for fun." Hoven shook his head, "Your attempt to get me to think about your naked body is just a reminder of their cruelty."

Hoven revealed an intense, unwavering gaze, "Alice has never once tried to manipulate, control, or hurt me. She's only been kind, gentle, and caring of me from the moment we met. Even if I was tempted, which let me make it abundantly clear, I'm not, I wouldn't do anything to hurt her in any way. So, no, I don't care that you are naked underneath that shirt. You could be sitting there without any clothing on, and I still wouldn't care. The only body I care about the details of isn't here right now and I would do anything to protect what she wishes to remain private."

"Okay..." Cara hadn't expected that, "Wow... Heard a lot about you but didn't expect that." She smiled, "I like it, glad to know that she's safe around you." Shifting topics, she asked, "So, you dropped the L bomb, huh? Bold move."

"L bomb?" Hoven shook his head slowly, "If you're referring to me telling my girlfriend that I love her, I guess she told you?"

"She's told practically anyone willing to listen." Cara laughed as she held out her hand in defense of what she expected would follow her statement, "First of all, don't be offended by this, I don't mean it this way, but when she came in here that night, she was glowing like a woman might after she had sex for the first time with a guy she likes. So, of course, I'm thinking, wow... You two..." She laughed, "I never said anything to her about that. I kept it to myself while I tried to find out what happened. Finally she explodes with this excitement of what you said to her. I should have known it was something cute and sweet, rather than what most people would be thinking. She's weird that way."

Hoven smiled, "One of many reasons I love her."

"Yeah, takes a special kind of person to love her in just the right way. Most people, like that crazy friend of hers, the sexy boy toy, he loves her like a little sister or even some sort of pet, I don't know. People may think she's cute, cuddly, like a puppy or kitten and so they end up loving her in that way." Cara studied Hoven, "With you, it's different. I can see it in your eyes. You would die to save her from harm, wouldn't you? No hesitation. You've got it bad for her, like devoted to her like some sort of knight protecting his queen." She nodded slowly, "I respect that."

Hoven laughed at the metaphor, "She thinks of herself as a queen, so I can go along with that. I would be honored if I could be her knight."

"Most men would say they would want to be a woman's king, not just a knight." Cara's brow furrowed in confusion, "Why not you?"

"I have a long way to go before I would be worthy of such a title. I'm not like that. I'm not confident the way a king should be, I'm certainly not powerful like one, I just... I don't know..." Hoven pressed his arms across his chest as he began to lose his earlier strength, "I'll stick to knight for now."

The door to the apartment opened to reveal Alice who carefully closed it behind her, locking it before turning to the scene in her living room. Her eyes flared wide when she noticed how her roommate was dressed. First, she addressed Hoven, "Thank you for responding to my request on such a short notice. I apologize for not sending a message telling you that I had arrived but I..."

Hoven stood, smiling warmly at the pleasure it was to gaze upon her. If he had been wearing a hat, he would have taken it off in her presence, "Are you alright?"

"Yes, thank you. I need to speak to you about the situation concerning my family." Alice made a small nod of her head, "If you would please be seated while I speak to Cara?"

Hoven quickly agreed, "Of course."

Approaching the seat Cara was sitting in, Alice asked, "Would it be alright if I spoke to you in private?"

Looking up, Cara grinned, "What? I can't stay?"

Alice didn't wish to be rude, the two women shared ownership of the residence and because of this she held no right to tell Cara to leave the space provided to both, "It will only be for a moment. If you wish to return to interact with Hoven and myself afterwards, I would not mind. However, the topic of our conversation may not present you much interest in that it involves my family."

After a lingering stare, Cara shrugged her shoulder, "Fine…" Sliding to her feet, she headed towards the back of the apartment, "My bedroom or yours?" She glanced back at Alice who followed, "Should we have our secret meeting in the bathroom?"

Alice was accustomed to her roommate's strange behavior, "I will let you choose. As I said, it won't be for long."

Choosing her room, mostly out of curiosity as to how Alice reacted to her personal space, Cara turned once in the center. Her roommate closed the door behind her before speaking, "I am uncertain of how best to approach this subject. I know that we made an agreement that the way we choose to lead our lives should not create conflict with the other within the boundaries of our apartment, but I do feel…"

Cara laughed, "You didn't like me being practically naked around your boyfriend?"

"I'm not concerned about him, his loyalty to me is unquestioned and I am certain he treated you as a gentleman." Alice struggled with what bothered her about the situation, "However, there is a certain level of modesty when a guest arrives that…"

Cara held up her hand, "Stop right there."

Alice felt terrible for bringing up the subject but at the same time, she needed to express her concerns, "I apologize if..."

"You're right, I shouldn't have done it and if it was anyone else, I wouldn't have." Cara sighed happily with a playful grin, "If it was your brother, I would have probably even dressed up for the occasion. That man is gorgeous... Like a prince from England or something like that, pure perfection and I would only want him to think of me as that level of perfect."

Alice felt insulted, "Then why would you ever treat Hoven with any less respect?"

"I had to know." Cara placed her hands on her hips, "Oliver, first time I met him was around his girlfriend, I saw the way those two are together and how he is completely devoted to her. You and your boyfriend are never around me at the same time, so I had to know. From what you've told me about him, he comes from a dark past, so I was curious just how badly that history of his left a stain on the man he is today. I thought, I was already dressed this way, might as well see his reaction to what I had to offer."

"You shouldn't have done that." Alice required respect from the situation, "That was inconsiderate of you and rude to Hoven."

"It's my apartment. We agreed we can do whatever we want within reason. I don't prance around naked like I would have done if I lived alone. It's my way of meeting you halfway." Cara grinned, "Besides, he didn't take the bait at all. He didn't even blink an eye when I told him I was naked underneath this." She laughed, "Which I'm not, I haven't been home that long and was debating on whether I wanted to go out again."

"If my boyfriend has proven his loyalty, trust, and devotion to me in your eyes, then do you agree you will begin to treat him with the same level of respect that you do my brother?" Alice wished for both men to be held with the same high regard in the eyes of her roommate.

"Fine, but I can still do whatever I want around Mitch." Cara motioned towards her body, "If that man shows up and you're not here, I get to answer the door naked."

Alice's eyes flared wide in surprise, "I do not know how to respond to that. From my understanding, this is not meant to be an insult to you. The only interest he may find in your nudity is the same way one would respond to a work of art at a gallery. He would not possess any attraction to you."

"First off, I like how you said that." Cara nodded slowly, "Me, a work of art, that's cool of you to say." She laughed, "The fact that he's not into what I have to offer is half the fun. I would love to see his reaction to that situation."

"That is most peculiar to me, but I believe Mitch would not be offended by the gesture. He may enjoy it on a level I do not understand as the two of you share a unique sense of humor that I do not grasp." Alice shifted to the previous topic, "Are we in agreement in further treatment of Hoven's visits?"

"Yeah, I just wanted to know if what you said about him is true." Cara smiled, "He's everything and more. Do you want me to apologize to him?"

"If you wish, but I will not request it." Alice nodded firmly, "This is your home as much as mine."

"He's your boyfriend and I should have been more respectful of what you two share and him." Cara grinned, "I'm not used to all of this formality that you brought into my life, but I have to admit, you've made me a better person because of it." She looked down, "I am definitely learning to respect myself more and what I have to offer the men in my life."

Alice responded in concern, "In the years we have lived together, I have not seen you with a romantic interest."

"Honestly, I almost gave up on dating, relationships, and men in general. I avoided it all because I didn't know how to approach the whole mess without jumping right back into everything that I hated about it." Cara stared at Alice's jade green eyes, "The more I learn about your approach, how you are with Hoven, I am learning how to find my own path to all of that."

Alice didn't want to keep her boyfriend waiting but at the same time, wished to address Cara's concerns, "Is there something you need to talk about?"

"Maybe later." Cara resumed her smile, "For now, get out there and talk to Sir Hoven."

"Sir Hoven?" Alice wasn't certain why she said that.

Cara laughed, "He'll understand." She motioned towards the door, "I'm going to log in for a while, lose myself in the four realms of the Age of Shadows RPG..." Seeing Alice didn't understand, she explained, "Online role-playing game? Remember?"

"Ah, yes, the fantasy world where you are..." Alice's brow furrowed as she tried to remember, "An elf?"

Alice laughed, "I'm an elf in the world of Mystical Alliance."

"Oh, another game you play?" Alice was embarrassed to not to know her friend's private life in more detail after being her roommate for so long, "I get them confused."

"I'm a werewolf in the western realm of Age of Shadows." Cara held up her hands like claws, "I'm a part of one of the biggest packs in the game, it's so awesome."

"I'm glad that you are enjoying your experiences." Alice hesitated, "Is there anything else we need to speak of before I depart?"

"No, you're fine." Cara grinned, "I promise to treat your boyfriend like I would your brother in the future, okay?"

"Thank you." Alice smiled sweetly, "I am sure he will be glad to hear that."

~

"Your roommate is weird." Hoven settled back in his chair with his hands folded across his chest in a defensive gesture revealing his discomfort.

Alice tried to politely respond, "Please don't be judgmental of her behavior. I requested that she treated you with greater respect than she did earlier in the future, so if you would return the kindness, I would greatly appreciate it."

Dropping his arms, Hoven stared at the floor, which to Alice told her that he felt ashamed, "I'm sorry, you're right."

"I did not mean to come across as scolding you. That was not my intent. It was a request on her behalf. I often do what I can to find an equilibrium concerning the various personalities in my life." Alice smiled, "She likes you though, if that makes you feel better."

"Likes me as a person or…" Seeing the flare of surprise in Alice's eyes he laughed, "Okay, cool, I thought I made it clear to her I wasn't interested in her in that way."

"I think she is intrigued by you, but not attracted to you." Alice looked down, a light blush crossing her face, "Not in the way I feel towards you."

"Good to know." Hoven smiled, avoiding eye contact himself, still adjusting to the idea of someone complimenting him often, "So, about tomorrow?"

"Oh yes, I am concerned about Oliver meeting with mother for the first time in what has been multiple years. The last they spoke was not on positive terms." Alice was uncertain of what to say, "I'm scared of what will happen. I do not wish to be thrust into a position of having to decide between the two of them, but of course I would choose my brother. However, I am also worried about his wellbeing and if this is the right choice."

"Did you ever pressure him to do this? Did you ask him to do it?" Hoven scowled in consideration, "From what you've told me, it was his choice. He wanted to do this. You're going with him as emotional support, the same way we provide that for each other."

Alice nodded in agreement, "Then, I suppose the reason for me asking for you to visit me at my dwelling is to comfort me in this time of deep concern. I need rejuvenation of my strength, courage, and determination concerning tomorrow's events and I felt that you would be ideal for aiding me towards that end."

"Okay, not sure what all that meant, but…" Hoven grinned, "What can I do to help?"

"You may think it's foolish of me to ask, but would you read me a story?" Alice felt embarrassed to ask this of her boyfriend, "I enjoy listening to the sound of your voice. You so rarely speak unless spoken to. I do not get the opportunity to hear you talk as much as I desire."

"Okay." Hoven didn't see anything wrong with the request, "I am not much of a reader, but I'll do my best."

"Excellent." Alice beamed with a joyous smile, "Thank you dearly for this." She stood before approaching a collection of books. Selecting one, she gave him a copy.

He studied the front for a moment before flipping it over onto the back. After reading, he looked up with a strange smile, "Time travel? Is this a science fiction book?"

"I thought you would enjoy that." Alice sat next to him, squeezing in next to him on the large chair, "It's also a romance, which is perfect for me. It is an ideal story for both of us."

"That's cool." Holding the book in his hands, he turned to the first page. Clearing his throat, Hoven began reading, "Did it work? Felicity could hear her heartbeat, the steady rhythm of her breathing, straining to hear anything else but there was stillness to the world." Closing her eyes, Alice allowed her mind to let go of her troubling thoughts, releasing any concerns or cares that once clung to her and allowed herself to slip into the blissful soothing caress of his voice.

~

"She's playing a game with me." Oliver stood behind a chair, one of eight surrounding a beautiful hand carved table. It was the only furniture in a large two-story room filled with books.

Shelves lined nearly every inch of the walls. Only the door leading into the enclosed room was uncovered. The two floors were divided by a small walkway allowing someone to move a mobile ladder along a track in the center. A second such ladder system consisting of one on each side of the room allowed access to the volumes of books available. The room was sealed off from sunlight and the artificial illumination was carefully controlled along with humidity and airflow to aid in the preservation of the collection.

It was one of the few fond memories Oliver had as a child. The books had been slowly collected over generations, his great grandfather being an avid reader as he began accumulating his wealth. As a child he was not allowed to read most of them but there was a peaceful tranquility to the room that he adored. "Why did she ask us to meet here of all places?"

The door to the room opened revealing an elegantly dressed woman with long blonde hair and crystal blue eyes. The dress she wore mimicked a gown worn by the queen of England during the late 1500s. It was the first time that son and mother had been in the same room together in years. The woman paused before reacting in curiosity, "I see that you don't approve of my choice of location?"

"Why here of all places?" Oliver's hands pressed against the back of the chair as he faced the door on the opposite side of the table. "Why not your throne room where you greet your guests?"

Oliver's mother glanced over her shoulder as the door was closed behind her before addressing the man before her, "I remembered this was your favorite room. I would often find you here, secluded from the others."

"You didn't find me, the staff who served you did. You never personally sought me out even as a child." Oliver refused to back down under the intimidating gaze of his mother, "I'm surprised you knew this much about my history here."

Oliver's mother didn't look away to acknowledge Alice's presence, she refused to give her the son of the satisfaction of feeling as if he had some level of control over this meeting, "I know more about you than you'll ever realize. I may not have held your hand or embraced you with gentle kindness, but I was fully aware of every small aspect of your personality, your strengths, weaknesses, passions, and desires. Even now, I know more about your life than those you would call your friends."

"What you can discover about my life is bits of information you glean from an invasion of my privacy." Oliver touched his chest, "You know nothing of what is found within here. You will never know of the soul that you abandoned so casually."

"Casually?" His mother smiled, "Is that how you remember it? I went to great lengths to investigate your fiancé. I presented you the facts of the situation, the truth of what she was, but you didn't listen. When I was proven correct, what she wanted to do with you and everything she desired to gain through marriage to you, it was too late. You had made your choice."

Oliver turned his focus to Alice, "I wish to have five minutes alone with her." He shifted his gaze to his mother, "That is all I will provide to you to make your case. She has spoken to me on your behalf, and I have agreed to be here but if you cannot convince me of whatever it is you so desire to express by then, it will be too late."

Alice shifted her gaze between mother and son before finally nodding in agreement, "I will be waiting for you when you're done. I will leave with you immediately the moment you wish." She concluded by speaking to their matriarch, "I have opened a door that would have been sealed shut without my aid. This is your last and only chance. Don't allow arrogance or pride to cloud your judgement. Know that the circumstances of what is about to take place will dictate the future of our relationship. Harm him and we will no longer be on speaking terms."

Amused by the show of strength but admiring what was said, Alice's mother smiled in response to her daughter, "Thank you. I shall heed your advice."

Alice turned back to Oliver but only after giving a small nod for him to acknowledge that he would be alright without her. She approached the door and knocked once. A moment later it opened with one of her mother's bodyguards standing patiently on the other side. Once she exited, the door was closed, and the mother and son faced one another in silence.

Oliver's mother motioned towards the table, "Would you please have a seat? If this is to be my last time within your presence, at least we can behave as civilized individuals."

Responding to the request, Oliver took a seat on the other side of the table. He kept his arms at his side, refusing to make any subtle gestures of defending himself against her. He felt it necessary to show strength, "Your time is limited, so make your presentation quickly. Begin by answering the question of why did you seek out this meeting? What is the purpose of this?"

"When I die, no one will attend my funeral. Not a single individual will be present, let alone someone to speak on my behalf." Oliver's mother stared into his jade green eyes, memories of his father at her son's current age flickering through her mind, "When I wrote you the letter that enticed your sister to visit with me, I spoke of a life-threatening condition. When she arrived, I spoke of it as a lie, a way to bring her before me to speak to me. The reality is that I indeed was inflicted with what could have ended my life but did not lead to such an outcome. I am not afflicted with a terminal illness, but I have begun showing signs of what this life I have created for myself is doing to my body."

His mother placed her hand above her heart, "I felt an uncomfortable squeezing pain. There was a shortness of breath before. I felt lightheaded to the point that I nearly lost consciousness. It was then that I was forced to confront my own mortality. I lead a strenuous existence, constantly combating others, vying for control to maintain my position of authority. It has led to a strain on my body which may have ended my life prematurely. That is when I wrote to you knowing that you would ignore my words, but Alice would be drawn to speak to me if only for one last time."

She continued in a firm, unwavering voice, "Your older brothers have withdrawn from me, distancing themselves the best they can, obvious about their intentions. I barely have seen my grandchildren, what I know of their growth is seen in photos, rather than meeting them in person. I have no friends in this world. There are those loyal to me but their interest in my wellbeing is due to monetary value. Without payment, they would quickly move on."

"I am not here to seek forgiveness. I will not request something that I know I will not receive from you. However, I do wish to correct the mistakes of the past. To begin with, I have arranged to fix the alteration I caused concerning your academic records. Your diploma and status as a graduate of the college in which you attended has been restored." Oliver's mother watched for a reaction, pleased to see that he didn't show any response, seeing such strength in those eyes that she had instilled within him, "Secondly, I know of your intentions towards Ms. Kensington and although I know you did not request it and have no desire to have it, I do give you my blessing to marry her. She is trustworthy, honest, and is seeking only what you are in this relationship from what I have been able to ascertain. Whether you seek my approval or not, know that I admire her ambition and strength of will to accomplish the goals she has set forth for herself."

"You're correct in that I don't want your blessing, nor do I care about your opinion of the woman I love. I never did before and I certainly don't now. You stripped me of the diploma that I earned through my work and perseverance. You arranging to grant me what I rightfully deserve is not a gift. It is returning what was stolen from me in the first place." Oliver scowled deeply, anger burning inside of him, "Is that all you wish to speak of?"

His mother asked, "Have you told anyone of your financial situation? Does Mina or Alice have any knowledge of just how close you are to losing your home? It is my understanding that it is worth a little less than half of what you purchased it at. There are extensive repairs required throughout the structure."

"You speak of your position as if you are a manager, earning a high enough wage to compensate for such a level of authority. The reality of the situation is that you are a glorified desk clerk, responding to the activities of the guests when the rest of the day staff has departed for the evening." His mother spoke of the situation in a matter-of-fact tone, not belittling his situation nor showing sympathy, "You are currently burdened with repaying a loan you took upon yourself when you purchased your home. Your vehicle was recently bought to replace your previous one that had severe engine troubles, putting you further under the pressure of debt. The past few winters have been severe leading to elevated heating costs, unforeseen damage done to your home that you had repaired in secret to hide the fact that your savings have been depleted. Your credit card debt is growing as you have been forced to make minimum payments due to your finances going towards other demands upon your income."

Oliver remained silent, not knowing how she had learned so much about his private life. He wanted to be angry, to lash out at her, yet to do so would not alter the facts that she had presented to him. Guilt over hiding these problems from Mina and Alice weighed heavily upon him. He refused to become a burden to them, to seek help from either to fix what was slipping out of his control. They each had their own concerns, their own problems to deal with. He had become so accustomed to dealing with his personal problems on his own, without aid for so long before meeting Mina that he didn't know how to ask for help. He refused to lie to her but struggled to confess the truth of his burdens.

"It does not seem like an ideal marriage when a husband is hiding so much from his wife when it comes to the financial aspects of his life that he would be bringing into their matrimony. When were you going to reveal the truth to Mina? Were you going to attempt to mask the truth while she was gone, find some way to fix these concerns before she returned? If you never did, what then? You become married and suddenly she learns of the severe financial burden you have brought into your union?" Oliver's mother watched his stoic expression with a blank face, "If you had been able to keep your diploma, enter a career path that was bolstered by your academic prestige, I would entertain the notion that you would be financially stable due to your elevated position in society. If anything, you would not be facing such debt that you do now. In a way, I am responsible for the circumstances of your current living condition. It is because of this, I am offering you aid in correcting this mistake. I can eliminate these debts that are weighing you down like chains. I see the strain of the mere mention of these concerns upon your thoughts causes."

Oliver moved forward, placing his elbows on the table as he clasped his hands together. Touching his lips to his hands he considered her offer before speaking, "What do you want in return?"

"Forgiveness cannot be bought with a single gesture. However, what I would request is the same open door of communication that your sister has provided me recently." His mother smiled, "The details of our agreement will be kept private. I will not divulge any information concerning my involvement in your life. It will be up to you to decide who learns of these events."

Oliver sat back in his chair, staring at the surface of the table in front of him as his mind churned with possibilities. He wished to begin the next chapter of his life with Mina. That was his priority. To do so, he had to correct the situation concerning his financial problems. If he told her about it now, she would help him resolve it by attempting to take on the burden herself. To bring such things into their relationship would be unfair to her, the guilt of doing so would weigh too heavily upon him and he would feel less of an individual. She was successful, driven to achieve remarkable things, while he remained behind, lost in his growing concerns, attempting to put on a smile, masking the truth from those who would be sucked into the dilemmas he had created for himself in the past.

"The house means nothing to me. I purchased it when I had financial stability as a part of this household. When I lost that, I took upon myself a debt I was not prepared for. It was meant to be a humble existence for my new wife and me. Now it is a reminder of what was denied to me both by you and the woman who once claimed to love me." Oliver looked up to meet his mother's crystal blue eyes, "Purchase the home from me. Provide enough money in your possession of the property to pay off my mortgage in full and handle the financial aspects of it and legal documents concerning the sale. I would not have attempted to take upon myself to gain ownership of such a home if I knew I was going to be rejected by this family. The stone you dropped into the water, my troubles with my current residence was a ripple effect of what you did to me. Allowing me to regain the status as a college graduate, complete with all that I earned will be end of it."

His mother continued to smile, hiding any other emotions in response to his words, "So be it. I will take this burden off your shoulders and give you back what was stolen from you. Any other debts created due to your struggling with the mortgage you took upon yourself in honor of your previous fiancé, could also be eliminated. You free yourself from the shackles that hold you down. An opportunity to begin again, not only with the woman you love but in discovering the man you truly are."

Oliver's eyes narrowed in anger, "What do you mean by that?"

"You have always been lost, adrift in a sea of endless possibilities, even as a child. I gave you purpose, structure, a way to live your life and something to focus your keen mind upon. You're an intelligent man who is often clouded by his emotions, which is why you were so easily duped by that temptress." His mother held up her hand for silence to interrupt Oliver's outburst, "To be clear, I speak of your previous fiancé, not the woman you wish to passionately defend just now."

Lowering her hand, his mother continued, "From the guidance I provided, what I would have given to you, a new life in the loving embrace of a woman you cared for became your goal. When she betrayed that trust, you were adrift again, a ship without its rudder, nothing to guide you. It was how your friend, Trevor, manipulated you time and again, using you for his own personal ends. It was Mina who intervened and cut him out of your life on your behalf." She was amused by Oliver's reaction, surprised that she knew, "If you're curious, he contacted me."

"What he expected from me, that is an unknown, but once I knew that your connection to him had been severed, I made certain that the next mistake he made while driving under the influence of substance abuse did not go unnoticed by the authorities. No longer would his friends and family hide their dirty little secret." His mother was enjoying the range of emotions revealed on her son's face, "His license has been revoked, he has spent months in jail for his crimes that he thought his access to wealth would protect him from. Money is not power. It is merely a tool to gain it in a world dominated by greed." She was curious about something, "I thought you would be pleased to hear this news, to know that the man who treated you like a dog on a leash, who took advantage of your moments of weakness, received the punishment he deserved."

"Are you attempting to paint yourself as a heroic figure, mother? Justice served to the one who hurt me? Providing aid to me in my time of need?" Oliver scowled, "Is that what all of this is about? What did you do to my ex-fiancé? Did you ruin her life?"

"She did that well enough on her own without my interference. After you, she eventually found herself a man of great wealth to marry, providing her what she thought she wanted." All signs of humor faded as her smile vanished, "I will not speak of the details I have learned of the situation, but her life now is not a pleasant one. She got what she wanted, but in turn, she received what she deserved."

"Would you say the same thing about me? That I have received what I deserved?" Oliver sighed deeply, "I am groveling before you, asking for a way to fix my life before it harms others."

Oliver's mother stood, a blank expression upon her face, "Do not think of this as me having power over you or your life. This is not a gift I am giving you, nor a debt you must repay. Whether you wish to believe in the truth of this statement, know it to be true. This is my repentance for a mistake made in the past. You are not the only one in this world with a burden weighing heavily upon your shoulders. What presses down upon me now is suffocating to the point that I may draw my last breath before I am able to free myself of all that I am responsible for."

She studied her son carefully, "Your debts will be eliminated, documents concerning sale of your home will be sent to you within the next few days, and a meeting will be arranged for you to speak directly with the dean of the college from which you graduated. All that I have taken from you will be returned and the aspects of your life that are directly linked to the actions I took against you will be resolved. Consider it a fresh start for you as I attempt to find a new beginning for myself."

Chapter 9

"I need your help." Oliver touched his elbows against the table in front of him, his fingers interlaced with one another as he rested his chin against them in between speaking, "I would have invited you to my home, but I felt that you would be more comfortable meeting at a neutral location such as this café."

Hoven looked around at the restaurant. It wasn't filled completely but certainly enough customers to not feel like they were going to get unwanted attention, "I was wondering about that." He swallowed hard, feeling deeply intimidated by the man sitting across from him. He had the same color as Alice's eyes and there were small traits they shared in the face, just enough to make their connection as family members easy to see. "I hope you don't take this the wrong way, the only reason you would be asking me for help is if you had no one else to go to and your situation was seriously bad." Seeing a flicker of emotion in Oliver's face, he wilted visibly, "Wow, okay, yes to both."

"I'm aware of your life choices concerning where you live and how you've learned to survive in the city using unconventional methods." Oliver sat back, allowing his arms to drop to his sides, "I need for you to teach me some of those skills you've learned."

Hoven burst out laughing, looking around nervously. "This is a joke, right? Did Mitch put you up to this? I know Alice wouldn't, maybe her roommate would. Then again, if you're the man Alice says you are, then you wouldn't be involved with that sort of thing, either." He felt trapped, "I'm confused, so… Why?"

Oliver tried his best to approach the situation carefully, "I may have need of such experience soon. All of which I will reveal to my sister, but until then, I do request that what is said here is kept between us."

"No..." Hoven shook his head, "I don't keep secrets from Alice. If she asks what we talked about, I'm going to tell her, so maybe if you don't want her to know, then you should stop with whatever it is you're asking me about before I know too much."

"You're a good man for being that way and I apologize for asking you to withhold such information." A look of defeat reflected on Oliver's face, "You're a better man than I am. There is much that Mina is not aware of concerning my life, which I did so in the hopes of fixing the problems before she learned of them. My concern was that she would attempt to fix what was wrong that I feel I am responsible for, not her."

"Alice taught me that when someone cares about you, that means it's their right to choose whether they're going to help you. You can't stop them from wanting to offer you what you need. By not telling them, that's what you're doing." Hoven was confused, "She learned this from you, so why aren't you acting more like her?"

"Pride, arrogance, a need to take on the problems of the world by myself. If I don't then I am revealing a weakness that I deserve suffering caused due to my failures." Oliver bowed his head, "Teachings of my parents dominating my thoughts more so than I thought. I didn't have a role model. What I taught Alice is an ideal I created in my mind, one I hoped to live up to. I didn't have someone to inspire me to behave such a way."

"I know you would never do anything to hurt your girlfriend any more than I would do so with Alice. So, the idea of you cheating on her is out. You didn't do anything she couldn't forgive you for, right?" Hoven's imagination was running wild, "If you want my help, you have to explain what it is that you've done that will lead you to needing to…" He quickly jumped ahead, "What about your house? Why can't you live there?" Suddenly his eyes flared wide, "You're losing your house, aren't you? How? Why? I don't get it."

"I purchased the home when I was still financed by my family's wealth and influence. When I lost those things, I was still attached to ownership of the home. I was surprised mother didn't take it from me, claiming it was bought with her money, but it was a loan taken out in my name, the debt was my punishment from her. I have been unable to maintain the monthly payments for some time now. The need to purchase a replacement vehicle recently added to my problems." Oliver lowered his gaze to the table, "I am less than a year away from facing potential bankruptcy. My home, my vehicle, any number of things will be taken from me."

"Again, I'm confused. I get why I live in my car. I did before I met Alice and even then, I wouldn't even think about us living together as a couple. It would be awkward for both of us for several reasons, so yeah…" Hoven cleared his throat, feeling nervous, "Why don't you move in with Mina? I'm sure she could handle buying something bigger than what she has, or she could even pay for an apartment…" Suddenly it clicked, "Okay, I think I get it now. The pride, arrogance, and need to do things on your own thing, right?" He nodded slowly, "What you're telling me is that you're an idiot."

Oliver's eyebrows rose in surprise, "Excuse me?"

"You have someone that loves you that would do anything for you. Yeah, she's off in another country and it's been practically impossible to maintain a normal line of communication and all of that, but…" Hoven's mind was leaping all over the place, "She gave up her apartment to go to Europe for who knows how long. Why pay for space she wouldn't be using. So, she doesn't have a place to live. She can't exactly arrange for you somewhere to live while… Okay, I thought I had it figured out there for a second but no, lost it."

"Alice kept a secret from me, one that you were aware of concerning meeting with my mother. She withheld information that she could have been conveyed to me to protect me. Doing so created an immense burden upon her until she finally told me about what was happening." Oliver stared at the table, his mind churning through decisions that had been made, "I am in a comparable situation where I withheld information concerning what was happening in my life from Mina. It is my hope that by the time she returns, the problems I am dealing with will be resolved and I can offer her what she deserves."

"Alright, so let me get this straight. Somehow you hid from your girlfriend that you can't keep up with your bills. Instead of asking her for help, you hid that from her in the hopes that you could fix it on your own because I'm guessing that's how your mom or dad would have handled the situation?" Hoven narrowed his eyes in confusion, "Nothing about this entire thing you told me is right." He shook his head, "I thought you were a white knight, the guy who always made the right choices, and you're not."

Oliver started to respond when Hoven interrupted, "No! You don't get to say anything until I'm done." He glared at Alice's brother, "The only reason I'm able to talk this much right now is because I'm angry and once I calm down, I may black out. Like, seriously faint right here in this booth. So, until that happens, you must sit there and listen to my rant because I'm not even sure what I'm going to say until I say it, okay?"

With a deep scowl, Hoven leaned forward, "Alice admires you like a hero. When she keeps saying a true hero should do this or that, I think she's referring to you. You're her idol, mentor, that old guy in all those movies teaching the young person how to become a hero, that's you." He paused, shaking his head, "You're not old, of course, but you get my point. When Alice finds out about all of this, you'll break her heart and that makes me angry!" He pointed at Oliver, "You're going to hurt her and that..." He struggled to breath, "You just..." He fell back in his seat, "Now I have a headache."

Once again, Oliver started to speak and Hoven interrupted, "No! I'm not done yet." He sighed, "What was I talking about?" He muttered softly to himself, "You hurt Alice. That made me mad. I am mad at you for hurting Alice. Right, so... Now what?"

Finally Hoven gave up, speaking in a calm tone, "Sorry, the thought of someone Alice trusted betraying that faith she has in you and thinking about her being sad because of that made me angry. I'm not used to that, and I don't know how to cope with those kinds of feelings, so..." Finally, he nodded, "You're losing your house?"

"It could be as early as the end of the week." Oliver motioned towards Hoven, "Thus my request for aid in knowledge."

"You know what? I think I've been approaching this the wrong way. I thought I was dealing with someone more like Alice, but you're acting more like the people I grew up with. The difference was that they lied to everyone else around them to get what they wanted. You? You're lying to yourself. You keep layering on one lie and half-truth on top of each other until you get so confused and lost in that jumbled mess that you feel like you don't even know who you are anymore." Hoven laughed at the absurdity the situation, "You're me, or at least who I used to be, maybe still me now but at least I'm trying to fix it. To me, it just seems like you're doing everything you can to make things worse when you have everything you could ever want out of life. Congratulations, you screwed up big time. Now, before you ruin your life and end up where I was a few years ago, fix it." Hoven leaned back against his seat, closing his eyes, "I think I'm going to black out now, that's all I got left in me."

"Are you going to provide me any advice concerning living the way you do, or would you prefer the two of us concluding this conversation now?" Oliver was aware of Hoven's severe social anxiety and how it had affected him, "I didn't mean to cause you to feel uncomfortable."

"The way Alice talks about you, you're perfect. I was so intimidated by that, having to live up to that standard. She knows someone who is perfect, how would I ever be anything close enough to that to be worthy of her." Hoven struggled with the wave of thoughts striking him, "You always knew the right thing to say. You were this noble guy who always made the right decisions."

"As it has been revealed to you, she idealizes me, which I am flattered but there are certainly expectations I cannot live up to." Oliver sighed deeply, "I have failed in my life in multiple ways, which makes me doubt whether or not I am worthy of any positive traits concerning my own life."

Hoven interjected, "I don't think you realize just how bad this situation is. You are one of those stones at the top of an arch."

Oliver responded to clarify, "The keystone, the one that prevents the others from falling?"

"Yeah, that. You realize that because you are who you are, the rest of us don't fall apart." Hoven scowled, "I know, sucks that you have all that pressure on you, but it's the truth." He looked up from his meandering thoughts, "You don't hear that a lot, I don't think. Everyone either assumes you are the person you present to them, all calm and in control or they're too nice to you. They want to be nice to the nice guy. Which is cool, I get that. Alice is nice to just about everyone." His face scrunched up in disgust, "Even her mom, which I don't get, but…" Suddenly his eyes flared wide, "Which is your mom…" He laughed nervously, "Sorry if I said something wrong just now."

Oliver smiled in response, "It's understandable, go on."

"You inspired Alice to become the woman that she is, at least to find the strength to stand up against your mom, to lead a life away from all of that. If it wasn't you doing that, she would still be living with her mother and probably married to some rich…" A pained expression washed across Hoven's face, "Definitely not someone living in their car." He groaned, "This is so hard to do."

Concerned for Hoven's wellbeing, Oliver asked what he was referring to, "What's bothering you?"

Hoven began to explain, "Early on when we first met, Alice made me promise three things. The first, suicide is not an option. I can't think about it, I'm not allowed to consider it. I can't even make jokes about it. It's just not allowed. That was tough for me at first, I admit, but now it never crosses my mind, so no big deal there."

"The second rule was that I am not allowed to say anything about other people. Even your mom, who I have a lengthy list of things I want to say bad about her just because she hurt Alice, but I won't because I..." Hoven cleared his throat, dropping his tone to a whisper, "I love her..."

"Do you find it difficult to say that?" Hoven's startled reaction drew Oliver to follow up, "After my fiancé broke off our engagement, the pain I suffered from that experience made me feel as if I would never speak those words again. When I told Mina I loved her for the first time, it wasn't a fairy tale conclusion. She essentially said, I don't feel the same way about you."

Hoven cringed, "Ouch..." A pain struck his chest, "Did I hurt Alice by not telling her how I felt when she said that to me the first time? I feel horrible."

"Telling someone you don't love them can cause pain and suffering, yes, but telling them that you feel that way but secretly don't, that will be a far worse thing to do to someone. It is better to be honest, as you were with my sister and Mina was with me. She loved me. She just wasn't ready to express those feelings at the time." Oliver tried to be encouraging, "I'm sure you sympathize?"

"If that means I was in the same boat, yeah." Hoven scratched his head in confusion, "I never understood that. I am in the same boat. I don't get it. I mean, I know what it means, but... I don't know why it means that I guess." Realizing he was temporarily distracted, Hoven tried again, "To answer your question, it scares me every time I say it. I should be excited and happy, but every time I feel this fear clutching at my chest that I'm scared to say it out loud."

Tears formed in his eyes before he realized it. Feeling embarrassed, Hoven brushed his hand across his face, "I thought I've been in love before, but every time I told a woman that I felt that way, they turned me down, made fun of me, used it to hurt me, so by the time it came to Alice, I was afraid of being hurt again. I know I shouldn't feel this way, I trust her. If it wasn't for her, I wouldn't be alive right now. She's been kind and gentle with me every step of the way. She's exactly what I needed in my life, not just wanting someone like that, but needed her."

New tears formed at the mere thought of what crossed his mind, "Even if I lose her, if something bad happens to her..." Droplets slipped down his face, his eyes staring blankly at the visions of her funeral, "I'll continue with her memory guiding me. I made her three promises. I promised to keep my life safe. She gave me a reason to live, and I'll never forget that vow. She asked for me to not be rude to other people, I don't have to be nice, I'm still working on that, but I promised her not to make the world worse than it is because I'm here. I may not be well enough to add good to the world yet, but I refuse to make it worse. Lastly, she said I can't be mean to myself, and I won't. No matter what."

Oliver had to keep his breathing steady, to rely on his teachings of his mother to hide his emotions, to keep a firm grip on what he was feeling. He was afraid of losing control himself as he focused on a memory that echoed of what Alice had taught Hoven, "When you see her next, ask her about where she learned those three rules from and who taught her them." Hoven looked up, wiping away tears form his face as his eyes narrowed in concern, "That's all I will say on the subject matter. If she wishes to discuss the topic further, I will let her speak of it."

"That's just it!" Hoven pointed to Oliver, "That's what I'm talking about! You inspired her to become the woman she wanted to be. Then she helped me become the man I want to be." He paused, staring at the table again, "I'm working on it, work in progress, but I'm trying. That is what gets me up every day, what pushes me to move forward in my life. I want to be a better person and I want to do more with my life. I just don't know what exactly, but as I said, I'm working on that."

Oliver sat back in his chair, considering what Hoven was speaking of, "Before I met Mina, she made a conscious effort to be defiant of her parents and their wishes of her. Throughout her life, they would lay claim to responsibility for any of her accomplishments. If she proved herself to excel in a sport, it was abilities and talent that she inherited from them. It was their encouragement and pushing her to do well that she was able to be so well at what she did in life. After graduating college, she..." He was misled at the memory of Mina. Every subtle nuance of how she expressed herself comforted him. "She tried to hide from success."

"Weird..." Hoven's face scrunched up in confusion, "She never came across as someone that would rebel for the sake of rebellion. She refused to be a certain way because her parents wanted her to be that way. Wow..." He looked up at Oliver, "She's so confident, in control. She's like this powerful mythical figure the way Alice talks about her." He laughed, "Then again, so were you. The way you two were described, you're like Greek gods or something, perfect in every way, living up on Mount Olympus."

"You've been talking to Mitch, haven't you?" Oliver grinned, "He loves Greek mythology."

"Only because he hangs around with Alice and I tend to be just there at the same time. I don't think I've ever been alone with him before, which is good, because he scares me." Hoven quickly added, worried that his statement would be considered rude, "He's high energy, intense guy, and if you know anything about me, that is way overwhelming for me. I can't handle it for long without Alice kind of shielding me and giving me a chance to breathe." He sighed, "She always knows when things are getting bad even before I do. She just senses this thing about me and pulls me away from a situation, calms me down, helps me cope with my anxiety." He felt like crying again but he struggled not to do so, "I love her so much."

"I am glad that my sister has found someone that is an ideal match for her." Oliver smiled, enjoying the fact that Alice was happy and able to provide so much for a man who so dearly needed her aid. "She speaks highly of you."

Hoven avoided eye contact, "Could we not talk about me right now? This is getting hard on me."

"Sure, we can do that." Oliver quickly shifted back to what he was saying earlier, "Mina said that after we met, she was finally able to release her previous contempt for her parents and to…" He smiled at the memory, "…bloom like a flower on a cold winter's day for I was the sunlight that provided her the encouragement to become the woman she desired to be."

"I'm sure that's beautiful and all, but to me that just sounds bizarre. Flowers and winter, sunlight…" Hoven's face scrunched up in confusion, "You two have a weird relationship."

"Each couple is different. What matters most is if both people involved are happy and we are." Oliver casually moved on with the topic, "The way she described her situation was that if it wasn't for me, she would still be living the life of keeping her proverbial head down, trying not to gain too much attention for herself. She lived the life within a cubical hidden away among a multitude of others at an office building. She had the skills, the knowledge, the education, the drive to do something more, but she was so determined to reject the life her parents wanted for her, that she was missing out on what could have been."

"See? You made my point. Without you, Mina would still be resentful of her parents and in a way, they would still be ruining her life. Well, at least her potential. Alice would be stuck under the shadow of your mother and who knows where that would have led. Without your sister making the decisions that she did, she wouldn't have been there for me when I needed someone the most. I would probably be dead by now." Hoven suddenly realized, "I owe you my life." His brow furrowed in thought, "Thank you."

"I don't wish to lay claim to something that is obviously my sister's doing but thank you for what you've said of me." Oliver shifted the focus of the topic, "Why are you so concerned about me revealing myself to be a failure?"

"Think about it. You disappoint Alice. She becomes heartbroken and maybe even falls under the thrall of the Evil Queen just like in a fairy tale. Mina discovers what happened and what if things fall apart between you two. That's it, no more happily ever after. Then, when Alice vanishes from my life, I'll be dead inside knowing that the woman I..." Hoven stopped himself, "That sounded way cooler in my head, it being an awesome story involving a gallant hero, a wicked witch, and a good queen, and whatever it is I am in the story." His face scrunched up in thought, "Am I that woman with the glass slippers? Is that it? I get to marry the queen and that makes me a king? Maybe? I don't know. This whole thing is falling apart in my mind."

Oliver nodded slowly, trying his best to follow what Hoven was telling him, "I don't believe it would be as disastrous as you may think. If Mina truly loves me, she'll find it in her heart to forgive me and we'll be able to move forward in our lives. The same thing goes for Alice. She withheld information from me for a similar reason. I believe I can resolve things with her, also. Alice certainly would not agree to fall under the influence of my mother once more." He chuckled, "You would have been proud of her if you had heard what she told my mother if she dared to harm me."

Hoven sat up with excitement, his eyes flaring wide in curiosity, "What did she say?"

Oliver laughed at the other man's reaction, "Well, let me try to remember her exact words. 'I have opened a door that would have been sealed shut without my aid. This is your last and only chance, don't allow arrogance or pride cloud your judgement. Know that the circumstances of what is about to take place will dictate the future of our relationship. Harm him and we will no longer be on speaking terms.'"

"It sounds like her, but how did you memorize all of that?" Hoven leaned forward, studying Oliver carefully, "Are you sure you're not some sort of robot? Did Alice secretly build you and you've been posing as her brother this whole time? It would explain a lot if that were true."

"No, I'm not an artificial life form." Oliver laughed at the thought, "I don't believe Alice has any knowledge of robotics, either. However, I was taught at an early age how to memorize much of what I was meant to learn from my private tutors. Often, I was punished severely for any mistakes and failures, more so than I should have been. It motivated me to learn techniques that I would have otherwise not have access to." He concluded with a smile, "What she said resonated with me, inspired me. I may have inspired you, but she does the same for me."

"Sorry for calling you a robot." Hoven stared at the table in front of him, "Your whole family feels kind of weird to me. You and Alice, in a nice way. Your mom, your brothers, not so much."

"Imagine growing up with that." Oliver quickly shifted topics, "What would you have me do concerning my situation?"

Hoven's eyes flared wide, "What?"

"You seem to have a proper grasp on what is going on, your concerns for what may happen next are valid." Oliver hadn't decided as to what he should do next, "What would you suggest I do next?"

"Well, first we need a plan in place to fix your situation." A question popped into Hoven's mind, "Is the bank taking your house? Just how long do you have until you lose it?"

"Within a week or two, I have already begun moving my belongings to a storage space until I can either sell them or find a home for what I cannot fit into my vehicle." Oliver wished to avoid the truth of his mother's involvement, "I have arranged to sell it to an interested party. A realtor is handling the details."

"Wow, kind of knew all of this was happening for a while now, huh?" Hoven slowly nodded as his mind processed what was happening, "Okay, I think I have an answer and..." He burst out laughing at the absurdity of what was going on inside of his head.

Oliver leaned forward in curiosity, "Are you alright?"

"Seriously, think about it. You and Mina, you are these Greek gods, right? All powerful beings that are all perfect up in your mountain, I think it was where they lived?" Seeing Oliver nod in agreement, Hoven continued, "That means your mom is the evil queen, the villain of this story that's playing out in my head. Alice is the good queen. Good and evil queen fighting for control over the land. Mitch is... I guess..."

Suddenly Hoven's eyes lit up with excitement, "He's that guy that's in all those stories. Usually it's some old man, but sometimes it's a younger trickster type, comes in with knowledge to help the hero fix things or some object that is needed for a quest."

Oliver wasn't certain where this was going so let Hoven run with it. "Alright, go on."

"Well, that leaves me. One god is gone from this world. The other is losing his power and strength, no longer able to provide his blessings to the good queen. So, the evil queen gains power in the absence of the two gods. That leaves the good queen vulnerable. So, she sends her mentor to find her a hero to save the day." Hoven sighed, "Which, unfortunately, would be me." He shook his head slowly, a bewildered look on his face, "We're so screwed. If the fate of the world is relying on me, it's doomed. I give up. We might as well just say goodbye to everything."

"What was it that Alice told you? Don't be rude to yourself?" Oliver smiled, trying to encourage the man across from him.

Hoven muttered, "I was afraid you were going to bring that up." He sighed loudly, "Fine, as the hero…" He lifted his head to meet Oliver's gaze, "Reluctant, very much a reluctant hero in this situation, I must do what must be done." He frowned, "I'm not so good with words when I'm nervous." He tried to steady his breathing, "As the hero, I must consider how to save the day, right? So, with that said, the goddess of this story is not here to help. The god left behind needs to find a way to renew his power and help give his strength to the good queen to defeat the evil queen all the while providing the hero the strength he needs to not die."

Oliver's eyes narrowed as he tried to analyze what was just said, "Alright… I think I follow?"

"I need to help you fix the mess you created." Hoven tried again, "Also, try to fix what's wrong with me at the same time."

Oliver asked out of concern, "What's wrong?"

Hoven looked up with what little courage remained within him, "What if you and I got an apartment together? That way you're not homeless and I won't be living in my car anymore. Alice is worried about me, and I don't like seeing her like that. She would be happy to know that the two men in her life, those she cares most about, are safe." He shrugged, "That's my idea." He held out his hands, "What do you think?"

Oliver was surprised by the suggestion but was intrigued by the notion, "You would want to do that? I thought you enjoyed the freedom of not being tied down to a specific location."

"I do, but at the same time, I care about Alice more than anything in this world. I think she feels the same way about me. I think to myself, how I would feel if our roles were reversed. I would be worried sick all the time, like scared out of my mind that something would happen to her. I then think to myself, is that how she feels about me all the time?" Hoven sighed, "Then I realize that I'm punishing her in a way, worrying her like that. Also, if I'm safe, the man she loves is safe, and that makes her happy." He stared at his hands resting on the table, "I like it when she's happy. I'm happy when she smiles and laughs, and…"

Tears formed in the lower rims of his eyes as his anxiety began to build within him, "Before I fall apart completely right now, what do you say?"

Oliver answered quickly out of concern for Hoven, "Yes, I would be honored. I know how much of a sacrifice this is for you to make such an offer."

"Cool, awesome." Hoven pulled himself to his feet, feeling like there wasn't any air in the room. Taking in short, shallow breaths, his eyes watering, he quickly concluded, "I need to go." He made a small wave of his hand as he rushed out of the café.

Chapter 10

"I seek your forgiveness." Sitting in one of the chairs in the living room of his sister's apartment, Oliver bowed his head as he leaned forward. Resting his elbows against his legs, his fingers interlaced with one another, he felt humbled before her.

Confused, concerned, and curious as to what was happening, Alice asked, "I forgive you, of course, whatever wrongdoing you feel you are responsible for. I would do so otherwise, for you did forgive me recently for withholding information from you concerning my time spent with mother. I would be inconsiderate for not returning the same kindness you showed me in this regard."

Looking up into his sister's eyes, Oliver felt it necessary to get straight to the point, "I wish to blurt out everything but out of context or understanding of the situation, much of what I have to say may not make sense. I suppose starting from the beginning is the best approach."

He cleared his throated as he tried to figure out how to explain his situation, "Shortly before I departed our family home, I arranged for the purchase of a small house, the one I currently live in, as a start of a new life. It was to be a humble existence for myself, my future wife, and children that I hoped to have some day. Everything was already set into motion. There was no turning back after documents were signed, agreements made, requirements of obligations set forth when everything changed in my life."

Fear flickered in Alice's eyes. She didn't know the details of how Oliver had purchased his home, "I see, please go on."

"It was not paid for by money provided by our family. A loan was taken out, payments would begin shortly afterwards once I gained ownership of the home. It was a way to teach myself humility, to pull away from mother's influence. I didn't want her money to purchase it, it would be earned through my work and dedication." Oliver tried to sort out all the information in his mind as to what he wished to tell his sister, "I had recently graduated from college. I had already made several connections through avenues I pursued while still a student. Several careers were opening for me. It should have been relatively easy to handle the financial burden that I had taken upon myself."

A chill raced across Alice's skin, as if knowledge of what he was leading into struck her thoughts. She had the foundation, the root cause of what would be troubling him so, but wasn't certain what it had led to, what was the outcome of this series of unfortunate events, "Before I leap ahead and come to conclusions that may not be true, I will endeavor to let patience guide me."

"When mother eliminated my education from my past, so did the opportunities that were attached to it. It was as if my entire time in college did not exist. She made certain all doors opened to me due to what she believed to be her influence upon my life were closed." Oliver bowed his head, "Within weeks of losing connection with our family, as you know, my fiancé at the time ended our engagement. I was devastated as well. I quickly agreed to the first job that became available and began my new life. Since then, I have lost my initial job due to the company having failed and its assets having been liquidated to pay for its debts."

"From there, I took a position as a janitor, working my way up to a low-level position that..." Oliver hesitated to speak of what was a half-truth presented as something more than it was, "I manage the front end during the night shift, but it certainly does not pay the wages of a salaried manager. I am required to fulfill much of the responsibilities of someone of that elevated position but the company that employs me does not wish to compensate me for that added workload. I am a manager in responsibilities if not in other aspects, which I fear I may have misled you and Mina to think otherwise."

Oliver tried to quickly move forward, "My financial situation is not well. When I was forced to purchase a new car, I was pushed further into a debt I was struggling to keep up with as it was. Mina is unaware of what is going on with me, at least that is my understanding. I am certain that if she knew, she would have said something by now. I didn't wish to burden her with my concerns or you, in that both of you had your own lives, issues, and problems that you were each dealing with. Mother and father taught us to be self-sufficient, to not rely on others, and I feel that such a mind frame is to be blamed for what were my financial concerns."

"Were?" Alice picked up on the use of past tense, "What has changed?" Her eyes flared wide, "What did you and mother discuss in my absence? You said you would tell me later but have yet to reveal to me any details of your interaction."

Oliver eased carefully into his answer, "Mother will correct the mistakes of her past by reinstating my status as a graduate of the college I attended. She feels regret for such a harsh punishment."

A smile spread across Alice's face, "That's wonderful, I am happy to hear that she is staying true to her word in changing her negative behavior towards her children."

Oliver was uncertain of how she would react to the second piece of information involving their mother, "I made an agreement with her. She will purchase my home, eliminating that aspect of my debt. In my mind, I felt that everything she was responsible for either directly or indirectly would be resolved if she agreed to those terms."

Alice instinctively brought up her arms against her chest, each hand lightly rubbing her upper arms in concern, "Why did you agree to this?" She looked away, staring at a spot on the floor in front of her as her mind raced for a proper response not spoken in the heat of a surge of emotion, "Mina would have helped you. Mitch would have done what he could…" She looked up, pleading with her brother, "I would have done everything within my power to help you with your burdens. You did not have to do this."

"In my mind it was a way for her to resolve all that she was responsible for as well as provide me a fresh start in my life. I have considered speaking of such things to Mina, but the house…" Oliver bowed his head, "There were multiple problems occurring with the plumbing, the heating and cooling system, bills I could not afford to respond to were growing." He looked up into his sister's eyes, "In my mind it was the last remnant of a broken heart and a life denied to me. Yes, I'm grateful that the truth was revealed before we progressed further into marriage. I love Mina dearly. I am happy that I am with my one true love and not the woman that scorned me. However, the house is a memory of that pain."

Alice slipped out of her seat, soon kneeling before her brother. Taking his hands, she looked up into his eyes, "I should have considered that. You seemed happy where you were, I didn't realize that..." She gently pressed down with her fingers in concern, "If you feel certain that this was the correct decision, then I support you. However, what concerns me is that mother will use this against you in some way, leverage to gain some advantage over you."

"I wish to begin a life with Mina, one unburdened by the past. She deserves that and so much more. I felt that this was the best possible solution given my options at the time." Oliver closed his eyes, trying to imagine the future, "However, from this point forward, it will be a life in which both myself and Mina will proceed together with. No more half-truths, no misinformation or holding back. I have vowed to myself to be forthcoming both with her and you..." A strange smile played across his lips as he opened his eyes, "As well as my future new roommate."

Releasing her hold on her brother's hand, Alice pulled herself to her feet before stepping back, "Are you moving in with Mina?"

Joining her in a standing position, Oliver smiled, surprised that he had the opportunity to speak to her before Hoven had, "I will share a household with my wife, not my girlfriend. I will not share a living space with another woman in honor of Mina, of course. Therefore..."

Alice was surprised, her eyes flaring wide in shock, "Mitch?"

Oliver burst out laughing, "No, it was another who offered to become my roommate. He was aware of the growing concerns for his wellbeing in the eyes of the woman he loves dearly."

Tears formed in Alice's eyes, "He's going to get an apartment with you?" She rushed forward, wrapping her arms tightly around her brother's waist as she pressed the side of her face against his chest, "That is wonderful news! I have been so dearly concerned for his wellbeing, every day I fear that he is in danger. With you by his side, I know he will be safe. Thank you so dearly for this wonderful gesture."

Returning his sister's embrace, Oliver smiled, "It was Hoven who suggested it to me, he considered your feelings on the subject matter from your perspective. The next time you get the opportunity, thank him for this offering that he made, both on your behalf but for me as well."

Alice smiled, "I will, thank you. I promise."

~

"Why didn't you tell me?" Mina had the most incredibly beautiful view of Paris, the Eiffel tower lit up in the distance. Despite this, her mind was focused on the conversation, what he had just told her, and the feeling of her world was crumbling around her.

"It would be easy to blame the teachings of my mother and father, but I made the choice to heed their way of coping with problems. I put it upon myself to resolve what I felt to be personal concerns that I created, that I was responsible for before we met. I didn't want to burden you with my past decisions. I hope you can find it in your heart to forgive me." Oliver's tone fell to a near whisper, "I'm sorry…"

Mina knew that tone of voice, the short intake of breath, he was crying, "Oliver… I wish you had told me sooner."

Mina could hear it in Oliver's voice that he was falling apart, what little strength he had left was gone. It had taken everything out of him to tell her everything, from his financial concerns that he had been hiding from her to the deal he had made with his mother, and finally the agreement he had made with Hoven concerning moving into an apartment together. "It was a mistake. One I will spend a lifetime making up to you for doing so. If you do not wish to speak to me further, I understand. I betrayed your trust, potentially broke the faith you had in me, and I will understand if you…"

"I love you." Mina wanted to be angry with him, that was her instinctual response, that's how she typically would deal with a situation like this. Yet, all she could think about was the tears in his eyes, the sorrow in his voice, the suffering he was enduring, and she wanted to heal the pain he was going through. "No matter what happens, no matter how bad our lives get, I love you."

She closed her eyes as she leaned against the railing of the balcony that her hotel room opened to, "You should have told me. You know I would have helped you out, without having to involve your mother. It's a miracle that she is doing all of this for you, so I'll have to thank your sister when I get back for getting through to a woman that I still hate for all that she did to you. I refuse to forgive her for that."

"I have not forgiven her either. However, this is a small step in eliminating what has been a burden of my past that I would carry with me into the future. I don't want us to be weighed down by what happened to me long before we met." Oliver was sitting on the floor of his bedroom, his back against the wall. "I don't deserve you."

"Because you made a mistake? You tried to take on all your problems on your own without asking for help from those who care about you. Yeah, I'm upset that you didn't tell me sooner but some part of me thinks that I may have done the same thing in your situation." Mina turned away from the balcony, walking back into her hotel room as she felt the strength leaving her legs. She needed to sit down.

Relaxing on her bed, Mina looked up at the ceiling, "My parents were so quick to blame me for anything that went wrong while they took full credit for anything positive that I did with my life. Until I met you, I lived my life basically to spite them, to try not to be successful. You showed me that I should let go of the past, to move forward with my life and to live it the way I wanted to. That's why I'm here, Oliver, because of you. You inspired me to be myself and to let go of what my parents did to me concerning how I should live my life. So, yeah, what you did was wrong, but I know you regret your decision, that you won't do it again in the future and that hopefully this is you doing the same as I did. You're letting go of how we've had our parents telling us how to live our lives and finally doing things our own way."

Oliver had brought up his legs tightly against his body, his forehead resting against his knee. "Thank you for forgiving me."

"As for what you said about you not deserving me." Mina closed her eyes as she fought with her urge to say something more forceful, "Do you honestly believe that? Do you remember when we were dating, I told you I hated you. I was screwed up, broken inside, and despite all of that, you forgave me. You understood me."

"There are days that I feel like maybe that this is destiny intervening. It is trying to tell me that you need to move on with your life, that I am holding you back somehow." Oliver struggled to keep the threat of memories of his first fiancé rejecting him from influencing his thoughts, "I'm sorry, I just... I'm in a dark place right now. I want to be hopeful, but I feel trapped where I am, alone in dealing with all of it, and I feel like I'm becoming a burden."

"Oliver?" Mina's voice was nearly a whisper, "Every time you say something bad about yourself, that you're not the man I see you as, I'm going to remind you of this fact. I love you. I love who you are, and I love that you are in my life. If you asked me to, I would get on the first available flight to be with you. I wouldn't hesitate to be with you if you needed me to be there." At the offering of doing so, Mina sat up, her eyes coming into focus on the room around her, "It feels like that's what you need right now. I hate feeling helpless, not being there for you when you're going through all of this alone."

"I've come to the realization that I am too dependent upon another person to define me. I cling to someone else to give me purpose, to guide me either directly in the case of my mother or indirectly as was our relationship. First my father when I was a child, then mother after he passed away. From there I was drawn to the woman I proposed to. When she vanished from my life, I clung to a childhood friend that used me, manipulated me, but I gave in because I had no one else. Then you came along and..." Oliver's brow furrowed in concern, "My mother pointed out that I was on a boat without a rudder, adrift at sea."

Mina was upset that Oliver was taking advice from his mother, "Don't listen to your mother, she isn't…"

Oliver interjected, "Despite my feelings towards the woman, I am forced to agree with her assessment of the situation. You deserve a husband that is worthy of you. A need to find purpose in my life that is separate from all others I share it with. I need to find happiness in my life, fulfillment in who I am as an individual. That way, when you return, I will be able to share that life with you. As it stands, you fill an empty void, which is asking too much of you."

"Oliver…" Tears had formed in Mina's eyes as she leaned forward, droplets hitting the surface of her bed, "Am I going to lose you? Is that what you're trying to tell me?"

"I love you, Mina, more than life itself. You are the breath that sustains me, the heartbeat in my chest, and the warmth that protects me on a chilly night. When I speak of how I feel, it is your name that crosses my lips, for it is the embodiment of what I cherish most in my life." Oliver fell silent, his eyes closed, his mind lost in a waking dream as he strained to picture the woman he loved in his mind, "I wish to marry you, my dearest love. I know neither of us are ready for that now, we are not prepared for such a step in our lives. We may never. However, that does not take away from the fact that I desire to dedicate my life to you, mind, body, and soul."

Tears continued to drop from Mina's eyes as she pressed them tightly closed, "I can come home. I can't continue like this knowing that…"

"Mina." She fell silent at the sound of her name. Oliver spoke firmly, "I need to do this on my own."

Mina wanted to remind him that's how he got into this situation in the first place but knew that isn't what he was referring to. He needed to discover what he felt was missing in his life without her presence serving as a potential distraction, "I'll give you the time you need but only if you promise me something."

Oliver had closed his eyes, feeling exhausted from the emotional turmoil had endured, "What would that be?"

"Every time you start to feel like giving up, I want you to listen to me, hear my voice in your head. I love you." Mina desired nothing more than to be able to hold him in her arms, to feel the warmth of his body against hers, the comfort his presence brought to her, "Close your eyes and listen to your heartbeat. Remember that I'm always with you, no matter what."

Oliver cried, unable to hold back the surge of emotion flooding his mind, "I love you, my precious Mina."

Mina whispered softly, "I love you, my sweet Oliver."

~

"Rule number one. Don't allow myself to consider suicide as an answer. Rule number two. Don't be mean to others. I don't have to say something nice to them, but I shouldn't add to the damage done in this world. Rule number three. Stop being so negative about myself which was the hardest one for me to do." Hoven stared at Alice, trying to figure out the truth before he was forced to speak of it, "When I talked to your brother, he mentioned that I should ask where you learned that from. I couldn't help but think that he was implying that he was the one that taught you those three rules." His eyes narrowed in concern, "Which means he had a reason to do so."

Alice turned away, staring at her hands that were resting in her lap. Hoven had offered to drive Alice home from work. It wasn't until they were sitting outside her apartment building that he brought up the topic. She wasn't certain if she should address his concerns directly, "There is a question you wish to ask me."

Hoven leaned back in his chair, his arms resting at his side as she stared at the steering wheel, "I can't. If I do, it becomes real and the thought of it being true breaks me inside."

"On the bridge I saw a man who was beyond hope, who had given up, and thought it would be best for the world if you ended your life. I recognized that look on your face because I saw it in a mirror years ago. I told you then that just because you cannot see the scars upon my skin, it does not mean they don't exist. I believe you understood the truth about me then. You may not have considered the depths of my words at the time, for you were trapped within your own pain and suffering to consider what another had endured." Alice looked over at Hoven, "Where I was able to save your life, it was Oliver who saved me. He had created those three rules to help him cope with what was happening to him in his own life. I learned those rules for myself and it helped me survive what I felt to be a hopeless situation."

Hoven struggled to breathe, the idea of losing Alice, the memories of his own suicidal thoughts in the past weighed heavily upon him, "I'm sorry."

"All that does matter is that we are both alive this day, that our past did not claim us." Alice touched Hoven's upper arm, "We are together now, protecting one another from such a fate."

Hoven smiled, "Did he ever tell you about the whole fairy tale thing I came up with concerning his situation?"

Alice withdrew her hand as she turned her body as much as she could to face him, "No, he did not." She smiled, "However, I am most curious to hear more about it."

Feeling embarrassed, Hoven tried his best to explain, "So, I compared him and Mina to Greek gods, up on the mountain where they lived. That made you the good queen of the realm and your mother was the evil queen. Without the powers of the gods to give you strength, you were going to lose in your fight against the evil queen. Mina is gone and Oliver was feeling powerless, giving up hope. So, that somehow made me the reluctant hero."

Hoven looked over at the sound of Alice giggling at his comment. Seeing his startled reaction, she quickly apologized, "I'm sorry, I laughed because I never thought of us in such a way. However, in my eyes, you are a heroic figure that I admire greatly. What I laughed at was not at the thought of you fulfilling such a role." She paused before asking, "Was Mitch in this story?"

"Oh yeah, he's kind of like the messenger of the gods, since he's close to Mina and he brings their power to you, the good queen." Hoven returned to staring at the steering wheel, "So, as the hero, I had to save the god, which is Oliver from losing his power. So, if I could help him regain what he had lost, he would be able to give you the power you need to save the realm from the evil queen."

"Awe..." Alice blushed at the compliment, "You think of yourself as a hero who aids others who in turn provides the strength and power to help save the realm. We all play our parts in doing so."

Hoven nodded, "Yeah, I know I'm not strong enough to do it on my own, but I know Oliver can and since you stood up against your mom once before, all he needs to do is to inspire you and so, in the end, you're the hero that saves the day. I fixed things so that it would work out the way it should."

"It is a lovely sentiment and a beautiful story. I enjoy it immensely. We all play our part, connected as we are, providing strength to each other to protect the realm from the evil queen." Alice hesitated for a moment before adding, "However, she is not evil anymore. At least, I don't believe she is. My mother is making attempts to correct the mistakes of the past."

"Fine, the good queen of the realm found a way to send a small part of her good magic into the evil queen and it is because of that good magic that the evil queen is slowly becoming like her daughter." Hoven grinned, "How about that?"

Alice felt a burst of excitement, "I love you, Hoven. You are truly precious to me in every way. Thank you for being so supportive and encouraging of me. I can only hope that I provide you that and so much more in return."

Hoven tried to sound poetic, but struggled with the words, "You are my light that makes the darkness go away."

Alice gently touched her hand to his cheek as she stared into his dark blue eyes, "You are so beautiful."

Despite his attempts to avoid doing so, tears formed in his eyes as he tried to respond, "Thank you."

Alice smiled playfully, "Cara is at work and as we have proven that the both of us can fit into the largest of our chairs."

Uncertain of where that was leading to, Hoven began wiping away tears from his eyes, "Yeah, okay…"

"This is the first time I have used this word. Therefore, I hope that you understand my meaning. Some would believe it to symbolize more than I would intend, but you know me well enough that I believe you will grasp my intention." Alice tried to find the bravery to speak of such a thing, "Would you be interested in…" She looked away, worried she wouldn't have the strength to say it. Finally, she steadied her breath before looking over at her boyfriend, "Would you be interested in… A…" She covered her face, feeling so embarrassed. Only after regaining her composure did she look up with a blushing smile, "Snuggle?"

Hoven felt his breath trapped in his chest as he stared at Alice. He gasped for air, soon hyperventilating, taking in a series of quick breaths. Startled by his reaction, Alice grasped his hand, "I'm so sorry, I didn't mean to… Oh goodness…"

Feeling her hand holding his, a soothing sensation washed across his body, a lightheaded feeling making it difficult to think. What had been tension worked into every muscle of his body, Hoven felt a sudden relaxation that nearly led to him passing out. Leaning back against his chair, he spoke in a whisper, "Yeah… That would be… That… Would be…" He turned his head to face her, "I would like that."

Alice kissed her fingers before speaking, "I love you." She touched her fingers to his lips. Before she could pull away, Hoven instinctively kissed her hand which made her heart feel as if it skipped a beat. Blushing deeply, she smiled, "Oh goodness…"

Feeling embarrassed for doing so, Hoven spoke in a hushed tone, "Sorry, that..." In response, Alice took his hand and brought his fingertips up to her lips. With a playful smile, she kissed them softly. As she did so, he spoke softly, "I love you."

~

"I need your help." Oliver smiled before he added, "Thank you for coming on such a short notice, I appreciate it." He laughed, "Sorry, my mind is racing ahead a mile a minute, it's hard to keep up with what should be proper protocol in greeting someone."

Mitch grinned as his eyes wondered around the room, "Wow, you're almost all packed up and ready to go, aren't you?" He shifted his gaze back to Oliver, "Before we start out, is it true that you made a deal with devil? You didn't have to sign in blood, did you?"

"If you're speaking of my mother, then yes, I made an agreement that she would purchase the house from me, eliminating any lingering debt connected to this building and the plot of land it resides on." Oliver hesitated to go into detail, "It's a long, complicated situation that I feel..."

"Short version, the job you had lined up that could afford it fell out from underneath you because your mom screwed you over." Mitch held up his hands, "I shouldn't talk that way around your sister, for some reason she still defends your mother in her own polite way. But you? She stabbed you in the back and kept twisting, so my question is why did agree to selling your soul to her?"

Startled by the harsh terminology used, Oliver did his best to proceed, "Her intervention in my life was at a pivotal time led to a loss of several job opportunities and connections I once possessed."

"Like I said, she..." Mitch sat back in the chair he was sitting in. The two men were having a discussion in Oliver's living room, "Sorry, I can't stand the woman. I almost cussed her out and that was the only time I met her face to face. I don't want to use the word hate, that kind of feeling is like a nasty bit of bitterness that no one should hold onto, but... She is right up there, threatening me to break one of my rules of not hating anyone."

"According to my sister, she's attempting to reconcile with those she has harmed in the past." Oliver considered Mitch's viewpoint, "I agree with you in that making this kind of agreement could put me in debt to her, giving her some sort of leverage over me. How, I'm uncertain. Legally, I'm sure she could find something in the sale of the home as a contract to hold over my head, but I am putting my faith in Alice, not my mother. She told me to trust this offering of peace between us, so I am doing so."

"Fine, when you put it that way. I'll refrain from trash talking your mom." Mitch sighed, "Let's just say that three ghosts visited your mother one night, even though its months away from Christmas, and she's learned the error of her ways. Whatever caused her to change her mind about what she was doing with her life, she is now trying to make up for all the garbage she dumped on people."

Oliver nodded, realizing the reference Mitch was making, "I don't believe the ghost of a dead partner intervened on her behalf, but the concept I believe is similar."

Mitch was concerned about his mother's claws digging in, "Other than fixing the terrible things she did to you in the past, taking this house off your hands, what else is she doing for you?"

"refuse to accept any further help. In my mind, she is fixing the past and allowing me a chance at a future that was denied to me." Oliver quickly shifted the focus of the conversation, "Which brings me back to the original request of aid."

"Yeah, word travels fast, you and Hoven are going to be roommates?" Mitch's brow furrowed in thought, "Never would have imagined him rooting himself in one place let alone offering to do so with you." He touched his chest with his fingertips as he grinned playfully, "Me, I love the idea. I have barely gotten three words out of the guy since we met that were directed at me. I've heard him talk but only because Alice is around him at the time. So, for me, he's a bit of a mystery beyond what Precious tells me."

"My conversation with him that led to us becoming roommates was the first I had with the man one on one." Oliver smiled, "It should make life with him rather interesting in that this is his first apartment and solid structure he's called home since he was a teenager."

"The ladies have told me practically everything concerning your situation, what's going on with you, which both of them are scared out of their minds by the way." Mitch pointed at Oliver, "Shame on you for making them both cry."

Oliver hung his head in shame, "Yes, I know, it is a burden I will carry with me until I can feel that I have made it up to them."

"Oh whatever, they both love you. Both Kitten and Precious have already forgiven you." Mitch leaned forward, "What you need to do now is the hard part. You must learn to forgive yourself. Until you do, it's just going to hang over you like a dark cloud."

"Which brings me to my point." Oliver wasn't sure how to approach the topic, "I don't know what to do with my life. As it has been pointed out to me, I have been drifting aimlessly from my parents' home, to playing the role of a fiancé, then being defined by my pain of that betrayal. I felt I had healed from those experiences by the time I met Mina, but then I fell into the role of boyfriend with few to no other facets of my life." He struggled to find the right words, "I am Alice's brother. I am my mother's son. I am soon to be Hoven's roommate. I am Mina's boyfriend."

"And you're my friend, it's okay for you to say it." Mitch tried to be encouraging, "Yeah, we've had our rough patches in the past, but that's behind us. We're cool with one another now, right?"

"Yes, thank you for forgiving my earlier behavior concerning hurting my sister's feelings." Oliver scowled in concern, "I overreacted at the time."

"You were being a protective sibling, that's normal. I have a little sister too and despite her being a roaring beast of a woman…" Mitch burst out laughing, falling back in his chair, "She's like, five-foot-tall, barely ninety pounds, but she is a fireball! Penelope is a famous writer in her part of the world. If you're not into comic books, you would have no clue who she was, but…" He abruptly stopped himself, "Sorry, getting off track." He resumed a serious expression, "My point being is that I get it, you're protective of your sister even though deep down you know she doesn't need someone to fight her battles for her or be her hero to save the day."

Oliver smiled, "Do you remember once Alice asked us how one defines success?"

"Oh yeah, I remember that." Mitch thought back to his memories of the experience, "Turned out to be a lot harder than I would have thought it would be to come up with an answer."

"I wish to become worthy of the woman I love. She has her career, a stable relationship with a man that loves her, and an incredible collection of companions in which she shares her life with." Mitch touched his chest with his hand as he smiled wide, fanning himself as if someone had just given him an esteemed award and he was dramatically thanking those who made it possible. Oliver laughed at his reaction before he assumed a more serious tone, "She has everything. I don't know anything that is missing from her life that she wouldn't strive to attain."

Oliver lightly rubbed his hands together in thought, "Meanwhile, I am as my mother stated correctly, a boat adrift on a sea of endless possibilities without any way to direct my path. I don't know what I want to do with my life."

Mitch sat up, leaning forward as he gave Oliver a lingering dissecting stare before speaking, "What are you passionate about? Life is all about finding passion. Mind you, this is bigger than just what do you like and what do you enjoy doing. Sometimes what we're passionate about takes work and determination to make it happen. Me, I love my job. I love pushing myself to do better in my career and I love my social life." He grinned, "That's what I was bringing into my relationship with Michael. I was a man filled with passion and desire to make my life as wonderful as possible. He was the same way with his own life. Now we are sharing two incredible lives together, making what was great to amazing status."

"That's the dilemma I am facing now. Mina is bringing so much into this relationship that…" Oliver struggled with what was happening in his life, "When we first met, we were both hiding from the world. Since then, she's bloomed like a flower in spring. Meanwhile, I am hidden away in a seed, afraid to grow into what could become the full potential of my life."

Mitch grinned happily, "I love the way you talk, all poetic. As much as I love my boyfriend, he does not talk as romantically as you do about your lovely lady."

"Other than Mina, what am I passionate about? What do I feel is akin to a way I feel about her? Nothing would ever compare to the love I have for her, of course, but…" Oliver sat back in his chair, "I haven't been involved with what would have been my career in so long, I've practically forgotten how to do so. Even with my degree returned to me, I don't have the experience I need…"

Mitch asked out of curiosity, "Mina has been tight lipped about all of this, so what exactly did your college degree do for you or would have if it wasn't for your mother?"

"I was going to be an architect, designing buildings and various structures and I was excited about bringing a new level of innovation to the field. When my life fell apart, so did my desire to create anything, let alone attempt to try to regain a new degree which I've certainly had time to do so since then." Oliver shook his head in consideration, "That was a lifetime ago."

"Doesn't sound like you're passionate about that anymore." Mitch didn't want to find the answer for Oliver, it was something the man needed to do on his own. "What is it that…?"

Suddenly Oliver's eyes lit up with a strange look of confusion and excitement, "Some part of me has been drawn to it. I have immensely enjoyed being a part of that experience in the past, but I am not sure how I could pursue this interest of mine." His brow furrowed in concern, "I certainly couldn't turn it into a career."

"Career and money can come later. Even then, that's nowhere near as important as finding your spark." Excited to hear what Oliver was thinking about and how something he had said earlier linked to it, Mitch asked, "Well, what is it? What is your thing? What helps define who you are, what you're passionate about, what is…?" He motioned towards the man sitting across from him, "You?"

Oliver smiled wide, "I want Mina to be the first to hear what I have in mind, if you are alright with that?"

Falling back in his chair with a load groan, "What! No fair!" Laughing Mitch concluded, "Fine… Whatever… But only because I love that woman." He grinned, "Nowhere near as much as you do, but she's my Kitten and I can't wait until she comes back home."

Chapter 11

"They want to sign you on for the full year with plans to bring you on permanently. This is the opportunity of a lifetime. In two years, you went from a low-level position in a cubicle to your own office, to aiding in the expansion of the company. You've proven yourself time and again that you are willing to make tough decisions and sacrifices to be on a fast track to being head of this branch of the company." Roy was in his late fifties, thinning hair with hints of gray sprouting throughout what remained. He led a comfortable life outside of time spent at work, which was practically consuming every moment of his life. He compensated by spending his money on elaborate meals and what Mina considered a luxurious lifestyle. All of which led to a rounded body that now sat in a chair that creaked under his weight as he spoke to her.

"Six months, Roy. That's what I signed up for, that's it." Mina leaned forward in her chair, giving the man across the desk an icy stare, "They practically had to beg me to extend my stay for another three months and now you're asking me to not only sign on for another three months, but possibly never go back home?"

Seeing resistance, Roy tried a gentle approach, "We were at a crucial juncture, in the final stages of setting things into motion. If you had left, it would have fallen apart. You are the keystone in all of this, without you, everything would come crumbling around us."

"I do the work of three people." Mina felt a growing anger with the situation, "I should know, my team started out with three of us handling what was being asked of us. What happened to them?"

"This is a tough business, demanding hours, you know that. This is a marathon, not a sprint. It takes endurance and strength of character, just like you have. We haven't been able to find anyone that comes close to meeting our expectations, the bar that you have raised for the position you now hold." Roy was quick to hint at change, "Now that the expansion is complete, new revenue will come in, and within a few quarters, we will be able to add to your staffing and alleviate the pressure that I'm sure you feel."

"You have been slowly witling me down to nothing while still paying me the same." Mina scowled, "As people leave, you don't hire new ones to take their place. You claim you can't afford to bring on more staff until the new branch of the company becomes profitable which may take a year or longer to make up for the loss it took to buy out the facilities we're now using here in Europe. I keep being given these promises that things will get better, the workload won't be as bad, and I'll be able to finally enjoy my life here. I've been all over Europe from England to France, Spain and Greece, never once do I get a chance to enjoy the sights or experience the culture. I'm shuffled from one building to the next to meet with people I barely had a twenty-four-hour notice in advance beforehand to prepare for."

Mina sighed in frustration, "I have fulfilled all the requests made of me and my position here. I have no interest in renewing my contract in this sector or extending my time here. I've barely seen my boyfriend six or seven times in the last nine months. I feel completely out of touch with what used to be my home and it feels like all the lives of my friends are moving on without me."

"I was hoping I didn't have to bring this up, but…" Roy cleared his throat, "Your previous position has been filled in your absence, it was a necessity. When you agreed to an extension, the man filling the position temporarily was given the option to take on the responsibilities permanently. We assumed you were showing interest in a long-term commitment to the company here at the European branch."

"You assumed? No one felt like communicating this to me?" Mina sat back in her chair, a deep scowl revealing her growing frustration, "Let me guess, some fine print in my contract that I either overlooked or more than likely, misinterpreted as meaning something else that is being taken in a separate way due to specialized wording that favors the company's interests at the time?"

"You are a valuable employee and due to your commitment to the company, I have been authorized to compensate you for whatever it is you wish to negotiate for. Higher raise, an extended paid vacation, open communication and I can see what I can do for you to resolve this situation." Roy leaned forward, resting his arms against the desk as he smiled. There was a look on his face as if he were speaking to a stubborn child resisting the command of a parent rather than a woman he respected.

"I would say I want my old job back, but after today, I realize I made a mistake. I thought this is what I wanted." Mina smiled, "I've proven to myself and everyone here that I can do it. It's no longer about that. I thought this company was different, but it's just like all the others. You reduce the staff until each person is doing the job of three people and for what? Company profit?"

Mina stood, giving Roy a lingering stare before concluding, "I used to think this is the job I wanted, the life I wanted, but it's not worth it. It's obvious to me that this company doesn't respect me. You make assumptions about what I want, decisions for what is best for the business rather than those who you employ. You offer incentives only when you fear losing someone valuable. That's just it, though, you don't value me. You'll probably replace me as soon as I leave, find someone else foolish enough to try to take on the responsibility of three or more people just so you can pay them a single wage that certainly doesn't compensate for the strain to their wellbeing both physically and psychologically."

Mina turned, heading towards the door. Pausing, she concluded, "You'll have my resignation tomorrow. I'll be leaving by the end of the week. I'm going home where I belong."

~

"I missed you." Tears had formed in Oliver's eyes as he stared into Mina's wide eyed, stunned expression. She struggled to breathe, having completely lost her breath during their first kiss after being reunited at the airport where he met her. Her heart was racing, her head feeling dizzy, and the rest of her body ready to collapse from the sheer passion expressed a moment before.

She lightly tapped his chest as she continued to smile, "Sit…"

Oliver turned, slipping his arm across her waist to help guide her and make certain she didn't fall. "You must be exhausted. Here, closest place to find a seat is this way." Concern etched itself into his features as he asked, "Are you alright?"

"Much better…" Mina leaned against him, touching the side of her head against his body, "Three months without seeing you, it's the longest we have ever been separated. I missed you too."

They walked in silence, enjoying the moment together as they found a seat where they could continue their conversation. Watching her carefully, Oliver asked, "Is there anything I can do for you? I feel as if I am greeting a soldier who has been to war, grateful that you are alive and well, afraid that what you've been through has changed you into someone I don't know." He suddenly covered his face, "I'm so sorry, when I started to say that it sounded better in my head. I feel horrible for…"

Mina silenced him with a touch of her fingertips against the soft texture of his lips. Everything about him was a collection of contrasts. He was as soft and gentle as the petals of a flower and the gentle caress of the wind upon one's cheek. Yet, a single touch of his body underneath her fingertips revealed that he was true to his word in that he said he had been eating a healthy diet and jogging in her honor, since that was the lifestyle that she had left behind to pursue her career. She never had any time to keep fit the way she used to, and meals were luxurious offerings at formal meetings or room service in at the hotel she stayed at. Firm to the touch, such strength behind every flex of his muscles.

It's what had first attracted her to him, a beautiful blending of strength and determination with a gentle kindness. He was able to not only stand up to her when need be, but challenge her, push her to be a better person. All the while he was offering her sanctuary, a place to let her guard down and feel loved.

"I must look awful." Mina had cut her hair shorter than what it had been before, nearly the length his was. It was easier to maintain during her hectic schedule than her longer hair had been. Her eating habits were dreadful. When she did well, it was at formal events, taking whatever was offered which was rare. The rest of the time she took quick bites to keep from starving, often passing out in her bed at her hotel before she ate much of anything. Breakfast was practically non-existent. She knew she had lost weight, no longer the vibrant strength she once possessed, now appearing withered, pushed beyond her limits.

Oliver gently touched his hand against her cheek, "You are as you have been from the moment that I first was given the blessing to gaze upon you, a radiant soul imbuing life to a magnificent woman that I feel humbled to call my own." He took her hand in his, gently kissing the back of it before smiling, "I love you, Mina."

"I love you…" Mina leaned forward, doing her best to wrap her arms around Oliver despite the arm rest separating them. He reciprocated, allowing her to touch her forehead against his shoulder. She could have fallen asleep at any moment they embraced, to lose herself in the world he created for her through his presence in her life. Pulling away, she looked up at his handsome face, the depths of kindness and warmth to be found in his gaze, and the gentle sweet smile that she felt was reserved just for her. "I think you're right. I feel like I've been to war in some far-off country, alone and isolated for too long. Meanwhile, everyone here has moved on with their lives, growing and changing without me." Tears had formed in her eyes as she looked away, "I have missed so much."

"I've kept you up to date with everything happening." To his surprise, Mina stood drawing Oliver to his feet, "What can I do to ease your suffering?"

Without looking back, Mina held out her hand, her fingers separated in a silent request. Following her gesture, Oliver interlaced his fingers with hers. She gently pulled forward as she began walking towards the area of the airport where she could claim her bags that she had traveled with, "I know you have and I appreciate it, but…" She sighed, staring at the space a few paces ahead of her on the ground, her mind lost in a torment of thought, "Alice and Hoven are going to be celebrating one year together. I've missed so much as how they've possibly changed and grown together as individuals and as a couple." She smiled, laughing at a thought, "I feel like a parent that missed out on nine months of their children's lives."

Gently squeezing her hand, Oliver smiled, enjoying the small gesture of feeling that connection with her, "If it helps you feel better, they are still who they were when you left, but more comfortable with one another. Alice is still rigidly formal about the progress of their relationship." He smiled, thinking about his experiences as a roommate, "Ever since I moved in with Hoven, finding a balance between the two of us has not been difficult, but it certainly has been a unique experience. However, I certainly don't think of either him or my sister as my children."

Mina leaned over, slipping her free arm around Oliver's, hugging it for a moment, "You would make such a wonderful father." She released her hold as she resumed walking with him, "I'm worried how I would be as a parent."

"There is no rush." Mina was suddenly brought to a stop when she realized Oliver had halted his movement. Turning, she looked up at his eyes, seeing concern and worry, "I'm sorry, that's horribly rude of me for saying."

Confused, Mina asked, "I love you, but sometimes you confuse me, so if you wouldn't mind explaining what's going on in that wonderful mind of yours?"

"I said, there is no rush to have children. That was implied expectations of what you desire to do with your body." Oliver swallowed nervously, "That is your choice, not mine. If you don't want to have children, I completely understand, and I will respect your wishes."

Mina reserved her response concerning a facial reaction by keeping a neutral look, "You would be alright with us never having children even though I know you've dreamed about what it would be like to have a son or daughter?" To her shock, he knelt in front of her, holding her hand. Her eyes widened in fear as she blurted out, "What are you doing?"

"Mina, you are the most important aspect of my life and will always be. What you desire, what you want from your life is of utmost importance to me. You are an incredible woman leading an astonishing life and I feel blessed each day to share that life with you." Oliver smiled, "I can only hope that the life I share with you in return provides the same joy and excitement that you do for me."

Leaning forward, Mina whispered, "Are you asking me to marry you?" She noticed people walking by had noticed what Oliver had done, some pausing thinking they may see a marriage proposal.

Oliver reacted in confusion, "I wouldn't do so in the middle of an airport surrounded by strangers. You deserve it to take place where you are most comfortable, at peace, and happy. You just arrived from a highly stressful situation and need time to adjust to life back home. This isn't the ideal time for such a momentous occasion, my love."

Feeling embarrassed from the unwanted attention of those nearby, Mina continued to speak in a hushed tone, "Then why are you kneeling like this? You do realize what other people are thinking right now?"

"I don't care what other people think, your opinion is the only one that matters to me." Pulling himself to a standing position, Oliver watched her in concern, "I'm sorry, I was trying to show my sincerity concerning the topic of our future together."

"That's fine and I appreciate it..." Feeling relieved, Mina smiled as she patted him on the chest, "It's just..." Suddenly her mind became distracted by the firm feeling of his body underneath her fingertips. She laughed before asking, "Do you want to go swimming?"

Confusion etched itself into Oliver's face, "Why?"

"It's one of the few times you'll run around without your shirt off." Mina made a small motion of her hand across his chest, "Right about now, I want as much of you as you're willing to give me." She grasped a handful of his shirt before she took a deep breath, letting it out slowly, "I feel your love in my soul. I can hear your words and listen to your thoughts in my mind. Those things I can experience anywhere in the world. However..."

Mina's hand slowly slid up Oliver's chest until her fingers began gliding towards his neck, "This part of you, I can only get in person and moments I've had a chance to be with you like this have been rare in the past few months and I am having serious..." She bit her lower lip as she concluded with her free hand finding a spot in the center of his back, her own body pressed against his. When she spoke, it was with a playful smile, "I miss all of you..."

"Oh..." Oliver hesitated, a part of him having forgotten what it felt like to be so close to his girlfriend after so long, "I see..."

Mina pulled away, staring up at him, enjoying every moment, "There is the man I truly love, right there."

Confused by the statement, Oliver asked, "I'm sorry, I don't understand."

Mina lightly touched her hands to his chest, "This... Is wonderful, I want this part of you too, but that beautiful, shy, bashful man that gets nervous when his girlfriend gets flirtatious with him about wanting to be with him intimately... That's the man I love so dearly. That is the man that invited me into his life, and made me feel safe, protected, and loved." She made a motion towards their surroundings, "Out there, I have to be strong, I have to be driven, and I have to prepare myself for whatever life throws at me."

She touched her hands to the sides of his waist, "Here, when it's just the two of us, I can be whomever I want to because with you, I'm home."

~

"Welcome home." Alice held Mina's hands firmly as she gazed up into her eyes. "I am so glad that you have returned."

"It's good to back." Mina glanced over at the room full of people, "I didn't realize I knew this many people until I started talking to them again after so long. Suddenly all these faces I recognized are saying hi to me and hugging me." She turned her focus to Alice, "I'm sorry, this is all surrealistic to me. I've been gone for so long. It feels like I stepped out of reality for a little while. Like I've been in a long sleep and just woke up."

"In some ways, much has changed. In other ways, it hasn't." Alice released her hold on Mina's hands before clasping them together behind her back, "I hope that you are well informed of all that has transpired."

"Yeah..." Mina looked across the room at Oliver who was doing his best to help Hoven navigate the social setting. "It's like hearing about the facts of history, but not experiencing what it was like to actually be there." She turned back to Alice, "There is a lot Oliver hasn't told me because he doesn't know the details of." She gave the other woman a concerned expression, "Your relationship for instance, it's been nearly a year since you two first got together. It appears that everything is going well." She laughed, "I don't mean ask about your private life or anything, it's just you two have such a unique relationship, I was hoping there wasn't any obstacles that you were facing that might be a problem?"

The party was being hosted by Mitch and his boyfriend who had gathered everyone together at his apartment. It was not the first time and certainly wouldn't be the last when a large group of people was together in his personal space. He loved planning, arranging, and being the cause of parties such as this one.

"There are things I must tell you in private." Alice glanced over at the collection of people, "I don't feel comfortable speaking of such things in a public forum such as this."

Mina's eyes flared wide in surprise, a hint of concern, but certainly dominated by curiosity. "That's not something I can wait for later." She grabbed Alice's hand as she gently guided her through the group of people who had gathered for the party. When asked what was going on, all she said was that she needed a moment to speak in private.

Mitch directed the pair of women to his bedroom for them to talk but asked after doing so, "What's going on?"

"Nothing." Mina grinned, "Just catching up."

His eyebrows rose in curiosity, "Are you going to tell me later about what you two ladies are needing to talk about so urgently?"

Mina glanced back at Alice who averted her eyes as a light blush crossed her face, "No."

Seeing Alice's reaction, Mitch pouted, "So not fair." He winked before concluding with a serious expression, "I understand, though, you two catch up. I'll distract the guests until you return."

"Thanks." Mina continued into Mitch's bedroom. Once she closed the door, she gave Alice a long, dissecting look before she asked, "What happened?"

Alice glanced back at the door, "Are you certain no one will hear what I have to say?"

Mina replied with something she didn't wish to know, "Don't ask me how I know, just that this room is practically soundproof."

"Alright then, if that is the case, I will tell you." Alice lightly rubbed her hands together in growing anxiety for revealing such a truth, "Hoven and I…" She steadied her breath, feeling lightheaded just thinking of the experience let alone speaking it out loud, "The two of us…" She brought up her hands to lightly rub her upper arms, "Our relationship reached a new stage of intimacy."

Mina's eyes flared wide, it felt as if her heartbeat had frozen in her chest just so that there would not be any distracting noises as to what she was about to hear next, "And?"

"It is a word that I feel embarrassed to even say out loud." Alice struggled to focus her thoughts, she was overwhelmed by what had happened, "I'm so sorry… I was taught that a man and a woman should not do such a thing before becoming husband and wife."

Mina's heartbeat returned along with the breath she had been holding onto. She didn't want to jump to conclusions, especially concerning Alice, but it certainly sounded as if… "What is the word you are afraid to say?"

"It begins with an S." Alice covered her face with her hands, "It was a moment of unbridled passion that drove us to do so. I yearned to be close to him, I was not thinking properly but to feel the warmth of his body…"

Mina wanted to scream for Alice to say it already but knew doing so would possibly ruin her chance of learning of what happened. Unlike Mitch, she didn't want the details, only confirmation of what the other woman was hinting at. Knowing how to handle the situation, she calmly said, "If you aren't comfortable telling me, that's fine. I understand. I know it's hard to…"

Lowering her hands, Alice held her arms firmly at her side as she announced the word, "Snuggle."

At first the word didn't register. It wasn't one she had heard often enough for it to sound normal to her. Finally, she blurted out, "What?"

"We snuggled." Alice lowered her gaze, staring at the space in front of her, "There is a large chair in my apartment, one that can easily fit the both of us due to our unique size in comparison to others who taller and wider than we are."

Not certain where this was going, Mina asked, "Okay, and?"

"We sat next to one another, our legs touching, our hips connected, I believe even a part of my…" Alice started to turn, glancing down behind her before returning to her original position as she concluded, "…toosh may have possibly brushed up against his." She began fanning herself with her open hands, "At one point, he put his arm around me…" She smiled wide, "It was more wonderful than I ever thought it would ever be. It was pure joy. I cried when it happened, I felt so embarrassed, but he was so comforting to me in that moment. I think he was feeling as shy and bashful as I was, it was a blissful, one that I shall never forget."

"How long ago was this?" Mina had learned to restrain herself in reaction to what other people told her. Now she fought back the urge to laugh at the pure delight that was Alice, something she missed dearly. She kept a serious expression, knowing that it was a topic of utmost importance to the other woman.

"A month ago." Alice quickly interjected, "We've only done so once, but I was wondering if I should do so again?"

"My advice to you is that every couple is different. What works well for one pair of people will feel uncomfortable for another. There is no standardized set of events that must be followed within a certain time frame for it to be considered normal for anyone. Some people move faster than others and that's okay. What's important is that both people involved are comfortable with what is happening. The other person stops and listens whenever anyone involved says they don't like what is going on. There should never be a feeling of regret or shame in what you do as a couple because each step taken is done so with careful consideration of the other person's feelings and happiness concerning the relationship." Mina smiled warmly, trying to encourage Alice to feel at ease. "I feel safe with your brother and our communication concerning intimacy is important to both of us. We often know what the other person wants or needs before we even realize we want or need it."

Alice smiled sweetly, "Hoven is the same way with me, he is attentive to how I react to him. I do my best to provide him that same level of trust and consideration of his feelings. I would not be here if it weren't for Oliver helping him out there. I know how he is around social events such as this, it can be overwhelming to him."

"Do you feel better about what happened?" What had been revealed answered a multitude of questions she had concerning Alice and Hoven's relationship.

"Yes, thank you." Alice rushed forward, wrapping her arms around Mina, "Thank you! I have dearly missed your wisdom and guidance." After giving the other woman a lingering embrace, she pulled away with a joyful smile, "You are like a sister to me."

"Well, if Oliver and I get married, you would be my sister-in-law." Mina shrugged, "Close enough, right?"

"Oh..." Alice stepped back, a strange look of confusion and curiosity flickering across her face, "Has he discussed the topic with you recently?"

What had been a happy moment a few seconds prior had suddenly turned into a cold chill racing across her skin, "Other than an incident at the airport when he kneeled in front of me to show his sincerity about how he felt, but made it abundantly clear that if he proposed, it wouldn't be in a public place like that, no?"

Alice struggled with something on her mind that she started to speak, stopped, fought with herself in an internal struggle before finally concluding, "It is not my place to speak of such things."

"Hey..." Mina instinctively touched her hand to Alice's shoulder, "What's going on? Is Oliver alright? He's not hiding something else from me, is he? He promised..."

Suddenly snapping out of her thought's Alice's eyes focused on Mina, "No! Of course not, Oliver..." She fought with herself, but it was a losing battle. Finally, she gave in, "He was going to propose to you shortly before you left for your business trip. A lot has happened since then, of course. I am uncertain of his intentions after what he has endured as of late."

"Oh..." Mina withdrew her hand as she nodded slowly, "I suspected that he was thinking about it, I didn't..." She smiled, trying to not allow her concerns to ruin the moment, "What I said about two people feeling comfortable about each step of a relationship applies to this situation."

"My brother loves you and, in my heart, I know that one day you will be wife and husband." Alice took Mina's hand, placing in between both of hers, "Remember what you have taught me, when the time is right, you will both be ready for that step in your journey together."

"Thank you." Mina returned her smile as she glanced back at the door, "We should probably get back to the party."

Alice nodded in agreement, "Thank you for taking this moment to listen to and provide me with heartfelt advice. I appreciate all that you have done for me."

Mina realized that the two women were the youngest daughters of each of their families. With a smile, she tried to conclude on a lighter note, "That's what sisters are for, right?"

~

"This is perfect." Mina was squeezed in next to Oliver, shoulder to shoulder in the back of his car. The seats had been folded down allowing them to lay out on a makeshift bed he had created for the pair to gaze out through the back window. Having parked at a downward slope, it created an ideal angle to look up at the night sky. It was a recreation of their first date they had been together during the colder months.

With his fingers interlaced together with those of his girlfriend, Oliver smiled, "I was hoping you would enjoy this."

"I love you." Mina shifted onto her side to look over at him. When they had first attempted the scenario on their first date, he had been shy, trying not to brush up against her. It was one of countless reasons she could not resist his heartfelt charm and kindness.

Matching her movement, Oliver gazed at Mina, "I love you."

They watched each other in silence, enjoying their moment together, knowing that words did not need to be spoken. They were holding each other's hands when Mina gently squeezed his. She smiled, "I want to spend the rest of my life with you."

Oliver's eyes flared wide in surprise at the statement. He started to speak, "Are you...?"

Mina shook her head, "I need to talk this out, just to clear my head of all of this." Seeing him nod slowly in agreement, she continued, "When I was gone, all I could think about was you. You got me through the hard days when I felt like I couldn't make it. It gave me the strength to stand up to them and walk away before they took too much from me. I don't want you to think that I'm depending on you for my happiness or that I'm needing you to..."

Mina struggled with her thoughts, speaking before she knew what she was going to say, allowing it to flow out of her, "I'm not happy without you. Knowing that you're in my life, even when you're not around is wonderful, but I need this. I want this, us together like this. You give me courage when I feel weak. You inspire me when I feel like I don't have the strength to continue. You make me laugh and smile when I feel like crying. Before I met you, I didn't understand what love was like, what it could provide me and how dearly it would affect me. I don't want to lose you again."

Mina's eyes slid closed as she was lost to waves of memories, "I remember when you first gave me that flower made from folded paper. It was with me on my trip, a constant reminder of what I left behind."

Mina opened her eyes to look at Oliver once more, "I want to spend the rest of my life…" She stopped herself, wincing, tears forming in her eyes, "More than that, I want to spend eternity with you. I don't know what happens afterwards, I don't care, I just want you to be there with me no matter what happens." She turned, rolling over as she pulled up her legs, whispering softly, "I'm sorry…"

Opening the door, she slipped outside, setting her feet down upon the road as she walked slowly around to the back of the car. She heard the other door closing behind Oliver as he rushed to meet her, "Are you alright?"

As she wiped tears from her eyes, Mina laughed at the absurdity of the situation, "I keep doing this to you. You set up something so beautiful like this and I become an emotional wreck, ruining such a romantic experience."

"The setting doesn't matter, what we do isn't important, all that does matter is that I am with you in this moment. That is all I need to make each moment of my life beautiful." Oliver concluded his statement as Mina moved forward, wrapping her arms around him, pressing the side of her head against his chest.

She spoke softly, "I don't deserve you."

"You deserve to be happy." Oliver gently brushed his hand across her hair, "Do I make you happy?"

New tears formed, soon vanishing into the fabric of his shirt as she answered, "Yes… More than words can say."

"You deserve that and so much more." Oliver held Mina in his arms, speaking softly, "A happiness that will last for eternity."

Chapter 12

"I want to marry him." Mina sat in the living room of Mitch's apartment as he watched her from a position next to her. Seeing little to no response, she asked, "That's it? I just made that statement, and you just stare at me like its whatever."

"Sweetie, I've wanted to marry that man from the moment I heard those honey coated words of beautiful poetry come out of his luscious mouth and I know perfectly well he's only into a certain lady I cherish with all my heart." Mitch sighed, "Do you mind me asking what changed your mind?"

"A lot of things." Mina turned away, staring at her hands folded in her lap, "You know me. I've been against the idea of marriage all my life. Relationships, sure, love I thought might happen, but never marriage. After what happened in college, I gave up on love too but obviously Oliver changed my mind about that." She smiled, "When I was gone for so long, all I could think about was him and this constant reminder that he wasn't there. I thought to myself, is this enough? Can I handle a lifetime of us being apart like that? Would I be okay with us living on two sides of the world?"

Tears formed in her eyes as she thought of those nights where she felt so isolated and alone in a place so far away from where and who she thought of as home. "I want to say, no, that would never be enough. That's why I came back but that's not it." She fought with herself, struggling to find the right words, "It would be enough. To know that Oliver exists, that somewhere in the world he was thinking about me. He said that…"

Teardrops fell onto her fingers, "He said... He would talk to me even though we weren't on the phone and knew that I couldn't hear him. When he felt sad or frustrated, he would speak to me for comfort. When he was feeling good, he would tell me about his day as if where I was, that I could hear him." She looked up, struggling to breathe, "He said that he knew that wherever I was, no matter what was happening to me at the time, my soul would hear him. I would feel him there within me, his presence, thoughts, and feelings. It would be a reminder that I wasn't alone."

She turned away, struck by a painful sensation that wracked her body, the mere thought of losing Oliver was torture. "He said that even if something happened to him, that I should not weep because he would always be with me, no matter what, for eternity." Mina tried to wipe the tears from her eyes with her hands as she continued, "I want him for eternity. I thought of marriage as contracts made between two people, legal documents binding them together. Maybe it is in the eyes of others, but not him. I don't care what anyone else thinks of the word, all I can think of is what he feels it represents."

Mina looked up at Mitch, "Marriage for Oliver is two souls bound together for eternity declaring to the world of this union. We are already connected in this way. I can feel him there with me in every beat of my heart. Sometimes I hear his voice talking to me, an echo of a memory to me, it's as if I'm listening to him all those times that he said something to me knowing I was in another part of the world. Wedding vows are a declaration, a symbol of what existed long before they said, I do."

Mitch fanned himself with his opened hands, tears in his eyes as he listened to Mina's heartfelt words. "I'm speechless. Me, of all people, I don't know what to say." He laughed, "I'm sorry, I just don't…" He wiped away tears as he tried to contain himself, "I love you two so much! I'm so happy for you!"

After the two friends shared a lingering embrace, Mina smiled as she regained her composure the best she could, "I think he's afraid to ask me after all this time. He knows how I used to feel about marriage and that's what held him back before. Now with his confession of hiding so much from me, maybe he thinks he's not good enough for me, that he made himself unworthy of me." She shook her head, "You know Oliver, he may think of himself as some knight who made a mistake and needs to go on a quest to redeem his honor or some such thing like that."

"I love that man, dearly, but yeah, he's…" Mitch sighed, "He's a lot more damaged inside than we ever knew. You were broken inside, and he helped heal you. He's on his own journey to make himself the man he thinks you deserve."

Mina felt like crying again but was able to contain herself momentarily, "He is the man I deserve. Right now. He doesn't need to do anything else. I want to marry him. I want to spend an eternity with him. I want to…" She fell back against the couch as she wilted, losing what energy that had been keeping every muscle in her body tense a moment before, "I would propose to him today if he didn't have this old-fashioned viewpoint of the man having to do it."

Mitch sighed in frustration, "Seriously? What is the key to any good relationship?"

Mina took in a slow breath, letting it out slowly, all the while glaring at Mitch, "You're making me feel stupid for having to say this, you know that, right?

Mitch laughed, "Sometimes we know the answer, but we need someone to confirm what we know is true."

"Fine, I'll say it." Mina muttered, "Communication."

Mitch raised his hand, cupping it behind his ear, "What was that again? I couldn't hear you."

Mina grinned as she spoke up, "Communication."

Lowering his hand, Mitch replied, "Exactly. Just talk to him about it. Don't play games, don't expect him to read between the lines and figure it out, don't put all this pressure on him to realize the truth when you can just come out and say it." A thought struck him, "How about this, tell him that you want to marry him. Give him this beautiful speech you just gave me about how you feel. People can change their minds on things, so just come right out and tell him. After that, conclude by saying something like, know that when you're ready to get married, I will say yes. That will be telling him that there is no pressure for him to get married right now either. For all we know, he's not ready yet to propose, he may have been before but he's dealing with a lot of stuff right now."

"That's perfect." Mina smiled, "I know I am going to regret saying this, but you're brilliant."

Mitch began pulling his phone out of his pocket, "Hold on, I want that recorded so I can make it as my ring tone." He held up his phone with a playful grin, "Now, say something like, Mitch, you are a brilliant man that I think is a complete and total genius."

Mina laughed, "I'll make you a deal. I will say it at the wedding reception. You can record it then, alright?"

Lowering his phone Mitch stared at Mina in open mouthed shock, "Are you serious?"

"Promise." Mina hugged her friend tightly, "Thank you so much for everything."

Mitch responded in a hushed tone, "Does this mean you're going to name your first baby boy after me?"

Pulling away, Mina punched him in the arm, "Just couldn't enjoy the moment, could you? You had to push it just a little bit too far." She pointed at him, "Shame on you."

"Hi, I'm Mitch." He held out his hand as if they were going to shake in greetings, "Have we met?" Lowering his hand he laughed, "You act like you're shocked by what I just said."

"In all seriousness, thank you for helping me through this." Mina smiled, "Besides, Oliver and I have already picked out names for our children, so…"

"Oh! How scandalous, you and him choosing baby names before you're ever getting this whole marriage proposal in the history books." Mitch acted shocked, "Alright, tell me, what beautiful names have you two picked out."

"It's something I'll let him tell you if he wants to, but it's kind of our secret." Mina smiled, "Another reason I love him."

"Speaking of secrets." Mitch noticed Mina's concerned expression so quickly moved forward, "Oliver said he had an idea of what passions in life he wanted to pursue but wouldn't tell me because he was saving that gem for his lady love. What was it?"

Knowing the answer Mina burst out into a fit of laughter, "He didn't tell you?" Once she regained her composure, she smiled wide, "I didn't think he was keeping it a secret from everyone." Suddenly her eyes flared wide as a realization struck her, "Good thing I didn't tell anyone else. Wow…" She reached for her phone, "Hold on."

Quickly dialing Oliver's number, she waited a few seconds. It kept ringing which made her think he was busy, and she would get her voice mail. Just as she was about to give up, she heard him answer, "Hi, it's me. Yeah, I don't want to bother you, but Mitch just asked me about what you told me concerning what you're doing, he said something about passions in life?"

Hearing Oliver's voice but unable to discern what was being said, Mitch was forced to wait as Mina nodded slowly before answering, "Would it be okay if we come by? I would love to show him in person. Mostly because I want to record the moment when he learns what you've been up to lately." She laughed, "I think it would be funny!"

Even though her boyfriend couldn't see her, she reacted with sad puppy eyes, as if he was there, "Please?" There was laughter before agreement that she could record their mutual friend. "Thank you, we'll be by there shortly." She paused before adding, "I love you, Oliver." Mitch felt like he was going to explode, seeing the level of just how much Mina had changed due to her boyfriend being in her life. She was practically glowing when she heard his response.

"Why did you just give that poor boy the sad puppy eyes?" Mitch wanted to scold her for what she had done.

"Oliver is more than happy for you to see what he's been doing for the past few weeks, so that isn't what he had concerns about. He thought it was mean for me to record your reaction when you saw it for yourself." Mina laughed, "He finally gave in and said it would be okay, only if you were alright with it."

Mitch touched his hand to his chest, "See? That's why I adore that man, willing to stand up to his lady love to protect the honor of his friends and show us such wonderful respect." He held out his hand, "Now give me your phone to remove temptation to record something I know will end up on some social media page or video channel. Just my luck, my video goes viral, and I'll be known as that guy who freaked out over what his friend's boyfriend has been up to."

Mina clutched the phone to her chest, "No!" She laughed, "It will be for my private viewing only, promise!"

"Fine..." Mitch quickly moved to his feet, "Come on, let's see what your sweetie baby has been hiding from me."

~

"See, this is why I wanted to film you." Mina laughed, "However, I will settle for photos." She had her phone held up in front of her, taking reaction shots of Mitch's wide-eyed, open-mouthed response to what he was seeing.

Mina had driven the pair to a building with the markings of *Movement of the Soul* on display across the top. It didn't appear to be much, a renovated older structure without much to draw the attention of those walking by beyond the bold lettering above the doors. Not knowing what he was getting into, Mitch entered.

After moving down a corridor and up a set of stairs, Mina guided him to a door that opened to a large room. Once inside, she closed the door silently behind her as she took photos without a flash to accompany it. Thankfully the room was well lit, so she didn't need it. She didn't want to interrupt what was playing out before Mitch's eyes.

In pairs of two, the majority of which was one man with a single woman, but there were some that were of the same gender. Not all were couples, but all were students learning of a style of dance that was often used at weddings and other formal occasions. It was clear that they weren't experts of their craft, many fumbling with their movement, but they weren't completely inexperienced either which led Mitch to lean over and speak softly. Thankfully, the music playing masked his speech from those who were focused on what they were doing. "How long has this been going on?"

"A few weeks. I did the research, made the connections, offered to set up a meeting with the woman running the studio. We met with her. She asked for Oliver to show his skills at formal dancing and within a few minutes she was more than happy to sign him on to help. It doesn't pay well, but he doesn't do it for the money. He's using the skills he learned when he was younger, a formal education of his mother to embody styles of dance typically known to royal families. To say that she was impressed with his skills is an understatement." Mina smiled as she resisted the urge to laugh at the memory of the woman's shocked expression, "She said that she could learn a few things from him."

Mitch quickly agreed, "I can see that."

Mina slipped her phone into her pocket, leaving her thumbs hooked on her belt as she watched with a wide smile. When Oliver moved it was graceful, fluid, almost like he embodied the music playing. Each note guiding his muscles in perfect synchronization. He was currently dancing with a young woman who seemed entranced by the focus he was keeping on her dark blue eyes. He was trying to teach her to not rely on watching where she was moving, to allow her body to respond to the music and the person leading.

For some, watching their boyfriend dancing with other women would be a concern. Mina was never the jealous type to begin with. She didn't care what he would do when she wasn't around even if it was with others who were interested in him romantically or intimately. Secondly, she knew Oliver was devoted to her. He would never cause her harm by doing something inappropriate with someone else.

It was a question she had been asked by several women who attended his classes. Was she comfortable with him dancing so close to other women? In Mina's eyes, the answer was easily seen with the way he was with others. He was formal, although he appeared relaxed and comfortable with his students, in her eyes she could see how rigid he was. He was instructing, not trying to make a personal connection with his partners.

When he danced with her, it was a unique experience. He held her close when he could. His hands caressed her body, where with others he would lightly touch them when necessary. There was a yearning to be with her that he did not reveal with anyone else in dozens of small, subtle ways that delighted Mina.

"I know that look." Mitch had leaned over, speaking just loud enough to be heard over the music playing nearby, "You're thinking about your first dance, aren't you?"

"Yeah…" Mina didn't hide her emotions towards Oliver. She used to, but after being separated from him, she felt foolish for holding back for so long. She didn't know how long she would have to be with him, a moment could take him away as did her job offer. She wanted to enjoy every moment she could to the fullest. Smiling she glanced over at Mitch, "It was the first time I ever wanted to…" She laughed, "I felt this intense desire…"

Mitch quickly placed his hand over her lips, "Wow, take it back a few notches. Did you forget that there are about a dozen people right over there?"

Mina laughed as he pulled his hand away, "He's made new friends, people who he met through his experiences here. It has given him the opportunity to explore what he enjoys and to socialize where he has something to offer others who are eager to learn."

"Are we going to get a chance to talk to him or is this an inconvenient time?" Mitch wanted to speak to Oliver, but it felt like he would be interrupting what he was watching.

"Not anytime soon. I called him shortly before his class began. I wanted to show you what he's been doing lately." Mina grabbed onto Mitch's arm, "Come on, we can meet him afterwards." She gently tugged at him until she reached the door, pulling them both to exit the room. Once in the hallway, she closed the door gently behind them as she began speaking, "He said you inspired him to do this and the other thing that you told him to do."

Not knowing what she was referring to, Mitch asked, "Wait, what? What other thing?"

Confused that he genuinely didn't know, Mina's eyes flared in surprise, "I thought you knew about that at least, you were the one…" Her eyes narrowed as she studied the bewildered look her friend was giving her. Typically, she would assume that he was joking around with her, but he honestly didn't know. "Wow… I thought…" She laughed, "I love him so much right now."

"You love your boyfriend because he's keeping secrets from me?" Mitch folded his arms across his chest as he dramatically pouted, "I'm hurt that he would do that to me and more so that you're enjoying this so much!"

"Of course, I'm enjoying this. Normally you're the first to know about everything, you find a way to get it out of them even when people try to keep secrets. It's frustrating." Mina smiled playfully as she turned way, heading down the hallway, "I'm glad to know that I'm the first to learn about these things." She glanced over her shoulder, "Not even Alice knew about either of the two things he's been doing. He waited to tell me first."

Mitch quickly caught up, "Wait, Alice knows?" Seeing Mina nod in agreement, he sighed in frustration, "Of course Precious knows, those two shares more things with each other second only to you and Oliver. I should have known." He shook his head in frustration, "This is a first for me, being the one on the outside looking in, not knowing what's going on before everyone else does."

"Now you know how I feel most of the time around your other friends." Mina grinned, "Welcome to my world."

Slipping his arm across her shoulders, Mitch smiled, "I'm sorry, Kitten, I didn't know we were making you feel like you didn't belong. You are always the center of my attention second only to my cuddly cutie I have waiting for me at home."

Mina laughed, "Are you talking about your dog or your boyfriend?"

Not realizing a comparison could be made, Mitch bit his lip to not respond with his initial reaction, "I was talking about Michael, but my adorable corgi would fit the bill quite nicely now that I think about it." He laughed, "I didn't know I had two cuddly cuties! That's adorable, I love that!"

Mina had slipped her hands into the pockets of her pants, a rare find that allowed her to do so, "I've thought about getting a cat or a dog, but that would make it harder for me to find an apartment and limit my options since a lot of places don't accept pets."

"You've got the money. You can probably live off your savings comfortably for the next year, especially if you keep rooming with a certain gorgeous man who loves having you at his place. The landlord and I are like best friends, so her giving it an okay for you to stay for a while hasn't been a problem. However, knowing you, you want to move forward in your life." Suddenly he stopped, grabbing onto a shoulder as she turned her to face him, "Wait, are you stalling in finding a place on your own?"

"No…" Mina studied his face, "Why would you think that?"

"Is there going to be a special event involving a Kitten and an Angel soon?" Mitch looked for any hint of details that would be revealed in her reaction, "Is there something you need to tell me?"

"No..." Mina sighed, "No! You would be..." She hesitated, "Well, the first person I would tell, not sure if you would be the first person to find out. Alice may learn about what happened before you, but that's just because she's family."

"If I find out that his mother knows before me, I'm going to scream." Mitch released his hold on Mina as he stepped back, "Fine, just saying, I need to know as soon as possible, don't spare the details of what happened either when the time comes."

Mina smiled, "Fine, all the dirty details."

"Oh!" Mitch touched his hand to his chest, "My favorite kind of details!'

Resuming a more serious expression, Mina turned away as she headed towards the exit of the building, "Oliver just moved in with Hoven and I think they need time together in this stage of their life. Hoven is learning to live in a place that is more stable, to feel like he doesn't have to be on the move or a quick escape from his life like he did before. Oliver needs to grow as a person, to..." She smiled warmly at the thought, "...bloom like a flower in the spring warmth caressing its petals."

"Sounds like something he would say." Mitch grinned, "When he speaks, it's like poetry." Mina laughed at his statement drawing him to ask, "What was that for?"

Mina grinned, "Nothing."

"Anyway..." Mitch glared at her, knowing he wouldn't get any additional information if he asked, "How are they doing?"

Mina wasn't sure how to best answer his question, "They have found a way for it to work."

Mitch gave her a deep scowl, "That doesn't sound good."

"It's a unique situation, just like Alice and her roommate have with their living setting." Mina shrugged, "I would have never put those two men together as roommates, but somehow they're making it work."

~

"May I come in?" Alice stood at the doorway to the joint living space of her boyfriend and brother. She had participated in helping the pair of men move in but had not been involved in the unpacking process and was curious about how they were doing. It was the first time she had visited their home since that first day.

"Sure, yeah, of course." Hoven stepped aside, feeling self-conscious about his personal space. "Sorry, I'm not used to visitors."

As Alice entered, her eyes slowly swept across the main living space as she spoke, "Has Mina not visited recently?"

Hoven laughed nervously, "No, they go somewhere else. I'm like, she can visit, and you can do whatever it is you want to do here. I mean, I have a girlfriend myself so it's not like a big deal." He shook his head, "I think they treat me like a little kid, it's weird."

Alice refrained from smiling, often she felt the same way. However, she didn't wish for her reaction to come across as derogatory towards what Hoven was feeling. "They are at a different stage in their relationship than we are. Possibly they believe public signs of affection may make you uncomfortable."

"It's not like I'm going to hang out in the room they're in while they're together." Hoven shook his head slowly as he sighed, "Whatever. Life of the reluctant hero."

Nearing the center of the room, Alice turned slowly with a smile, "Reluctant hero?" As Hoven approached her after closing the door behind her, she touched her hand lightly against his cheek which sent shivers of excitement across his body, "You are a hero. You survived ordeals that would have broken most in your place. You have made sacrifices of your comfort to aid others and to provide a sense of serenity in those you love." She withdrew her hand as she asked, "May I?" She touched her fingertips to her lips before lightly tapping her cheek.

Smiling nervously, Hoven nodded, "Yeah." Instinctively he closed his eyes, his shy reaction taking over as he turned his head. When Alice kissed his cheek, he felt the strength in his legs begin to give out on him as all tension in his body relaxed. "Thank you."

Sensing the need for him to do so, Alice suggested, "Would you like to sit down?" Most of what filled the public space of the apartment was from Oliver's house which provided enough seating for four people.

Opening his eyes, Hoven looked towards the back of the apartment, "Would you like to see my bedroom?"

Alice's eyes flared with surprise at such a bold statement. "Oh goodness."

To Hoven, his bedroom was nothing more than a contained space where he slept. It was his secluded area where he could decorate it as he saw fit and had complete control over who visited. When he made the offer, he didn't realize the implications as to what it may mean for his girlfriend, "Sorry, I just thought…" His gaze fell to the floor, "There was just something I wanted to show you."

"It is I who should apologize for reacting as I did. I know you would not imply that we engage in intimacy without discussing it beforehand." Just the mere mention of the word connected to a couple's personal desires for one another made Alice blush. "I would be honored to accompany you to your private quarters."

Hoven grinned, "I like the way you talk. Makes me feel like I'm royalty."

Alice smiled sweetly in response, "In my mind, you are my future king. You are worthy of such admiration."

As Hoven escorted her the short distance to his bedroom, he replied, "I'll stick to your loyal knight, my queen." Clasping her hands together in front of her, Alice was practically glowing with joy as she approached the door to his bedroom. "I know it's not much." He paused before opening the door, "Thank you for talking me into getting an actual bed."

"You were going to sleep on a cot most often used for camping." Alice shook her head, "You deserve to enjoy comfort after all you have endured." She took his hand in hers as she smiled, "What is it that you wished for me to see?"

"Before you see it, don't freak out on me, okay?" Hoven hesitated, "I just, I'm not used to having a space to decorate or do anything with, so…" He turned, opening the door to his room before stepping aside.

Forced to release her hold on his hand, Alice moved cautiously forward, curious as to what she would see. She was barely a step inside when her hands moved quickly to cover her mouth, "Oh Hoven!" Tears formed in her eyes as she smiled.

Hoven avoided eye contact, feeling nervous, "I hope you don't think I'm weird but it's all I could think about putting up."

Alice had forgotten to breathe. She was in such awe of what she was observing. The room was empty, only a bed was set into one corner. Everything Hoven owned was put away in the closet or stored in a cabinet in the bathroom. Across the four walls were two rows of framed pictures that were eight inches wide and ten inches tall. She could see that Oliver had helped decorate in the room in that each frame was evenly spaced apart, approximately six inches separating them.

Within each frame was an image of her, pictures that he had taken of her since they had first met. Despite her posing for a multitude of images, she noticed that these were ones that were in the moment, as if he had caught a still frame of life as it was happening. "This is so beautiful, thank you dearly for this." Tears began streaking her face as she did nothing to remove them, "I know I have said this before, but you are an incredible photographer. You have a natural talent for this craft."

Hoven stared at the floor, his arms pressed against his body, "You don't think this is weird?"

Alice became concerned, "Why would you think that?"

Looking up, he realized she was crying, "I'm sorry, I didn't mean to upset you, it's just..."

Touching her cheek, Alice smiled, "These are tears of joy, my dearest Hoven. I am honored that you did this."

"Cool." Hoven wasn't certain how to respond so fumbled his way through it, "I just thought, you make me happy, so..."

New tears formed as emotions bubbled up within Alice's chest, "I am in awe of you." She hugged him tightly in attempt to relieve the concern he was feeling. "This is a beautiful thing you have done, thank you." Releasing her hold on her boyfriend, she stepped back to look into his blue eyes, "What inspired this?"

"I like looking at you, thinking about you, and I was honestly scared to move into a place like this. I lived in my car because buildings make me feel trapped, like a prison. So, when I agreed to do this with your brother, I did so without thinking too much about how it would make me feel. When I first moved in, I couldn't sleep at all. I was so stressed out by just being here, I was feeling suffocated. Oliver noticed I was awake all the time, sleeping in my car rather than in here. He said I should find something that helps me deal with the stress and I thought of you. So, he helped me create what you see on the walls."

Before he had a chance to speak further, Alice resumed hugging him, pressing the side of her face against his shoulder as she cried, releasing the floodgate of emotions. Hoven returned the embrace, not sure what he had done to cause what was happening but was happy to provide her comfort. He wasn't sure if he should say anything but blurted out what was on his mind, "I should be the one to thank you. Without you in my life, I wouldn't ever have the courage to overcome my fears of being in a place like this. I know I did it to help Oliver, but… I don't know, I just wanted to say that I don't know, I just… I'm not good at talking like you are, sorry."

Pulling away from him, Alice smiled, "I feel ashamed that I don't have more framed images of you where I live."

Feeling embarrassed, Hoven nervously smiled, "It's okay, you don't need me to give you courage the way I need you. You're strong enough on your own, like a queen. I wish I were more like you, able to talk like you do and have the strength you do."

"I will tell you a secret to my courage and strength. I become scared just as you do. I hesitate sometimes when I shouldn't. What gets me through these moments is thinking about the people in my life that I admire and look up to. My brother, Mina, Mitch, and most importantly, you." Taking his hands in hers, Alice smiled, "I admire you for the man you are. Many who endured the hardships that you faced before we met would have changed them into a nasty sort of person that were like those who tormented you. You chose not to become like your abusers, you rose above it, staying true to the man you wanted to become. You may not have shining armor, nor would I want you to be adorned in such a manner, but you are certainly my hero, my knight, my dearest love."

Releasing the hold on her hands, she touched her fingertips to her lips, "May I?"

"Yeah, of course." If he could do so, Hoven certainly felt like he was blushing at the thought of her kissing his cheek once more. Turning his head, he closed his eyes.

To his confusion, he felt her fingertips on the side of his face that were turned away from Alice. Keeping his eyes closed, he turned his head in confusion. Just as he was about to speak, he felt her lips touch his.

Chapter 13

"True love's kiss." Oliver walked alongside Mina, holding her hand as he spoke, "It is said that it is the most powerful magic in all of the world, that it can break any curse, heal a broken body, and even bring someone lost back to you."

Mina smiled, nodding at the memories of stories her grandmother would tell her, "Are you saying we're in a fairy tale?"

Oliver calmly replied, "When I first saw you, I thought I was in a dream. A woman such as yourself asking for help in a dangerous situation. I guess in that moment I was the hero saving a damsel in distress from a despicable villain." He nodded slowly, "However, the next day when I was trapped outside my house and later when I was walking home, lost in the middle of the night, you became my knight in shining armor rescuing me from a fate that would have been most unfortunate."

"Hoven would think we are in the pages of a book, our story worthy of legends, fairy tales, and myths. The way he sees it, we are a god and goddess living high upon a mountain peak looking over the mortal realm. My mother is an evil queen, Alice is the good queen, and he is the reluctant hero who wants nothing to do with being the protagonist in this tale." Oliver laughed at the wild look in the other man's eyes when he had first come to his original theory, "He is Alice's loyal knight, faithful and true, while Mitch is a messenger of gods, speaking to mortals and the divine alike."

Mina grinned, laughing at the thought of Mitch with little wings on his feet, "That's my favorite part of the story."

"I've felt like I've been in a fairy tale, not the real world that is our lives. When I'm with you, it feels like magic exists, dreams can come true, and if we wish hard enough for something, it will become reality." The couple approached a familiar building, having parked close by and they walked to their destination. Mina had a feeling that this was where she was being led to. "Speaking of which... There was something I wanted to show you, a surprise I have been working on shortly after you left for Europe. With a lot of time on my hands, I thought it would be an ideal thing to focus my time and energy on."

Mina's eyes narrowed as she studied what should be darkened windows of a restaurant that she was familiar with. It was the same location that Mitch worked at, it should have been completely shut down nearly an hour ago and yet it appeared as if there were signs of life inside. Turning back to Oliver with a playful smile, she asked, "Did he have something to do with this?"

"He leveraged several favors according to him to make this happen. It was sold to the owner as a private party, since I needed a location to properly display what I was needing help with." Oliver nodded slowly, "I have much to thank Mitch for in arranging this."

Mina glanced over at the front door, "There isn't a bunch of people in there going to yell out surprise, are they? My birthday is months away, so that can't be it." Curiosity flickered across her face, "Or is it? Are you making up for my last birthday when we couldn't be together until like a month later?"

Oliver held up a key in his hand, "We will be alone. Mitch gave me keys to the building after he locked it after leaving."

"Okay, you've piqued my curiosity." Mina bit back what she wanted to say, to ask a question that may ruin the moment, "How many people were involved?"

"As a magician once said, a man of mystery and magic, I wouldn't want to give away all my secrets. It may ruin the fun of the grand reveal." Approaching the door, Oliver quickly unlocked it before stepping aside, "Ladies first."

Grabbing onto Oliver's arm on the way through, Mina playfully tugged him forward with her, "Mr. Kent, if you're going to be a part of my life, you need to learn to walk beside me, not in front or in back. I want a companion in life, not a leader or follower."

Joining her, they moved through the main lobby which was well lit as if the business was in operation. The last time she had visited, it was brimming with people waiting to get in. Standing near the hallway leading into the main eating area, Oliver held out his hands for Mina to take, "Would you please close your eyes if only for a moment."

Giving into his request, she let herself to be led through the corridor that separated the main lobby from the dining area. When he came to a stop, she asked, "Is it okay for me to open my eyes yet?"

"One moment." Unknown to her, Oliver was inspecting what had been done on his behalf by his sister, Hoven, Mitch, and a group of Mina's friends. He had done the arduous work in creating what his girlfriend was about to see, but he wanted to make certain everything was perfect. Finally, he turned back to her, taking in a deep breath. Letting it out slowly, he finally answered, "On the count of three. One... Two... Three..."

Mina revealed her gaze as shock washed over her. She wanted to speak, but her mouth opened and closed without a sound escaping. Just above eye level were a series of strings spread across the length of the large room. Interconnected with the architecture of the open space. Each had been carefully tied into place before what Oliver had created was attached to be seen by the two-person audience now standing before them in the center.

"When we first met, I folded a piece of paper into the shape of a deer. When we were began dating, I created a flower out of paper to represent my sincerity in how I saw a future between us. One of my favorite moments was when I presented to you an entire bouquet of carefully folded flowers for you on our first anniversary." Oliver fought the urge to cry at the memory, the pure joy in Mina's eyes was beautiful. "When I realized that I would have a lot of time on my hands when you left, I thought of a Japanese legend concerning the folding of paper."

Taking a step back, Oliver opened his arms wide to collection now on display, each carefully separated from one another across the vast array of strings placed throughout the room. "What you see is nine hundred and ninety-nine origami paper cranes."

Mina's eyes drank in the details as she turned slowly. They were a vast array of colors, different shades of each, as if he were able to find a different tone for each one. "That's incredible." Turning back to him, she asked, "Why? Why did you do this? Why cranes?" She stopped herself, "I'm sorry, this is beautiful, it truly is, I just am wondering what it means?"

Olive grinned, "I was about to explain…"

Feeling embarrassed, Mina cringed, "I'm so sorry." She approached him, taking his hands in hers, "Go on."

"Legend says that if someone folds a thousand paper cranes, you are granted one special wish." Oliver motioned towards a nearby table, "That piece of paper there will be number one thousand. When I finish, I will be given the chance to ask for anything."

Feeling a chill racing across her skin, Mina fought back tears, "This is…" She struggled to breath, "I don't know what to say."

"You don't have to say anything just yet." Oliver approached the table and began work on carefully folding the piece of paper into the shape he desired. Mina stepped up close to him, watching his slender fingers delicately move with practiced skill. After folding so many, he was an expert at the task. When he was finished, he held it out before Mina, letting it rest in hand. With his empty hand, he made a silent request for her to take it. When she did, he began what he wished to express to her, "I spoke of magic, the power of true love, and the fact that we can create our own fairy tales and make the impossible a reality in our day to day lives. We just have to believe with all our heart and soul."

Both were on the verge of tears, each fighting against giving into a sign of emotion just yet, "Think of me as your genie, here to grant you a single wish. I have invoked this magic. It is mine to give it to the woman I cherish with all my soul. I must ask you, what does your heart desire above all else? How would you like this magic to take shape in your life? What is your wish?"

Tears fells down her cheeks as Mina asked, "Would you marry me?"

Unable to hold back any longer, tears quickly fell down Oliver's face as he lowered the crane in his hand, "Your wish is granted." The crane dropped to the floor at their feet as he caressed her cheek in his hand, "Yes, my dearest Mina. I have wanted to marry you from the moment I first said the words, I love you." They kissed, a nervous laughter soon followed as he asked in a near whisper, "I hope there is enough magic left to grant two wishes."

Mina was crying, not caring about holding back her expression of emotions, "What would you wish for?"

Oliver smiled, not making any movement to wipe the tears from his face, "Would you spend an eternity with me, both in this world and beyond, two souls forever bound together by true love?"

"Yes..." Unable to hold back any longer, Mina moved closer to Oliver, wrapping her arms around him tightly, pressing the side of her face against his chest as she clung to him, desperately not wishing to ever let him go in fear of that beautiful moment from every coming to an end. "I love you, my sweet Oliver."

Returning the firm embrace, Oliver touched the side of his cheek to the top of hair, "I love you, my precious Mina."

~

"I am so happy for you both." Alice hugged Mina before pulling away to embrace her brother. Finally, she stepped away from the couple as she clasped her hands behind her back, "I feel overjoyed. I knew it would go well. I have known the both of you to be deeply in love with one another and each wishing the same things to be with one another in matrimony. I am most pleased to know that you are now betrothed to one another."

"One day you'll have me as a sister-in-law." Mina grinned, "I had an older brother, but never a sister. I like the idea of having one in my life." She cringed, realizing how bad that may have sounded, "I have felt like you're a sister to me long before now, but now it will be more official."

"In the eyes of the public, yes, I will be a part of your family through your matrimonial union." Alice giggled, "As is your heartfelt love for one another now revealed to all, you have taken this momentous step towards a future with one another. However, as the two of you knew and those who cared about you likewise were aware, you have felt this way long before the moment that you became engaged to one another. Your marriage will a proclamation of what already exists in each of your hearts."

"Speaking poetry runs in your family, I see." A thought flickered across Mina's face. They were visiting Alice at her apartment, given a chance at privacy since her roommate was currently at work and wouldn't be home for hours. "Speaking of which…" She wasn't sure if she should bring it up but felt it would be needed to be addressed eventually. Since she had essentially those that she considered family with her, it seemed like the ideal time to speak of the topic, "Who from each of our families are we inviting to the wedding?"

Oliver and Alice exchanged worried looks before he replied, "In all honesty, I am not close to either of my older brothers or their families. As far as I'm concerned, they won't be attending. As for my mother, I don't believe it would be appropriate for her to be involved in my private life."

"I haven't spoken to either of my parents in years, not since I moved out. They made some attempts for about a year to keep in contact, but I ignored them, so obviously they're not going to be there." Mina squeezed Oliver's hand, "I'm sorry, we should be excited, and I brought up all this negative stuff."

"Just because we don't want to speak of these concerns, doesn't mean they'll go away." Oliver kissed her softly on the cheek, "We will have to address all concerns eventually. I think it would be best that we get those out of the way early, so it doesn't ruin our enjoyment of our engagement in the future."

"If you don't mind an intrusion into your personal discussion?" Seeing the couple focus their attention upon her, each showing signs that it was acceptable for her to continue without appearing to be rude in the form of an interruption, Alice asked, "If you are not inviting any members of your families, myself being an exception of course, who will you be inviting to your wedding? I am assuming Mitch and myself, with our significant others. Is there anyone else you wish to include?"

Mina laughed nervously, "We're still in the announcement stage of all of this, the whole tackling the planning aspect of it, terrifies me." She looked over at Oliver, "I'm not one of those women who had this perfect wedding planned out years before the time came. This is all unknown territory for me."

Oliver caressed her cheek with his free hand, softly kissing her on the forehead, "Whatever we decide to do, we will do so together. I refuse to be the type of man who sits idly by and forces his fiancé to do all the work. This is a partnership."

Mina smiled sweetly as she mouthed the words, "I love you." She bit her lower lip for a moment as she gazed into his beautiful eyes before speaking, "Well, Mitch loves planning parties and I would think he would consider this the ultimate party planning opportunity. You know how I said something about women who plan out their perfect wedding? I think Mitch was a little boy planning out his perfect wedding, so he may be able to help us out." She grinned, "Besides, I did say he was going to be the second to know of our engagement if and when it happened after Alice was informed of our decision."

Alice giggled at Mitch's strong reactions lately, "He has been rather perturbed that he is not the first to learn of tidbits of personal information concerning his friends as of late."

~

"I'm just going to lay here for a little bit and enjoy the glow of this moment." Mitch was on the floor of his apartment, his arms pointing away from his body with his legs spread apart as if he was creating a snow angel on his carpet. He would not be doing such a thing in anyone else's home, but he was meticulous in keeping his home exceptionally clean.

Mina laughed, "Best reaction ever, thank you." She lightly clapped her hands together.

"I don't care if you're being sarcastic or not, I'm not going to allow that to spoil my moment." Mitch sighed happily, "It's like I've been waiting for this from the moment you first started talking about your Angel. I knew you were madly, head over heels in love with the guy then and there. I'm so glad that you two are getting hitched."

Oliver, who was standing close to Mina who was holding onto his arm, asked, "Getting hitched?"

Mitch sat up, bracing his upper body with his arms, "I'm so sorry. I love my parents to death. They are wonderful people but sometimes the way they talk bleeds through. My sister and I do our best to not allow our roots to surface our day-to-day speech, but it does from time to time. One time, I used the word fixins in a conversation with my manager, I was so embarrassed." He shifted to a sitting position as his face lit up with excitement, "Speaking of my famous little sister, would it be okay if I invite her to the wedding? I think it would be an amazing experience for you to meet her and her roommate."

Oliver looked over at Mina, "It would be fine by me, but I don't want to assume that..."

Mina grinned before answering, "Oliver needs to meet her. I love being around her, she's incredible."

Doing a small roll onto his feet, Mitch shifted his gaze between the two individuals before him, "So, do you have a date planned or are we still in the initial stages here."

Oliver laughed nervously leaving Mina to answer, "As we told Alice, we're just announcing our engagement at this point. We don't have anything planned yet."

"Oh, so I was second on the list again, which is fine..." Mitch touched his hand to Mina's shoulder, "You did warn me and Precious is family, so I forgive you." Withdrawing his hand, he continued, "Let me guess, you assume that because I'm good with parties, I would be ideal choice to help with the wedding?"

Mina revealed a sheepish grin before looking over at Oliver. Finally, she returned her focus to her friend as she answered, "Yeah? I thought, since you're good with parties, a wedding is pretty much a big party, right?"

"Oh sweetie, there is an enormous difference between throwing a party, arranging a get together for friends, or even setting up a major social event, and that of planning a wedding. It's like comparing Oliver and I. Sure, we're two gorgeous men that anyone would be blessed to be with, but obviously there is a laundry list of details that makes us different." Mitch laughed, "The most obvious difference being our eyes." He touched the spot next to his eyes, "Brown eyes..." He pointed to Oliver, "Green eyes." He concluded with a wink, "See my point?"

"Cute." Mina shook her head slowly, "Anyway... I guess that puts us back at not knowing where to go from here." She turned her focus to Oliver, "Maybe I can begin research into it? Find out some details and then we can discuss what I've found?"

Oliver was feeling optimistic, "I can meet with some of the students I work with at my dance classes, ask for advice, maybe get some information based off experiences."

Mitch touched his hands to each of their shoulders, "I admire your attitude, but I'm not about to let two novices go fumbling around in the dark without a flashlight on your major life event." His face scrunched up in anger, which was rare for the man, "I hate it when someone says it's the most important day of your life. As if everything that follows is sliding down hill and that your wedding day is where you peak and it's just going to get worse from there."

Stepping back from the couple, Mitch apologized, "Sorry, call it a pet peeve, just bugs me." He gave himself a small pause to calm down before continuing with a smile, "Anyway, enough of that out of me. This is all about your special day. I want you to speak with an expert on the subject matter. She is brilliant at what she does. She even makes wedding gowns from the ground up, so it will be unique and perfectly fit to your desires. She could go full time wedding planner if she wanted to but let's just say she has run up against too many doors slammed in her face just because she's not what they expected. Their loss, if you ask me, but I digress."

Mina smiled to reassure Mitch, "If you suggest her to help us out, that's good enough for me. I am not about to judge someone because they're different than what I'm used to."

"I know and I love you for that." Mitch blew her a kiss before addressing the couple, "Her name is Tonia, and she did me a favor once and made me a dress to prove a point to Precious."

Oliver's eyes lit up surprise, "Oh! I remember that. Alice told me about your adventures walking around the city."

Mina laughed, "I still have the photos saved on my phone. You were amazing."

"Oh, go on, flattery will get you everywhere with me." Mitch grinned, "She'll help you out, trust me. With her guiding you, your wedding is going to be glorious."

~

"Excuse me, I think you two stole something of mine that I would like back." Tonia stood in the middle of her workshop as she slowly shifted her gaze between Mina and Oliver.

Oliver reacted in confusion, "I apologize, I believe there is a misunderstanding. We would never…"

"Come on, you can give me my breath back any time now, because you just stole it the moment you two walked in the room." Tonia giggled at her private joke, "I thought Mitch was exaggerating, but you two are the most beautiful couple I've ever had the blessing of working with." She quickly added, "That is, of course, if you choose me to help you with your wedding plans."

Mina laughed at the odd behavior concerning Tonia's reaction to them, "We had only begun announcing to our friends and family about getting married when we thought Mitch would be an excellent choice in helping us arrange everything. He laughed at us for suggesting it and then mentioned you."

"Love that man to death, always sending potential clients my way." Tonia turned, motioning towards the large room in which she worked from, "I know, it doesn't look like much, but…" She had taken three steps away from the couple before turning slowly, "Did he tell you everything about me? Full disclosure, no secrets, I don't want you backing out at the last minute because something about my private life makes you uncomfortable. I've put a lot of time and effort into creating magic only to have someone vanish like a puff of smoke the second they learn some little tidbit they don't like."

Oliver gently patted Mina's arm as he pulled away from her. Taking a step forward, he extended his hand, "I am Alice's brother. I have not had the opportunity to thank you for all you have done for her. She was at a turning point in her life, willing to relinquish all that made her who she is when you intervened."

Tonia's eyes flared wide, "Oh goodness..." She took Oliver's hand, expecting a firm handshake as if it were one man greeting another. Instead, he gently cradled it in one before placing his other over hers as he would greet a woman that he highly respected, "It was Mitch who did all the work, I just helped out with the dress."

Gently holding Tonia's hand, Oliver smiled warmly, "Mitch may have set events into motion, but it was something you said that Alice refers to when she speaks of that point in her life. Whether you realize it or not, you are her role model and a heroic figure in her eyes. You are one of profound influence in helping her discover her confidence in being a woman in a world that wishes to dictate how one in her position in life should behave. You provided her the strength to be herself and I cannot thank you enough for that."

Tears formed in Tonia's eyes as she looked past Oliver, "He's going to make me cry. I see why you want to marry this fine gentleman."

Mina practically glowed with the radiance of her smile, "He has that effect on people and yes, I consider myself blessed to have the chance to be with him."

Releasing her hand, Oliver stepped back to rejoin Mina. Tonia wiped away tears, careful to not cause disturbance to her make up, "If that's how you feel, then I would be equally honored to be working the both of you. I would like to get a chance to meet and greet, get to know the both of you before we proceed, if that's alright with you? I feel like every wedding should be crafted to fit the personalities of those about to be wed."

Oliver exchanged a quick glance with Mina before answering, "Of course, when, and where?"

"If you two aren't busy, as soon as possible and at your favorite place to mingle with someone you just met, your choice." Tonia grinned, "Consider it the first step in getting to know you." There was a short pause before she added, "However, before we begin, I like to get this ugly little detail out of the way. What exactly are we looking at concerning a budget?"

Oliver reacted in concern, worry quickly took shape across his face as he looked over at Mina, "I am not sure."

Mina lightly touched his cheek, smiling sweetly, "We'll figure something out, okay?" Turning to Tonia, she continued, "We're both in a point of transition in our lives."

"Don't worry about it. Consider me your genie here to grant your wishes. I'll find a way to make every dream come true." Tonia shifted her gaze between the pair, "There is a website that one can set up to help fund projects, get help with emergency situations, stuff like that. From what Mitch has told me, you have a lot of friends that would be more than happy to help with this special occasion. Every little dollar here and there can help, so if you would be alright with doing so, I'll set it up in your name, have all the funds transfer to you. I'll just be doing the leg work, getting people to notice and try to entice people to help." She paused with a curious look, "What do you think?"

Mina nodded in agreement, having heard about such websites, "Yeah, that sounds a great idea."

Oliver added, "Already you've done so much for us."

"You are so charming, adorable, and handsome as can be." Tonia shifted her gaze from Oliver to Mina, "And loyal. As much as I hate to confess this, some of my previous clients, I could tell were in for a short-lived union. I almost turned them down, but they insisted. Either the man or the woman just wasn't in it a hundred percent, their eyes wondering, their thoughts on other things, I could tell it wouldn't last and I was right."

Tonia held up her hands as if defending herself, "Not you two, though. I see in your eyes a couple that love each other unconditionally and the loyalty to one another is unquestioned. I love that about the both of you and I am excited about your future. Don't think of this as the beginning of a new life together. Think of this as a new chapter in each of your lives, one where you are going to share in this experience that begins with a wedding and continues throughout eternity."

~

"We have a problem." Mina was entering Oliver's apartment after he greeted her at the door. She was about to ask if his computer was on, but she remembered that Hoven never used it and it was rare that her boyfriend had any need of it. When it wasn't in use, he was careful to shut it off. Clicking the power button, she turned her back to it as she waited for it to start up, "You know that website that Tonia set up for us to help fund our wedding?"

Oliver quickly ran through a list of concerns but quickly considered the most obvious problem concerning the situation, "We took a chance for this to help our financial situation concerning the event, we weren't relying on it to help us."

At first Mina was confused as to what he was alluding to when her face lit up with recognition, "Oh! No, that's not it." She paused, "Have you checked it at all since she set it up for us?"

Oliver slipped his hands in to his pockets, a sign that he felt ashamed, "I'm sorry, no, I was afraid the news wouldn't be good."

"Then this is going to come as a surprise to you." Slipping into the chair in front of the desk, Mina quickly brought up the website, filling in the necessary information to log in. Finally, she chose the option to reveal the funds that had been raised so far. "See the problem?"

Oliver's mouth hung open in shock as he tried to wrap his mind around what he was seeing, "It must be a glitch of some sort, that can't be…" He was trying to think of anyone who had that kind of money, "Would Mitch do this?"

"He's generous, I love him dearly, but he doesn't have that kind of money to give away." Mina folded her arms across her chest as she leaned back in the chair, "Who else do you think has that much to invest in us?"

A cold chill raced across Oliver's skin, "My mother."

"I know you told me everything about your meeting with her, but I thought you two were done. She did a favor for you and fixed what she did to you in the past. You are moving on from what happened so you can start a future with me, right?" Mina moved slowly to her feet, "She's not letting this go, is she?"

Oliver shook his head, "I don't know what kind of game she's playing with us but is there a possibility to reject that donation? That way we can show her that we aren't interested?"

"If we do, she may end up dropping off cash at our front door." Mina saw Oliver's amused reaction, "What? You think I'm joking? I don't know what kind of lengths she'll go to try to manipulate you, get involved with our lives, who knows? After what she did to you, I don't trust her at all. I'm still in shock that you agreed to meet with her, especially after what she did to Hoven to try to drive him and Alice apart."

"Weird thing is that Alice forgave her for that." Mina turned to find Hoven having stepped out of his bedroom, his hands buried in his pockets, his eyes staring at a space in front of him, "I was going to tell her everything eventually, I wanted to be totally honest with her, but what your mom did wasn't cool."

Mina lowered her tone, having realized it had raised in volume as she became more agitated with the situation, "I'm sorry if I woke you, I didn't know you were here." She looked over at Oliver, "I should have asked."

Hoven shrugged, "It's cool. I don't exactly have a lot of places to go when Alice is at work, and I have the day off." He nodded slowly, "Is the evil queen up to something again?"

Surprised that he would use such a bold choice in front of Oliver, Mina turned quickly to see her fiancé's reaction. He nodded slowly in agreement, not appearing to be upset, "It would appear she is attempting to gain the favor of the gods by bestowing upon them an offering in the form of a portion of her grand wealth."

Confused, Mina turned back to Hoven who grinned, "Tricky one, she is, that's for sure. Turn her away now, and she may attempt another way to interfere with the divine union."

Mina quickly darted her gaze back to Oliver, "When did this happen?"

Oliver smiled, acting innocent, "What do you mean?"

"This secret code of yours. I know about the fairy tale that Hoven told you about that led to you two moving in together, so I'm guessing it's based off that?" Mina turned back to Hoven, "Right?"

Hoven avoided eye contact, "Yeah."

Oliver touched Mina gently on the shoulder, "When he doesn't think about the reality around him, more so a character in a book, he's more comfortable handling stressful situations."

"Oh..." Mina nodded as she whispered, "Am I allowed to play along or is this just something you and he do together?"

Oliver addressed Hoven, "What say you, can the virtuous goddess of wisdom and courage participate in our narrative?"

Hoven grinned without looking up, "Of course, the divine is always welcome to share her blessings upon this humble mortal."

"Great hero..." Hoven acted as if had just been insulted forcing Mina to ask in a whisper, "What did I do wrong?"

Oliver leaned forward, speaking softly, "He's a reluctant hero, he doesn't feel great yet, even though we all know the truth."

"I'm sorry, reluctant hero, how would you suggest that the divine gods respond to this gesture made by the evil queen?" Mina was trying her best to work with Oliver's roommate.

Hoven looked up to gaze upon Oliver and Mina, "The evil queen showed no respect or care for the good queen until she confronted her adversary. It is time for the gods on high to meet with this darkness upon the land."

Mina wasn't certain what Hoven had said at first, her mind deciphering the metaphor before she turned her focus to Oliver, "You said something about how she liked me?"

Oliver nodded, "She said she highly respected you and the work you've done as well as the woman you've proven yourself to be when dealing with obstacles in your life."

"She respects me, and yet she's doing this. Either she's just trying to manipulate you, or she thinks I want her gifts." Mina sighed deeply, "Mitch told me about his encounter with her, she was vicious with him. Yet, Alice speaks of her willingness to change her behavior, so no telling how this is going to play out."

Oliver was growing concerned, "Are you sure you want to do this? The last time I visited her at her home, she had every advantage over me."

"I don't plan on playing this game on her terms. If she is so determined to be a part of your life and to an extent, our future life together, then she's going to do things my way." Mina turned back to Hoven, "You have proven your wisdom, reluctant hero, but the gods will not step down from the mountain peaks to speak to the evil queen. It is she who must humble herself before the divine if she so desires to have audience with us."

Chapter 14

"You wish for me to tell my mother..." Alice sat across from Mina as the two women met with one another at a small café to share a cold beverage and to talk. "I wish to clarify before I proceed with this discussion."

"Your mother made a sizable donation to our wedding fund on the website that Tonia set up for us. I know that she's trying to change her behavior lately, but you must understand our mutual concern for her interest in being involved in our wedding. We wanted to know what is going on and you're the only person that is in communication with her." Mina hated to use Alice in such a way, but she wasn't certain of any other way to relay the message.

"I see." Alice revealed a faint scowl as she considered the situation, "I don't believe my mother's intentions are malevolent in nature, but I will speak to her on your behalf." With the immediate concern addressed, she felt it was acceptable to proceed with the conversation, "Is there anything else that you wish to speak to me about?"

Mina smiled, "There was something else I wanted to talk to you about of immense importance." She hesitated, laughing nervously, "I'm not sure how much you know about weddings."

"I am well versed in multiple topics, the formalities of weddings being among the things I was taught when I was still under the tutelage of my former household." Alice was relieved the topic was moving past her mother, "Did you need my help in planning your wedding?"

Mina laughed, "Yes and no. Tonia is doing an amazing job planning out everything we want for our wedding, but there was something that I have discussed with Oliver and we both agree. That is, of course, if you say yes."

Uncertain of what Mina was alluding to, Alice asked politely, "If you and my brother are in agreement, I trust you both with my life, therefore my answer will be yes."

"Will you be my maid of honor?" Mina saw Alice's eyes widen with shock as her mouth hung open for a moment in surprise. "You don't have to…"

"Yes! Of course! I would be honored!" Alice clasped her hands together in front of her before pressing them tightly against her chest as if she were about to explode from sheer delight, "Thank you for making this request of me, I am without words to properly express the happiness I feel in this moment." Tears welled up in her eyes, "I find it a struggle to breathe." After attempting to steady her breathing, she held up her hand, "One moment."

Closing her eyes, Alice thought of all that Hoven had taught her concerning how to respond to a panic attack. Although, her circumstances were not the same, she certainly was exhibiting similar signs of distress that needed a calm mind to respond to what was happening to her body. After she regained her composure, she opened her eyes, taking the clean napkin resting in her lap to lightly dry her eyes. "I apologize for the outburst, what you said came as a surprise to me."

"Why?" Mina realized how rude that may have sounded, "I meant to say, who else did you think would be the maid of honor?"

"Mitch, of course." Alice clutched the napkin in her hands, as she rested them in her lap, "I did not believe you would restrict yourself to specific gender roles and he is your best friend."

Mina smiled, nodding slowly at the thought, "Before I met Oliver, Mitch would often joke about how if I ever got married, he would wear a dress and everything to be my maid of honor. However, we felt he would be better suited as Oliver's best man in that he doesn't have a man to be there for him the way I do." She quickly added, "Before you ask, yes, we thought of Hoven, but we knew that he would not like at all. The pressure of standing up in front of a group would be too much for him to handle."

Alice slowly nodded her head as she spoke, "Yes, I hadn't thought of that, but you are correct. It would be too much of a strain on him to be a part of the wedding party." It was then that a thought struck her, "I don't mean for this question to be considered inconsiderate, but I am curious, who will be attending your wedding if you don't mind me asking?"

"Well, so far we have you, Mitch, Hoven, and Tonia." Mina tried to remember who else was included, "Oliver doesn't feel that he is close to any of his coworkers at his job, so he wished to extend an invitation to some of the people from his dance classes, especially the woman who gave him the opportunity to teach there. I have several friends that you may not have met."

A memory surfaced leading Mina to smirk, "Mitch said he wanted to invite his family. I have visited them with him on the holidays before I met Oliver since I didn't have anyone to spend that time on a few occasions, so it would be great for them to be there."

Alice considered their extended family and hesitated to bring up the topic, "What of my other two older brothers and my mother? Are they not invited?"

Mina sat back in her chair, assuming a defensive posture by folding her arms across her chest, "I will let Oliver decide on that, but..." Dropping her arms, she suddenly sat up as she thought of something she hadn't considered, "Wait, is that what's this all about? Your mother buying into the wedding? If she pays for it, we're obligated to invite her, is that it?"

"As I said, I don't believe my mother's intentions are malevolent in nature." Alice felt uncomfortable defending a woman who in the past only had motivations based upon personal gain, "You must realize, she is accustomed to getting what she desires through force of will. She commands something to happen, and she expects others to fall in line. However, in this change of attitude towards others, the concept of how to be nice, which comes naturally to people like you and me, is difficult for her. She doesn't know how to behave with benevolent intentions, for it does not come naturally to her. She may believe her wealth is a way of showing kindness, by providing what you need, she may earn a positive response."

Mina spoke firmly, "Tell her I'll meet her in the park, by herself. If she's got this small army of people following her around responding to her wants and needs like some sort of queen strutting around with the common folk, I'm leaving. She meets me on my terms. Oliver won't be there, I'm not about to put him through that again. She hurt him and I still hate her for every tear shed and moment of suffering she's responsible for in his life."

"Agreed." Alice felt as if she had betrayed Mina by showing kindness to a mother that had caused so much pain in the lives of others, "I know why you feel the way that you do, but please provide her an opportunity to prove to you that she is indeed worthy of salvation. Not all lives lost to the darkness should forever be damned for the mistakes they have made in their past."

"Bringing the devil into the light of day doesn't make him an angel." Mina considered the future with a heavy heart, "She has one chance to prove herself. If she makes one mistake with me, I'll do everything in my power to make sure she not only doesn't harm Oliver, but if we have kids, they won't even know she exists."

~

"Do you mind if I sit here?" Mina looked over at a woman wearing a pair of jeans, a dark green button up blouse tucked in with a thin black belt keeping her pants firmly in place. A generic looking baseball cap came down just above her eyebrows.

Mina didn't think anything of it, "Yeah, sure."

"You look as if you're expecting someone." Mina wasn't sure why a random stranger desired to strike up a conversation with her, but she was accustomed to it. For whatever reason, be it attraction to the way she looked, some sort of aura she gave off that created a sense of trust in others, she had heard multiple theories as to why, but having people approaching her was normal.

Mina sighed, "You could say that." Her dark green eyes were on the lookout for a woman wearing a fancy gown, something that stood out from the usual crowd of people coming and going, "I don't think she'll show, though."

"Oh, a woman? A friend, relative?" There was something about the voice that left a tingling in the back of Mina's mind. A British accent was not common to hear.

Turning her head slowly, Mina gave the woman sitting next to her a longer, more discerning look. Suddenly her eyes flared wide in shock, "You…"

"I find your reaction both flattering that I was able to mislead you with my appearance as well as disappointed that your keen mind did not detect the truth sooner." The woman held out her hand, "I don't believe we have been formally introduced. My name is Katherine. It is a pleasure to finally meet you, Mina."

Mina glanced down at the hand extended towards her, "I'm going to skip formalities if you don't mind."

"As you wish." Katherine rested her hands in her lap, despite the casual clothing choice, her rigid posture refused to relax, "It is a beautiful day to have our meeting, don't you think?"

Mina's eyes narrowed as she studied the woman sitting next to her, "Is this a disguise to blend in, to test me to see if I would know who you were?"

"My role as queen is a costume, the image I present to the world is a mask. What you see before you is humility in physical form." Katherine turned her head, glancing over at Mina, "That is what you wanted, to draw me out from the protective barriers of my household, away from my guards, to make me as vulnerable as possible. I am not attempting to blend in, merely show you that who I am is not limited to my appearance. The outer shell that all who see is no more than a façade."

Mina admitted to herself that she greatly underestimated Oliver and Alice's mother. She expected to either have her request ignored or she would arrive in all her finery. The idea of a woman dressed up like some royal queen walking around the park seemed absurd but considering the fantasy world that Katherine had built up around her, she wouldn't be surprised if that were what happened. Her appearance dressed this way was an unexpected move, "You're not what I expected."

Katherine smiled, revealing her amusement without laughter, "Did you expect me to arrive in a full gown, a crown set upon my head, a scepter in my hand?" She turned her intense focus to Mina, "You don't think highly of me, do you?"

"You hurt Oliver, for that alone I hate you. You hurt Alice, another reason for me to hate you." Mina kept her expression blank, refusing to allow the other woman to gain any advantage, "Mitch told me about how you talked down to him and insulted him. Three reasons why I don't trust you. I want nothing to do with you and the only reason we are having this conversation is because I am concerned about what you plan to do next that may harm those I care about and will protect with my life."

Turning away, Katherine gazed across the grass filled stretches of open space where people played games, had picnics, enjoyed time with their families and friends, "Interesting speech, one that felt prepared beforehand." She smirked, "I should know, I am often reciting such words in my mind before I address others. I have carefully crafted a specific image for those I interact with that a single mistake could shatter the illusion of what is the truth."

Mina wasn't about to give Katherine the opportunity to lead her along in the conversation by forcing her to ask what she was speaking of. It was because of this that she remained silent until the other woman continued, "I see why Oliver chose you. You appeal to both the man I raised him to become and the fragile, gentle soul that I nearly killed in my attempt to make him strong enough to endure the horrors of this world."

Katherine turned her body slightly, her hands resting in her lap as she addressed Mina with her full attention, "You think of me as an inhuman monster, an atrocious being worthy of your hatred and loathing. That is the masquerade I have been living for so long that I nearly forgot how to be any other way. Consider a potential outcome of what would have happened if I had not intervened with Oliver's first love, shall we?"

"I knew she was interested in only his wealth and social status. I had encountered countless individuals such as herself when it came to my experiences both in my youth and through keen eyed observation concerning his two elder brothers. By the time she introduced herself into his life, snaking her way into my garden, I was fully aware of her ultimate intent." Katherine locked her gaze upon Mina, giving her an unwavering stare, "Oliver was naïve, head over heels in love with a woman who didn't care about him, only what he had to offer her. That gentle soul that you think I have little regard for, I knew existed. He was that way since he was a little boy, as was Alice."

Katherine shook her head slowly, "He trusted her, put his faith in her, and loved her. I knew she would betray him eventually."

Katherine raised her hand interrupting Mina's question that she was certain was to be asked, "Why did I not intervene? I attempted to do so. He had no interest in listening to me. The only way to pry that succubus from my child was to prove to him what she was. The only way to do so was to remove that which she was seeking from him, the wealth and social status that she desired. It was my intent to bring him back into the family, to forgive him for the harsh words that he spoke to me, of the insults he wounded me with. However, once he stepped away from my influence, he never turned back. There was no yearning to be under my protection."

Mina scowled, studying Katherine's blank expression, "Is that how you would describe what you did to Oliver and Alice? You saw it as protecting them?"

As if ignoring the anger being shown her, Katherine calmly replied, "I saw myself in their eyes when they were children. Naïve, trusting to a fault, blindly agreeing to those who would sway their opinion." She looked away, her gaze focused on a stand of trees in the distance, memories flickering across her mind, "Their two older brothers were more like their father, I was forced to assert myself in their presence, make certain they knew I was in control and would be until my death. If I had not been firm with them, carefully controlling what they had influence over, they may have grown to enjoy power, to be corrupted by it as their father had before them."

She smiled as she looked over at Mina, "Power did not corrupt me, it did not transform me into what you know of me. Circumstances of my life forced me two options. Bend to the will of others and submit to their authority or assert my strength."

Despite the warmth of the day, a shiver raced across Mina's skin. She tried to hide it, but it struck so suddenly it was hard to mask its existence. Katherine gave a small nod, "You know exactly what I speak of. Your parents were like that, controlling, manipulative, selfish, their only desire was the fulfillment of their own self-worth. Your former employers misled you to think that they thought highly of you, of the position they provided to you, and that they were treating you with the respect you deserved. From what Alice has told to me of your situation…"

Katherine raised her hand to silence Mina before she interrupted, "Do not think ill of my daughter." Lowering her hand, she continued, "She speaks of you as a heroine, a mythical figure she admires, often attempting to emulate. She told me of you asserting yourself shortly before you submitted your resignation. It is one of multiple reasons why I too admire the woman I now share this moment with. You have done so on your own, as yourself and not some conjured disguise where I could not."

Was Oliver's mother showing humility? Confused by the sudden shift in attitude, Mina was wary as to let her guard down. It wasn't the first time she had played a mental game with someone. Typically, men thought they could mislead her before pursuing what they secretly were wanting of her.

Katherine lightly brushed at her pants, as if to smooth out a wrinkle she observed, "I was like Oliver and Alice in my youth. Hopeful, trusting, a heart yearning to be cherished by my family who had little time for me. It was like what you endured. I was an extension of my parents, nothing more in their eyes."

"At the age of eighteen, I met a young man who would have been gladly accepted as my partner in life in the eyes of my family. His wealth and the influence of his own kin made him an ideal match. It was not this that drew me to him, it was the same fragile soul that I saw in the eyes of my two youngest children." Katherine's eyes narrowed, a moment of anger flickering across her face, "He made grand gestures and promises that we would be wed one day, that his heart belonged to me, and he would never break that trust."

"His parents had other intentions for his future. A more suitable wife had been selected, one of actual royalty, a baroness that flaunted her inherited title as if it held much meaning in the modern world. A man who would speak poetry one day, turned an icy stare upon me within days of his sudden engagement to this other woman who had been introduced into his life." Katherine looked over at Mina, her emotional revelation fading from her face, "It was because of that scenario that I learned that power is not wealth or social influence."

"All too often those who inherit a substantial sum of money are spoiled brats, spineless cowards, those who immerse themselves in hedonistic behavior of self-pleasure. There is no strength of will or dominance to be found in their eyes beyond peacocking, all show, little substance. Strip away their vast wealth and what remains tells the true tale of the individual's worth." Katherine watched Mina's subtle reactions in curiosity as she continued to speak, "Royalty rose to power at the tip of a sword, conquerors and grand leaders who fought against threats to prevent the loss of a civilization. Kings and queens throughout history have been forced to prove their mettle."

A smile formed, which startled Mina as Katherine stared into her eyes, "You have done that throughout your life, each step proving yourself worthy of the admiration you have garnered, the companions in your life that have pledged their loyalty to you, and the love of a man who is worthy of you."

"The queen I present myself to be is a representation of who I am, how I see myself to be, and I wish the world to respond to me. That is how I forced others to see me, as a powerful presence worthy of admiration and if not that, respect of my authority." Katherine turned away, thinking of another memory, "When your companion, the vocal male that confronted me alongside my daughter, arrived I knew of his type. An alpha male who was accustomed to being in control of a situation, their first inkling is to assert oneself as the dominant power in a potential confrontation. I knew that's how he saw my meeting with Alice, for he had assumed a defensive position concerning her."

"Alternatively, he was a protective guardian, seeing himself as both her shield to protect her from me but a sword that would attack in her place, preserving the purity of how he saw her." Katherine revealed faint signs of concern, a pain revealed in her eyes that led to the breath being caught in Mina's chest, "I had not spoken to my daughter in nearly two years. I knew of the life she was leading, who was a part of it, and a small fraction of knowledge concerning the woman she was developing into. So, when that man entered my home as if he were a knight there to slay a dragon, I would not stand for it." To the surprise of her audience, Oliver's mother laughed, "He proved to be quite entertaining."

"Before you scold me for my actions, I will apologize for what was said. I did so not only to fend off a man who would dare see himself as my superior with his brash attitude, but also to test my daughter, to see if anything of what I taught her remained." Katherine continued to smile, "I had not thought it possible, to not only preserve the precious soul that she was as a little girl, but to retain what I taught her concerning an inner strength to not only defend herself on her own terms, but to do so with respect of those she encountered. She did not fight fire with fire. She did not attempt to stop the flow of a river, but gently guide it to a new path away from her. She showed me that there was a third path, one not of weakness or dominance, but an ability to assert oneself without the need to take control over a given scenario or those involved."

"Where do you think Alice learned how to do that?" Mina felt like Katherine was carefully building up her daughter while ignoring her son, "Oliver taught her how to deal with those who may harm her without becoming like them. You barely talk about him. Is Alice the only child that's important to you?"

"I love my son, as I do all my children." Recognition flickered in Katherine's eyes, "Ah, yes, the story of the boy that exists purely because his father desired a female child." She nodded slowly, "An interesting narrative that developed to further paint me as the villain of this story. That is just one of many that took a tidbit of truth and was used to create an elaborate illusion that best suited what they desired of me."

Mina studied Katherine, trying to figure out if she was lying to her, "If that's not true, then why allow him to think that?"

"If you and Oliver choose to have children, you will learn there are times that a parent must become the villain in their narrative for what is best for them. Denying a small child candy in favor of food that will nourish their growing body, will paint you as a cruel dictator for denying them simple pleasures." Katherine lowered her gaze as she looked away, "Tell a young man that the woman he loves is not who she claims to be, that she does not reciprocate, you force him to choose between love and family."

"The truth is, he would not exist if it weren't for his father's desire to have a female child. I did not love him, despite the occasional moments when I felt a close kindship with the man, my relationship with him was more akin to an arranged marriage than one born from love. Those that my parents considered suitable for me were quickly being snatched up one by one, the number of bachelors who were ideal in their mind was dwindling." Katherine turned slowly, focusing on Mina, "I had been betrayed by someone I trusted once with my life, an event I am certain you can relate to. You were lucky to have found my son, the heart of ice that refused to beat within your chest finding life once more. I had no such destiny in store for me by the time I was introduced to Oliver's father. Our relationship was mostly a convenience for both of our families, one I accepted for I had given up on anything greater."

"My two eldest children were much like their father. Each possessed dominant personalities, I knew that as they grew mature enough to do so, they would quickly take their place at their father's side in the family business." Katherine scowled in reflection, "That is when I lost all hope, giving in completely to my fate."

"I would have refused the man to touch me again if I could have done so, he had already shown interest in other women, other lovers. I was almost welcome to the thought of him no longer visiting me in my bed, for at the time we spent most of our lives apart." Katherine met Mina's eyes, "I'm not telling you this for sympathy. I consider such frivolous emotions as signs of weakness that I have no desire for you to see in me. I do so, for you to understand who I am and why I became the woman I am today."

"Alice's father desired a daughter, one born from his legitimate relationship, the one the public knew of. I was forced to endure his presence once again." Katherine turned away, staring at children playing in the distance, a smile tugging at her lips, "That is when Oliver was born much to the disappointment of his father who quickly left the room once he discovered the reality of yet another male heir. That is the truth buried underneath the narrative that he may have told you."

"What neither of you know is that before Alice was born, I looked into my little boy's eyes and saw myself staring back at me." Katherine's smile grew in intensity, memories flooding her, "All those years of being drained away, bled dry by the viciousness of this world until I was nothing more than an empty shell. My heart long since frozen, having become a stone block, a weight in my chest. I had nearly forgotten who I once was, who I was meant to be. There he was, staring back at me with such hope, joy, warmth, kindness…"

Katherine turned back to Mina, "It is my conclusion that these are the same qualities that you fell in love with, am I right?"

Mina nodded slowly, distrust blended with confusion, a peculiar look on her face as she spoke softly, "If he was all these wonderful things that reminded you of what you lost, why did you try to change him?"

"For the same reason you extinguished all emotion to protect yourself." Katherine's smile faded, "Alice does not know and did not need to reveal the intimate details of why or how, just that it occurred. You are not the woman that first met Oliver and yet it is obvious you have not discarded that strength completely, either. That is why I taught him to be the man I desired him to become, to protect this fragile soul that I knew would be broken if I did not intervene. He needed to learn to protect himself from a hostile environment that would shatter what remained of the purity of who he was. Without my guidance, he may have fallen prey to the same suffering I endured that which transformed who I was."

"Before you ask, I did the same for Alice, both were so much alike. If it weren't for the span of time separating their two births, one would think of them as twins. Such strength and resilience protecting the truth of who they are." Katherine reconsidered, "That isn't true, either, is it? Alice has proven that one does not need a sword to combat that which would threaten who she is. All one needs is a shield to protect oneself, to turn away threats, to stand their ground but not push back when pressed for a response. The world told each of them to step aside, to become like so many others who came before them, and they refused to give into the demands of this society." She smiled, pride seeping through her expression, "I have much to learn from them if they provide me the opportunity."

"I became who I am because the world threatened to strip away everything until nothing remained. I had thought at the time the only way to respond to such portents was with a mutual show of strength." Katherine's brow furrowed as in concern as she thought about that chapter of her life, "My husband wished for me to be silent, a shadow to follow behind him, present when he needed to show me off to the public but otherwise ignored. He died due to complications of alcohol consumption from an early age. He did little to alter an abhorrent lifestyle and disregard for his wellbeing despite warnings of his physicians."

"After his passing, it became clear to me that his business associates had no interest in my continued involvement in the company despite my inheritance of controlling influence upon its activities. My two eldest sons were teenagers at the time, already showing signs of belligerence and a disregard of any respect that they may have held for me in the past." Katherine's gaze turned downward, anger burning in her eyes, "That is when I considered queens of old, of the woman I was tossed aside for in favor of by a man I once loved. It was the only way to garner the respect and fear, if necessary, to assert myself."

Katherine concluded, "I quickly reigned in the attitudes of my eldest sons, presenting a fiercely dominant matriarch that would not have them speak unless spoken to in my presence. Any signs of rebellion were quickly and firmly responded to. Knowing that the world would destroy the lives of my youngest children, I began to indoctrinate them towards a midframe that would protect them from the broken existence I had found myself trapped within."

There was a lingering silence before Katherine turned to face Mina, "There you have it. All the answers you were seeking. From the starry-eyed little girl to the heartbroken young woman, to dutiful wife, and finally into the woman you felt you knew from the tales told of me from my children. I know the only reason you agreed to meet with me was due to the donation I provided, which if it would please you, I will withdraw. I meant it as a gesture of kindness, to provide you what was denied to me. Namely that of a wedding filled with cherished memories, rather than the pomp and circumstance that was my own exchange of vows."

Mina sat against the back of the bench, staring at the various scenes playing out before her eyes throughout the park. Her mind processed the information that had been provided by her future mother-in-law. Just how much should she believe was true? Should she allow skepticism to taint her viewpoint of what was just revealed to her? She let out a slow breath before responding, "I met with you because I was afraid of what you were going to do to Oliver, how you may try to influence our lives once we were married and maybe, one day, how you would attempt to work your way into the lives of our children."

Despite the seriousness of the situation, Mina abruptly laughed, "I came here wanting a fight, just as Mitch described his experience with you. I expected that from you. I thought you would arrive with this attitude of being better than me, attempting to tell me how things would be. I was going to not only defend Oliver but do what I could to make it clear to you that I would protect him from you. As I told you, I hated you and everything you stood for."

"I get it. I don't want to, but I do. I hate the fact that you had to become this..." Mina made a motion of her hands towards Katherine, "...other version of you to survive. Forced into that situation, I may have done the same. I want to tell myself I would be strong enough not to get involved with someone like Oliver's father, but honestly..." She fought back tears at the mere thought of what she was about to say, "If you hadn't made that sacrifice, he wouldn't exist. He would have never been born, and I would still be the woman I was when I first met your son. Maybe worse."

Standing, Mina took three steps forward before turning slowly back to Katherine who remained in her seat, "This is too big for me to deal with alone. Besides, you need to tell them everything you told me." She did as Katherine had responded to her multiple times earlier by holding up her hand to interrupt the other woman from speaking, "Maybe not your older two sons, I don't know anything about them so that's up to you." Lowering her hand, she concluded, "However, you need to tell Oliver and Alice everything. They were the ones who were hurt the most by your actions."

~

"I knew of the truth. I was certain of it in my heart but without proof, something to refer to specifically, my feelings on the subject matter were limited to what I feared to be misguided hope." Alice smiled, tears streaking her face, "Thank you for telling us this, mother. I am grateful that you felt comfortable to speak of this to each of us." She looked over at her brother as he continued to stare at the woman sitting across from him with a blank expression. After a lingering silence, she spoke to him, "Oliver?"

Mina lightly patted his hand which was beginning to squeeze her own so tightly it was beginning to hurt, "Oliver." She spoke in a firm tone to get his attention.

His gaze darted over to his fiancé, his grip on her hand instantly releasing its tight hold, "I'm sorry."

"It's alright." Mina lightly rubbed his upper arm with her free hand, "I understand."

No tears were shed, anger kept such emotions from being revealed, "You destroyed my life to protect me. You did all of this to prevent someone from hurting me and yet, in doing so, you did just as much harm to me in your efforts to shield me from what she was going to do." His eyes narrowed, an intense fury focused on his mother, "Why should I forgive you?"

Katherine was wearing similar casual clothing as she had met Mina in nearly a week earlier. Alice had arranged for them to meet at her apartment on a day her roommate would be out of town visiting family. Her blue eyes met the intensity of her son's gaze as she replied calmly, "I don't want you to forgive me." The statement startled Alice who began to speak only to realize she shouldn't interrupt. "If there had been another way where I would be certain that the outcome would lead to a more positive conclusion, I would have made that choice. However, I felt my options were limited and as with all decisions I have made in my life, I did what I felt was best. You would have been harmed one way or other, better you to hate me than yourself by being in a loveless marriage to a woman who would treat you the way your father felt towards me. I will carry the burden of my choices, ones I take no pleasure from."

Oliver shifted his gaze to Alice, "I need to speak with Mina in private. Thank you for arranging this meeting to take place in your home. I don't wish to disrespect you in my abrupt departure, but I hope that you understand why."

Alice nodded slowly, "Yes, I understand. Thank you for coming. I know you had your misgivings for doing so."

After gently squeezing his sister's hands in reassurance, Oliver turned to his fiancé, "Would you accompany me?"

"Of course." Mina quickly joined him, holding onto his hand to make certain he knew he wasn't alone in coping with what had just been revealed to him.

Oliver gave his mother a lingering stare before speaking, "I know why you did what you felt was necessary. However, I believe you approached the problem incorrectly, assuming the worst of all involved and thinking the only way to achieve your goals was through force rather than as a request. In some instances, I agree, your life did not provide you an alternative. However, when it came to Alice and me, you nearly destroyed all that you were attempting to preserve due to this mind frame of treating all scenarios with equal show of strength. All we wished from you, mother, is for you to love and protect us as any parent should provide for their children. Your attempts to do so made it appear as if you did not care about us, which nearly extinguished all hope."

The walk from Alice's apartment to the front door to the building in which it resided was in silence. It wasn't until Oliver and Mina had walked nearly a block away from their original location that he finally found his voice, "What am I to do?"

Mina had been watching Oliver in concern. When he spoke, tears began forming in his eyes, "When she first told me all of this, I was skeptical. She seemed to have the perfect answer for everything she's ever done. This could be explained in that she's used to preparing herself before giving a speech, organizing her thoughts, focusing what she wants to say beforehand to not show any signs of weakness in not being in full control of the situation." She hesitated to side with his mother on anything, "I wanted you and Alice to hear what she told me because I felt like it was too much for me to handle alone. I needed you there with me. I wanted to decide, but I wanted to know your opinion first."

Oliver turned to face Mina, holding her hands in his as he bowed his head, "I want to be an ideal husband for you, to fulfill every wish, desire, and need that you ask of me in our journey together. If we choose to have children, I want to be an ideal parent. I don't wish to repeat the mistakes of either of our families. I can't provide those things if I hold onto the past, clinging to that pain and suffering that I endured."

Mina wanted to avoid deciding something that her fiancé was struggling to do so, "I love you, Oliver. I will support your decision concerning your mother whichever way you decide."

"If we are to be married, life choices should be made together. Two people presenting their thoughts, desires, wishes, and viewpoints. It is then we make a mutual decision after discussing what we feel is the best possible choice provided to us." Oliver scowled, anger slowly fading, "My mother did not have that luxury. She had to make those hard choices by herself, for she was alone."

"Yes, she was, with what she felt to be the entire world threatening to take everything from her, including the beautiful soul that I love dearly." Tears formed in her eyes and Mina stared at Oliver, "I hate what she did to you. I hate the fact that you were hurt, but if it was the only way to save you, the man who gave me his heart, who saved my life not just that night we met, but from a lifetime of suffering in silence…" A tear broke free, dropping down the side of her face, "I am grateful to your mother for doing what she did, because if you had married that other woman, it would have been two souls lost to despair. You and me. I can't think… I don't want to…" She tightly gripped his hands, "I refuse to accept a world without you, the man that is now standing before me, the man I love, the man I want to spend eternity with."

Oliver embraced Mina, tears breaking free from his eyes as he spoke in a hushed tone, "I will always be with you, my love. Even when I cannot be in your arms, holding your hand, or there before your eyes, know that I am forever by your side." He pulled away, brushed his hand across her cheek before they kissed.

Chapter 15

"She is beautiful." Alice smiled with such excitement that she was glowing with joy, "Her wedding gown is exquisite, yes, but what makes her appear so radiant is the love she feels for you. It is in her eyes, her smile, the way she speaks of you, today, and of your union." Alice watched her brother, worried that he may collapse, he appeared pale in coloration, his breathing erratic, it was rare for her to see him so nervous. "Will you be alright?"

"I shouldn't be this anxious for my own wedding. I am not scared or nervous concerning my decision to be wed to Mina, and yet I'm still feeling this way." Oliver smiled, "I've had months to plan for this moment, I am marrying the woman I love, and I have no doubts in my mind that this is the correct decision for both of us." He laughed, "Why do I feel as if I may faint?"

Alice touched her hands to his shoulder as she looked closely at his face, "I believe I know the ideal person to talk to about this." Alice pulled a way, "One moment please." She quickly exited the room where Oliver was waiting for the guests to arrive.

Oliver had asked Mina to marry him on November eightieth. They wanted a wedding in the spring or early summer, so after much discussion on the subject, they chose to be married in late May on the twenty fifth. They had over six months to make the arrangements, plan out every detail they wished for, send out invitations, and prepare for the event. With Tonia's help, everything felt as if it flowed easily for them, falling into place, each detail feeling perfect in both their minds.

Now that the day had come, they followed some of the older traditions such as the bride and groom not seeing one another the day of the wedding until they met together for the ceremony. Oliver was dressed in a black tuxedo and white undershirt. He wasn't wearing a tie because it made him feel uncomfortable to do so. Mina had even stated that he didn't have to dress up so formally, but he enjoyed the attire. It made him feel like a gentleman of the previous century.

Staring at the mirror, Oliver lightly rubbed his hands across his face in the hopes of clearing his thoughts. He heard someone clear their throat drawing his attention. He was surprised to find Hoven standing near the doorway. He was dressed up compared to his usual attire. Black slacks, a matching button up shirt. Where typically he would leave it free, it was currently tucked in. He had done so not only to honor the occasion, but Alice had chosen the outfit for him to wear. Oliver remembered seeing the twinkle of excitement in his sister's eyes when she spoke of it, she was rather fond of the way it flattered her boyfriend's body.

Hoven gave a small wave of his hand, "Hi. Alice thought maybe I could help." He laughed nervously, "It also gave me a reason to get away from all the people out there."

They had gone for a smaller wedding party, close friends, and family. Oliver was surprised to hear that, "We didn't plan for a large crowd."

"There is like three dozen people out there. To me, that's a lot, so yeah…" Hoven tried to keep his breathing steady, "Alice said she thinks I could help you with ways to keep calm in stressful situations, I guess?"

"I think it was done so more for your benefit than mine." Oliver smiled as gestured towards one of the few chairs in the room, "If anything, a discussion with you may get my mind off things."

"I get why you're freaking out." Hoven slipped into one of the chairs, his hands clasped in front of him with his elbows resting on his upper legs, "Makes total sense to me."

"Oh really?" Oliver wouldn't have used the phrase, freaking out, but he understood the meaning meant by the words chosen. He moved a chair to be across from Hoven before joining him, "Why do you say that?"

"I was scared when I first realized Alice wasn't my enemy." Seeing Oliver's confused look and internal debate on how to respond to the statement, Hoven continued, "Seeing someone as a threat is easy, I put up my guard around them, and I react to them defensively. I know how to deal with bullies and people who are out to hurt me. As for people who are nice to me, that's when I get nervous and scared because I'm afraid I'm going to lose them."

Oliver nodded slowly in agreement, "I feel the same way concerning losing my loved ones." He wished to shift the topic away from darker tones, "However, I don't believe this is the case. I am not afraid of losing Mina on my wedding day."

"No, of course not." Hoven hung his head, "I'm sorry, this is not working out as well as I was hoping." He sighed deeply before looking up at Oliver, "You're nervous because of change. We get afraid of things changing because we know what is right now. If we're nervous about that changing, it means we like right now. Change can be good, like you are getting married, but yeah…"

Considering Hoven's words, Oliver took up the conversation after the other man fell silent, "You are correct that I'm happy with the relationship I have with Mina. She is the first major change in my life that was for the best, not a decline in the path of my life. I blame my past for being nervous, for fearing change, because it has often resulted in negative experiences."

"Not with Mina. Maybe you two are hiding something from Alice and I, but you two have always been stronger together, getting better with time. She's…" Hoven laughed, "When I first met her, she intimidated me, scared me, honestly. She was this powerhouse that freaked me out. I'm being told she was way worse before she met you from the way Mitch talks about her. Yet, after she was gone on her trip, she came back, and she was different. It was like she was softer, gentler, a lot less intimidating and scary, that's for sure."

Hoven motioned towards Oliver, "When I first met you, it was like meeting a butler. You were so rigid, like one of those guards at the castle in England. Those guys with the tall fuzzy hats." Seeing the other man laughing at the description made him feel less worried he had insulted him, "Now you're so relaxed, comfortable with who you are. Maybe it's you and your mom finally fixing things between the two of you, you're not carrying around this burden of pain you used to. I know all about that. Every day I'm with Alice, my own weight lifts a little bit more each day."

Oliver smiled, "I've noticed that about you, too. You're less timid than you were when we first met. You take more risks in speaking to others, you now stand beside Alice more so than…" Oliver stopped himself, "I'm sorry, I don't mean to be rude."

Hoven grinned, "You can say it, I used to be her shadow, following her around, afraid to speak up." A lost look that Oliver knew all too well as when the other man thought of his sister, "She brought me into the light. I was shrouded in darkness and when I was with her, I was somewhere in between, just a shadow." His tone dropped to a near whisper, "Eventually I stepped out into the light to be with her, rather than following her lead."

"I'm certain you've been asked this before, but since it is my wedding day, I thought you would tolerate my question." Oliver sat back in his chair, watching Hoven closely, "Do you see yourself as a husband some day?"

Hoven's eyes widened in surprise, his breathing quickly accelerating, "Oh, uh…"

Oliver didn't realize he would get such a strong reaction, "You don't have to answer that, it was just a curiosity of mine."

"Yeah." Hoven nodded, trying to regain his composure, "No… I mean… I see myself with Alice for the rest of my life, she wants that, and I do too. If we get married, yeah, that would be amazing, but not anytime soon. I have so much to work through, to become more stable and to figure out my place in the world. All I know is that a few years ago, I thought I would die alone, unloved. Now? I'm happy focusing on the fact that I have a girlfriend that loves me for who I am. That's all that matters. I guess…" He cracked a nervous smile, "When I see myself as a husband, that's the day I'm going to ask her to marry me because I'll know I'm ready."

"I love you." Hoven bolted to his feet, turning quickly to find Alice standing in the doorway, tears streaking down her face.

Oliver stood, responding to the questioning look Hoven gave him, "I'm sorry, I didn't know she was there, I was focused on what you were saying."

For the moment, her brother didn't exist, Alice was fixated on Hoven as she slowly approached him, "I apologize for not speaking up sooner, but curiosity is to be blamed for my intrusion. I heard your words and I desired to know what you were going to say." Once within reach, she touched her hand to his cheek as she held his in the other, "That was beautiful, thank you."

"It's how I feel." Hoven looked into her eyes, lost in beauty found within, the warmth and love that radiated from her gaze, "I love you."

"Oh my goodness, love is certainly in the air." Mitch cleared his throat loudly, "Excuse me, love birds, if you would not mind giving this handsome groom a moment alone, I do believe it would be best for you to conclude your interlude without an audience?"

Blushing deeply, realizing that she had almost kissed Hoven in front of her brother, Alice hid her face against her boyfriend's shoulder before looking past him, "I apologize, I am so embarrassed."

Touching his hand to her shoulder, Oliver smiled, "I understand all too well."

Clapping his hands lightly together, Mitch turned towards the open doorway, "Come on you two, I need someone to gossip with and a few witnesses to prove that I am not making this up. You are a fan of my sister's work, right? You'll understand what I'm talking about. Come on, let's get going, no time to waste."

With Hoven holding her hand, Alice walked down the hallway with Mitch, "What is it that you are so excited about?"

Mitch grinned, "You'll see. Trust me, you are going to understand when you see it."

Alice smiled, "There is much of your behavior I do not understand. However, I will keep an open mind concerning what you are intending to reveal to me." Once they entered the main group where the guests were gathering, Mitch quickly pointed to a trio of individuals speaking to Michael on the other side of the room, "There. You see what I'm talking about now?"

At first Alice didn't understand, "Your sister and two people I don't..." Suddenly recognition of the pair next to Mitch's sibling led to a wide-eyed expression of stunned surprise, "Oh goodness."

Mitch had to do everything he could to contain his excitement as he tried to maintain a whisper, "I know! She told me about what had happened leading up to them being together, but I was like, no way, but it's true!"

Alice looked over at Hoven who was visibility confused, "That is Mitch's sister in the dark blue gown. Next to her is her coworker, an artist. The two of them create a comic book series that inspired my quotes concerning the actions of a true hero."

Hoven grinned, "I love those." Early on in their relationship, Alice would often use phrases that began with, a true hero... What followed would be an inspirational statement that helped her through her struggles in life. She had mentioned being inspired by a comic book that was written by Mitch's sister. "So, basically, you're about to meet your heroes?"

Alice hugged Hoven's arm tightly, "I so dearly desire to do so, but this is my brother's wedding, I should not…"

Mitch grabbed Alice's arm, in turn tugging Hoven along, "Yes you should and right now. I'm sure Oliver and Mina would agree. If anything, I can enjoy the double dose of eye candy, like two scoops of delicious ice cream, lathered in hot fudge. My boyfriend and that beautiful divine beauty talking to him. I am in heaven."

Approaching the group, Mitch made the introductions, "Hello there, handsome." He let go of Alice as he slipped his arm around Michael's waist, "I see you've met my sister."

"You sure you two aren't twins? As if God stamped out two of the same personalities. Put one in a beautiful body of this man right here and the other in a gorgeous lady I've had the blessing of talking to." Michael noticed Alice and Hoven had joined them, "Before we continue, let me introduce everyone."

"This is my moment to shine, let me." Mitch gave Michael a pouting expression.

One of the two women, each only five-foot-tall in height, muttered, "My brother, always the diva."

Mitch held up his hand to silence his sister, "Shush." Lowering his arm, he began, "This is my sister Penelope, she gets all of her charm and personality from learning from me, of course." He pointed to the woman next to his sibling, "This is Kimberly, famous artist for Tagonist Comics. As for you, I just met you, so I may not know your name just yet."

Gray blue eyes met Alice's dark green gaze as the man smiled, "My name is Logan, it is a pleasure to meet you."

There was something in his gaze, even a passing glance at the woman next to him spoke of his heartfelt connection with her. Without realizing that what she was about to say may create an awkward moment, Alice spoke, "Beautiful."

Mitch whispered, "You're telling me." Michael immediately nudged him in the side, "What? Just because I enjoy a piece of artwork doesn't mean I want to take it home and put up on my wall."

Logan, accustomed to compliments, smiled, "Thank you."

Feeling Hoven pulling away, it was only then Alice realized her mistake, "I'm so sorry, I believe you all may have misunderstood me." She gently pulled Hoven closer to her as she motioned towards Kimberly and Logan, "What I see in your eyes is pure, unconditional love. It is what I find beautiful about you, for what you obviously share for her." She looked over at Hoven, staring at him as she continued, "He looks at me that way. I did not understand what true love was until I saw it in his eyes."

"Awe..." Penelope grinned, "You must be Alice." She glanced over at her brother, "She's exactly as you described her."

Logan held out his hand towards Hoven, "It is a pleasure to meet you, sir. As she said, I see in your eyes for her what I feel for my dearest beloved, Kimberly."

"Thanks?" Feeling awkward, uncertain of how to react, Hoven shook Logan's hand. He looked at Alice, "I don't know what to say here. Everyone is talking poetry and I don't..."

Kimberly smiled, speaking up, "Finally, someone who knows what I'm going through." She turned, patting Logan gently on the chest, "I can't keep up with him. I try, I really do, but..."

Mitch tried to explain, "What she's trying to say is…"

Penelope intervened, "Stop interrupting people. Let other people talk for five seconds, alright?"

Michael burst out laughing much to Mitch's overly dramatized shock. Kimberly grinned as she finished her statement, "What I've learned is that that some people express that side of them more easily than others. Logan is comfortable with that part of himself. He is incredibly expressive of how he feels, and he doesn't hold back in telling me or anyone else who is willing to listen."

"I know I just met Alice, but it feels like she's a lot like Logan that way. She's more comfortable expressing that part of her life towards you and others." Kimberly tried her best to be reassuring, "That doesn't mean you don't feel just as strongly for her in return. Sometimes, for some us, it's harder to show that part of ourselves. It doesn't mean we don't feel the same way they do. It's just we are still learning to reach the level of self-expression."

She cringed, "As you can see, not as good about talking about this as much as I would like to. The only thing that should matter is that the person you love, knows you love them. We may not be able to say it as easily, but they know."

"Eloquently stated." Logan lightly kissed Kimberly on the forehead leaving her to feel awkward in front of a group like that.

"See what I mean?" Kimberly shrugged, "Don't feel bad about not being as expressive, but enjoy what they have to offer. Appreciate what they do reveal to you, and that will make you both happy in the long run."

Hoven nervously smiled, "Thanks. I'll do that."

"Speaking of which, little sister of mine..." Mitch focused his dark eyes on Penelope, "Where is your plus one?"

"Not here because I don't have one." Penelope took a step forward, jabbing her finger into Mitch's chest, "You know what, being single does not mean something is wrong with me. Just because I'm practically the only single person here, doesn't mean anything about who I am. I am successful, I love who I am, and guess what, I just haven't met the right man. I am enjoying my life right now. If the perfect guy for me comes along, great, but I'm not putting my life on hold until he shows up and I certainly am not upset that I don't have the kind of love the six of you are enjoying."

Stepping back, Penelope smiled confidently, "Don't get me wrong, I am horribly jealous of all three couples. I love and adore what you have. However, I am just saying, nothing wrong with being single and loving life without romance being a part of it."

Mitch clapped his hand, "What a wonderful speech, did you make that just up just now or have you been holding onto that golden nugget of inspiration for a while now?"

Giving her brother a stern look, she playfully grinned as she slowly turned her gaze to her brother's boyfriend, "So, Michael, have you thought about trying to catch the bouquet? I know Mitch never will, I'm so afraid he's stuck in this bachelor mentality. Me, however, I am counting the days until I hear the news that you two are engaged." She concluded by giving Mitch a devious smile.

A song began playing which was a signal for guests to begin being seated. Mitch leaned over to speak to his sister, "You keep talking like that, I'm going to tattle on you to mom."

Penelope laughed, "Oh, whatever, she loves weddings and Michael, it's a perfect combination." She waved at their parents who were already seated, "Should I mention this to her now or…"

Mitch responded quickly, "Don't you dare get her started."

Penelope giggled, "Too late, it was practically all she talked about on the way here."

"Thankfully, I can avoid dealing with that until after the wedding." Mitch turned away as he called out, "I have to go check on, Kitten, make sure she's ready."

~

"Where have you been?" Mina stood in middle the room she had been waiting in when Mitch entered. "I was hoping my best friend would be here for me, not out there socializing with everyone else."

"Tone it down, Ice Queen." Mitch stared into the intense look of her eyes, "Oliver loves you." Frustration instantly melted away as her face shifted from a slight scowl to a glowing smile, "I just melted the queen right back to an adorable little kitten." He paused, "Or is that the magic of husband to be." He waved away the notion, "Fine, I'll give him this, no one else could melt you like that until he entered your life."

"I miss him." Mina slowly paced the room, "I get that he wants to do a lot of this traditional stuff, most of this wedding is for him more so than me. I don't like this whole not being able to see him at all last night and then most of today." She stopped to glare at Mitch, "Don't you dare say one word about me seeing more of him than I ever have before anything like that on our honeymoon."

Reacting with an open-mouthed shocked expression, Mitch took a moment before he burst out laughing, "Wow... For once, I wasn't even thinking that, and you were!" Seeing Mina's reaction, he couldn't let it go, "Oh my... Are you blushing? I don't know how today can get any better, but that just... I love it!"

"You're not helping." Mina turned her back to him, "You keep this up and I'll replace you as my best friend."

"If you do, who would you replace me with?" Mitch knew she was bluffing, "Hoven? He certainly can't handle you."

"Your sister." Mina had met Penelope on multiple occasions before and was comfortable with her stepping into the role, "We already discussed it. If you do something wrong to ruin my wedding day, she would take your place."

"Plotting against me like that. I'm so..." Mitch wiped away a fake tear, "I'm so proud." He grinned, "In all seriousness, what do you need from me? You have the dress on, you're looking beautiful. The guests are seated, everything is ready. Your equally handsome husband to be, a man who is madly head over heels in love with you, will be out there waiting for you to make your grand entrance with all the flourish of the divine goddess that you are."

Mina smiled as she approached Mitch, "Fine, you're still my best friend." She laughed, "Thank you for wearing a tuxedo, I appreciate it."

"Only because Michael said I can't wear a beautiful dress." Mitch sighed happily, "He said something about how I shouldn't try to outshine the stars in the sky with the radiance of the sun." He touched his hand to his chest, "I love him so much, such a romantic."

A soft knock at the door was soon followed by Tonia who peaked her head inside, "We're about to begin. Do you remember everything from the rehearsal?"

"We got this." Mitch turned to Mina, "Are you ready, Kitten?"

Mina looked up at Mitch, all signs of humor fading from her face, "I never thought I would ever get married. I thought so negatively about marriage. How is it possible that I'm standing here in a wedding gown about to walk down the aisle?"

"You met someone that showed you this beautiful world that he created around himself. One filled with hope, true love, and a belief that there is a magic in this world that makes life such a wonderful experience every day. All he had to do was show you the possibilities he thought could become real." Mitch took Mina's hands, "He unlocked something deep within you that existed all along. He helped you nurture that part of you, let it grow and flourish. You have been on this incredible journey with him, discovering so much about yourself and what you want out of life. You found this precious gift that you share with Oliver, one that so few in the world truly get the opportunity to experience. Cherish this moment as much as you do that first day your eyes first met.

Mitch squeezed her hands, "This is not the most important day in your life. Every day you'll spend with him from this point forward will feel like the greatest to all those who came before. True love grows, becomes stronger and more beautiful with every passing moment as you share an eternity together." He grinned, "Now then, as Alice would say, are you ready to see your one true love?"

Mina was felt as if she was glowing. She had to remember to start breathing again after hearing such a beautiful speech before she could answer, "Yes."

~

"Dearly Beloved, we are gathered here today..." Oliver felt his heartbeat resounding in his ears, drowning out what was being said. It was as if all other sounds faded into silence as he stared at Mina's dark green eyes. In his mind, he kept telling himself not to cry, he could feel his body wanting to form the tears, preparing itself for when he would lose control. Not yet, he wished for this to be perfect.

In a trance, fixated on the beauty he found in the eyes of his fiancé, the love and warmth that enveloped his soul, he was startled by the sudden touch of the hand of the man enacting the ceremony for the couple. He looked over to find a pair of dark, near obsidian eyes watching him with a comforting smile. An elder man with shoulder length white hair and a short cut, thick white beard covering most of his face, spoke softly, "It's time for you to speak." He lightly patted the groom on the shoulder, "At your own pace, of course. This is your moment and that of the lady before you."

Laughing nervously, feeling an obvious flush of coloration across his face in embarrassment. He first spoke to the elder man, "One moment please." He raised his voice from the near whisper he had been using to be heard by those watching the ceremony, "I had something I wanted to say, something I had memorized, but I did not anticipate forgetting everything I wished to say beforehand." Oliver fought back tears, "I apologize for the interruption."

He turned to find the best man standing close by him. There was a discussion of reversing the roles, his sister playing the part of the best man and Mitch being the maid of honor. However, Alice was so excited to stand by Mina that all involved quickly agreed that the various roles would follow a more traditional path. Handing him a piece of paper, Mitch grinned before he stepped back as Oliver thanked him, "Thank you."

Mitch was doing his best to hold back tears, but even he was forced to wipe them away from his eyes as anticipation of what was about to happen struck him. He steadied his breathing, trying his best not to ruin the moment for the happy couple. Finally, he cleared his throat to speak, "You're welcome."

Turning back to Mina, Oliver continued, "I believe this moment of silence, of losing all memory of what I wished to say is perfect for this moment. Often, I would think about what to tell you, some beautiful piece of poetry or to express how I felt in advance. Yet, when the time came, I saw you, the beautiful woman I now gaze upon, and all of my preparations would vanish." He smiled nervously, "I like to think that my mind removes all other thoughts, reserving as much possible space within me just for you."

He paused, thinking of something that flickered across his mind, "I realize now that I have always prioritized what is most important in my life and completely focus upon that which I care most about. When I see you, that is why the world fades away and there is only you in my mind. You will always be the greatest part of not only my life, but who I am, for within me, I feel your heartbeat. It is a reminder that you will always be there with me."

When Oliver touched his chest, tears fell from Mina's eyes, twin droplets sliding down her cheeks. He waited, watching the beauty of the expression of such heartfelt emotion until she was able to clear her eyes if only temporarily and give him a small nod to continue. "Long before I met you, I wrote a poem. It was born from hope of a young man that desired nothing more in this world than to find his one true love."

"In your eyes sparkle the stars. Which have granted an endless number of dreams. In your smile glows a warmth. Which caresses my soul with gentle tenderness. In your voice echoes the sound. Of countless children laughing with endless joy. In the touch of your hand against my cheek. Flows emotions that no words can properly express. In your chest beats a heart. That has never lost hope in true love. In your thoughts there is a purity. From which fairy tales are given true meaning. In your soul there speaks a language. From which only my own can truly understand. In your life exists the potential. To make any dream become reality. In every moment you share with me. A world forged in perfect light is given hope. In your words I am blessed." Oliver lowered his hand to stare into Mina's eyes, "My dearest, my beloved, my love."

Startling many of those attending, Mina stepped forward, ignoring tradition as she wrapped her arms tightly around Oliver's waist, pressing the side of her face against his chest as she wept without restraint. Behind the couple, the elder man raised his hand, touching the finger of his other across his lips in a request for silence and for none to disturb the moment. Lowering his hands, he clasped them together before him, his dark eyes watching with a warm smile.

Time was lost to Mina. She didn't know how long she held Oliver. She wanted to cry, to release the pent-up emotions she had been struggling to hold back. The idea of standing so close and not being with him in that moment frightened her. She didn't want to be alone. She had never felt more vulnerable in her life. She needed to hold him, to feel him close, for him to provide the strength and comfort when she needed it most.

That is what she found so beautiful about her connection with him. There were moments when he was feeling weak, vulnerable, and scared. He found strength, protection, and guidance within her. Other times in their lives, it was she who sought that comfort in him. Together, whatever happened in their lives would never be too much to endure, to overcome any obstacle.

When her body relaxed, the last of the tears shed, and she felt at peace once more. Mina pulled away from Oliver, looking up into his beautiful jade green eyes. She mouthed the words, unable to find her voice to speak, "I love you."

Oliver responded in silence, "I love you."

Mina glanced back over her shoulder at Alice who gave her an encouraging smile. She remembered days before when she was sitting in the apartment of her maid of honor when she asked, "What do I say? I know Oliver is going to have this beautiful speech, something so poetic I am going to cry. Should I just fumble through something before he says something?"

Should she talk about her journey to discovering love? No, too many painful memories. What of her realization that she wanted to get married? No, too much negative thoughts leading into that.

Mina remembered a speech that Mitch had given to her when discussing the blooming relationship between Alice and Hoven. It was then that inspiration for what she wanted to say was first discovered. She spent time trying to write out something formal in advance, to have it prepared but she wanted to speak from the heart, flaws and mistakes included. It was those tiny details that one doesn't expect when it comes to love that makes it beautiful.

"When I first met you, a part of me buried deep down inside of me wanted to explore the beautiful reality that you were bringing into my life. I was curious. Here is this beautifully handsome, charming, sweet, kind, and generous soul that desired nothing more than to love me. That has been the greatest gift and blessing that you have given me." Mina touched her hand to her chest, "With each beat of my heart, I feel you there, a pure, unconditional, wonderful feeling that goes beyond words to properly express how I feel."

"I look into your eyes and memories of every moment I had the joy of seeing you comes to mind." Mina smiled nervously, practically laughing with a burst of euphoria that struck her, "I am so incredibly excited for the future when there will be all these wonderful moments when I will be given the opportunity to look at you, to see the love expressed in every small detail of who you are."

Tears formed once more in Mina's eyes, "That is what you are to me. Love. If someone asked me to describe what love is, I would talk about you for hours, finding some new thing I want to tell them about that I adore about you." Taking a moment to wipe tears from her eyes, Mina steadied her breathing before continuing, "True love exists, and his name is Oliver."

"Once upon a time I first met you." Mina took in a slow breath, letting it out slowly as she finished, "As with every fairy tale, our journey together has been filled with beautiful experiences, challenges we've had to overcome, and discovering the truth about not only ourselves but those we share our lives with. I traveled to lands far, far away, spoke with queens, learned from wise men, and become the hero of my own story with you by my side. As we begin the next chapter of our lives together, I eagerly look forward to what the future will bring for us. What I do know, is that no matter what happens next, I have found my happily ever after."

Made in the USA
Columbia, SC
12 November 2022